CW01467905

COUNTERFEIT RELATIONS

BOOK 2

ALASKAN SECURITY-TEAM ROGUE

Jemma **WESTBROOK**

Counterfeit Relations, book 2 in the Alaskan Security-Team Rogue series. Copyright 2020 by Jemma Westbrook. www.jemmawestbrook.com

All rights reserved. No part of this publication may be reproduced, stored in a retrieval system, or transmitted in any form or by any means electronic, mechanical, photocopying, recording, or otherwise without the prior written permission of the publisher and copyright owner except for the use of brief quotations in a book review.

First printing, 2020
Cover design by Robin Harper at Wicked by Design.

CHAPTER 1

"YOU'RE KIDDING." BROCK stared down at the file in his hand. "They've only been gone twenty minutes." He shoved the docs back at Shawn. "I'm not interested."

Shawn made no move to take it back. "Wasn't really asking." He sauntered toward the fridge in the small kitchen and opened the door, scanning the handful of contents before turning back Brock's way. "Looks like it won't take you long to clean the place up before you go either."

Bess had spent the whole previous day cleaning up the small cabin he'd been sharing with her, Wade, and Parker for the past two months while she recovered from the gunshot that messed up more lives than just hers. "Bess thought I wouldn't clean out the fridge."

"Doesn't know you very well, does she?"

Brock shrugged. "As well as anybody."

"You mean any woman." Shawn snagged the single remaining bottle of water before letting the stainless steel door swing shut. "You need something to occupy your time while they're gone or you'll go crazy."

"I have plenty to occupy my time." It was a lie, but the last thing Brock wanted to do was whatever was in that file.

Shawn leaned against the counter. "Such as?"

It would figure the bastard would call his bluff.

"I have work to do on my place." Brock dropped the file to the counter, wanting it as far away from him as possible.

Shawn snorted. "That's a lie if I've ever heard one." The coordinator for Team Rogue straightened. "That cabin is pristine." He tipped the capped top of the bottle Brock's way. "And I'm a little pissed you haven't invited me over in a while. You're not the only one who needs to get away from all this bullshit sometimes."

"I don't want that job." Brock eyed the file. He hadn't worked without Wade in years and wasn't interested in starting now, especially not on one like this. "Give it to Nate."

Shawn shook his head. "This is a one-man show, and you're the only one without a partner."

Brock tossed the file to the counter. "Come on. There's got to be somebody itching to play house. What about Tyson? He would love that shit."

"Tyson and Reed are already on a different project." Shawn pressed his palm flat on the top of the file and shoved it Brock's way. "This job is yours whether you want it or not." He checked his watch. "You better get going or you'll be late picking Ms. Tatum up from the airport, and I'm guessing she won't be thrilled when her fiancé isn't there."

Thirty years he'd managed to go without ever having that word thrown his way. "I'm not her fucking fiancé."

"You are for now." Shawn gave him a wink as he patted the file. "Ring's in here and everything." Shawn started to walk toward the door. "I can't imagine she's expecting a grand gesture when you propose."

Brock flipped the front cover of the file and sure enough, stapled to the top sheet was a tiny plastic bag containing a ring. He snatched the plastic, tearing it free of the staple's metal grip. "This isn't real, is it?"

"What do you think?" Shawn didn't stop walking until his hand was on the knob to the door. He turned Brock's way. "The cleaning crew will be here in an hour and if you're still here we're going to have a problem."

Brock stared down at the stack of papers.

When he and the rest of the team voted to take Rogue on a different, more solidly moral path, he was expecting they would be doing more domestic jobs. Like the one that brought Bess and Parker to them.

He never imagined any of those jobs would involve pretending to be a strange woman's long-distance paramour.

"I'm not sure this is in my wheelhouse, man." Brock scanned the top page, looking at the information on Eva Tatum. "I'm not exactly boyfriend material."

He'd made damn sure of it, actually. Worked hard to ensure no woman ever wanted him to stick around for more than a little fun.

Not that he would have.

"I bet you surprise yourself."

"I bet I surprise her." Brock flipped the file closed. "What happens if Ms. Tatum is unsatisfied with your selection and wants a do-over?"

Shawn's expression cooled. "Then her safety is compromised." He pointed at Brock. "And it will be your fault."

Brock wiped one hand down his face. Shawn knew him too well. "You're a dick, you know that?"

"Harlow reminded me of it first thing this morning." Shawn shot him a grin that said he wasn't even a little upset at their new hacker's assessment of his personality. "Pack your shit up and take the red Rover."

"Red?"

"Half the point of this is being visible. Show the world, and anyone watching a little closer than they should, that Ms. Tatum is happily taken."

"Hopefully she's a good actress." Brock grabbed the file and shoved it in his bag.

"I guess we'll find out." Shawn pulled the door open. "Want me to leave the SUV running?"

"You worried I'm not going to show?" Brock grabbed the coffee he was half through when Shawn showed up to ruin his day and swallowed down the lukewarm liquid.

"Nah. I know you won't leave a defenseless woman stranded." Shawn stepped onto the porch. "It's not the kind of guy you are."

8

Brock glared at the back of the door for a good thirty seconds after Shawn left.

This was not how he envisioned these next few weeks to go. While Wade and Bess were in Florida visiting with Wade's mother he planned to head up to his cabin and bunk down.

Reassess.

Because the simple life he led was no longer the same.

"Fuck."

He rushed through getting ready and packing up the clothes and personal items he'd brought to the cabin, shoving everything into the suitcase he frequently lived out of, before dumping the hardside case into the back hatch of the cherry red SUV still running in the driveway. While the red paint screamed look at me, the heavy tinted windows made the act impossible.

"Stupid."

Brock locked up the cabin, resisting the urge to look around the space that held more happy memories than he cared to admit.

He needed this time to decompress, distance himself from the woman and baby who'd managed to creep under his skin without so much as a whisper of a warning.

And now he wasn't getting it.

Worse, he was going to have to live out his worst nightmare. Pretend or not, domestication was not something Brock wanted to ever touch, let alone bathe in.

He crammed into the Rover, immediately shoving the seat back almost as far as it would go, before skidding down the driveway, taking a little of his frustration out on the 4-wheel drive.

An hour later he was at the airport, parked in the garage and making his way to the doors as he thumbed through the file on Eva Tatum.

Maybe this job wouldn't be so bad after all. The woman sounded boring as hell. She served as CEO of a company called Investigative Resources in Cincinnati, Ohio which also sounded boring as hell.

Probably an accountant.

The amount of personal information Dutch was able to find on her was limited to a LinkedIn profile that only listed the bare minimum of information, along with a photo of her company's logo instead of a headshot.

Which would explain the next paper in the file.

EVA TATUM

It was printed in big bold black letters across the cardstock.

"You've got to be kidding me." Brock pulled out the paper.

"Shit. Damn. Hell. Sonofabitch."

The feminine lilt of the string of cursing did nothing to soften the edge of aggravation it contained.

Brock looked up just as a container of airport sushi bounced off the toe of his boot and a full cup of soda imploded between his feet.

"Christ." The woman who could line up a row of expletives better than most people he knew glared at him. "You made me drop my lunch."

"*I* did?" Brock turned his head from side to side, positive she was talking to someone else. "I'm just standing here."

The woman's brown eyes narrowed. "That's what they all say." She dropped down to pick up the plastic pack of rice and fish, turning it from one side to the other. "It looks like it survived." Her attention turned to the puddle of red liquid pooling between them. "More than I can say for my punch."

"You drink punch?" Brock leaned down to pick up the mostly-empty cup. He didn't know anyone over the age of ten that drank punch.

Definitely no curvaceous brunettes in—

Was that a New Kids on the Block t-shirt?

She snatched it from his hand. "Are you the fun police? You think women only drink iced tea and bottled water?"

"The fun pol—"

Her head bobbed on an animated nod that made the wad of hair banded at the top of her head bounce around as her gaze moved down his front. "The fun police. You look about as fun as—" her eyes drifted toward the long line of windows, "Alaska."

"You don't like Alaska?" Why was he still talking to her? He had an uptight businesswoman to find and babysit.

A woman who would be nowhere near as interesting as this one was proving to be in her 1980's t-shirt and hot-pink leggings.

"I'm greatly doubting it." The woman dropped a stack of napkins onto the splashed remains of her drink and used the sole of one silver sneaker to push them around as she tugged on an oversized sweatshirt.

"Can I ask why you are in Alaska then?" Brock scanned the people milling around the baggage area, checking for an early thirties woman who looked in need of saving.

"Business." She snorted out a scoff. "A forced work trip."

He should wish her well and go find Ms. Tatum. Leave this unique woman to her unwanted Alaskan adventure.

But there were no lone women wandering the lobby. No one who fit the profile of his next job.

"Ugh." The napkins made a hollow splatting sound as the woman dropped them into the cup. "They're probably going to have to mop." She stood and scanned the area.

"I'm sure they'll get it."

Her eyes found him.

He thought they were brown at first, but it must have been the bad airport lighting that threw him off.

Because these eyes were most definitely not brown.

Not completely anyway.

Rings of grey, green, amber, and finally brown circled her iris like a bullseye.

"Is that how you usually handle the messes you make? Just walk away and let them figure themselves out?" Her full lips pressed into a frown.

And for some reason that frown bothered the shit out of him.

Maybe because for the first time in years he was a one man show.

Maybe because for the first time ever he was dangerously close to doing something he swore never to do.

Or maybe it was because this woman was so fucking far off base it would be laughable if he was in the mood to laugh.

"I'm the one who cleans other people's messes up."

Her brows lifted. "Interesting."

"Is it?"

She nodded. "Very."

"And why is that?"

She tugged at the band holding her knot of hair in place, wincing as it pulled free. "I never get to see that part."

"What part?" He was having a hard time following their conversation as her fingers raked through the waves of dark hair falling wild around her face.

It was probably soft. Smooth.

"The part where the mess gets cleaned up." She shook her head a little and the hair he was struggling not to imagine touching tumbled past her shoulders. "I only uncover the mess." One of those shoulders lifted and dropped. "Then I pass it down the line."

"Down the line?" A faint scent tickled his nose.

Made Brock step closer so he could breathe it in as she continued to move the pile of dark strands around, kicking up the sweet smell of summer and sunshine.

Something he hadn't had much of the past few years.

One long-fingered hand waved in the air. "Just down the line." She looked down at the empty cup in her hand and sighed.

"I can get you another one."

His offer seemed to surprise them both. Her ringed eyes jumped to his, mouth twisting to one side. "I got it on the other side of security."

"Oh."

Why was he disappointed? Continuing to talk to this woman was the last thing he should be doing.

For a number of reasons, the primary one being that he was supposed to be finding Eva Tatum and taking her to—

"Shit." Brock flipped the file back open and scanned the pages to see where in the hell he was supposed to be taking his first fake girlfriend.

"What's that?" The woman leaned in close, bringing her summertime scent with her. The brush of her hair against his hand was everything he imagined it would be.

Brock slapped the file closed and stepped away.

He never missed an opportunity to be close to a pretty woman. Never passed up the chance to charm his way into her evening plans.

But this woman wasn't normal.

And that was a problem.

Especially right now.

He needed nice, uninteresting, normal Eva Tatum to show up and save him from this other, completely interesting, and definitely not normal one.

"I've gotta go."

Her lips quirked. "That was sudden."

He shrugged, trying to ignore the way her indescribable eyes were sizing him up.

Appraising him.

As if she was studying his every move. Every word. "Do I make you nervous?"

"No."

Her head tipped back in a belly-deep laugh. Loud and long. "You are a funny man." She wiped at the dark lashes framing her eyes. "Maybe I won't hate Alaska as much as I thought." She bent at the waist to dig into the leopard-print bag at her feet. One of the luggage claims started to buzz, catching her attention. She squinted down the row of carousels. "I believe that's me." She straightened and gave him a dazzling smile. "Good timing since you said it's time for you to go too." She pointed to the floor. "Don't worry. I'll let them know about the mess." She gave him a wink and turned, swinging her large bag onto one shoulder as she walked away.

And damned if he didn't hate to see her go.

Which meant he should have walked away from her sooner.

Brock tucked the folder under one arm and lifted the paper printed with Eva Tatum's name as a line of people started to file from the gates. He looked through the crowd as they passed. Unfortunately, his eyes immediately found a head of dark hair and a leopard-print bag. He watched as her head tipped back again in a long, full laugh. The old man she was with beamed at her as she took the bag he had looped over the bar of his walker and hooked it on her other shoulder.

Brock turned his back on the scene as another baggage claim buzzer started to wail. He squinted up at the flight list.

He needed to get Ms. Tatum and get the hell out of here. Far away from silver shoes with her sunshine scent and soul deep laugh.

He needed to get his head on straight. Get back to his normal self. The man who was always up for a good time.

And that's it.

He skimmed the list of flights until he found the one he was hunting.

Eva Tatum's flight had already arrived. Thirty minutes early.

"Shit."

CHAPTER 2

"YOU DON'T HAVE to do that."

Eva's new friend Elmer shifted in his orthopedic loafers.

"I know I don't have to do it." She smiled, taking his arm so he wouldn't waste anymore time arguing. "You sit down and relax and I'll bring your bag over. What does it look like?"

The old man chuckled. "It's neon orange. My granddaughter bought it for me so I would be able to find it."

"She's a smart girl." Eva gave him a wink. "I'll be back."

The bags from her flight were already racked and circling the belt. Elmer's was unmissable and she grabbed it as it came close, setting it at her side while she scanned the carousel for hers.

Luckily she and Elmer's granddaughter had something in common, and a second later her bag was in sight.

Eva rolled Elmer's bag along as she stepped in to grab her own suitcase, hefting it up and off.

"Over pack?"

It was almost freaking impossible not to react to the voice beside her. It took everything she had to act casual as she lifted her head. "There's no such thing."

The man who hadn't figured out she was the woman he was here for looked ready to argue with her.

Then his eyes landed on her suitcase. "Are you stealing an old woman's luggage?"

"Of course not." Eva tugged the handle up on her case and tipped both bags onto their wheels. "That's my Gram-Gram." She gave him a smile. "Now if you'll excuse me."

He nodded. "Enjoy your trip."

Enjoying this trip wasn't going to happen, but his arrival at the airport was certainly making it more interesting.

Eva resisted the urge to glance back at him. There would be plenty of time for that on the drive to the Airbnb she rented for the next few weeks.

Hopefully she was overestimating how long this stay would be.

By like, a lot.

Elmer was still sitting just where she left him, only now he had company. Eva grinned at the tiny woman with turquoise hair at his side. "Hey. I was just getting your handsome friend's bag for him." She passed the bag handle over to the other woman, giving Elmer a wink. "Stay warm out there."

He smiled wide. "Thank you, Miss Eva. You are an angel."

That was a first. Most people likened her more to the other end of the spectrum. Which was understandable.

She tended to have more to do with people's sins than their salvation.

Elmer's eyes drifted over one shoulder. He pointed at the spot. "You take good care of her. She's something special."

Eva didn't have to turn around to know who Elmer was talking to.

She could feel him.

The young woman with turquoise hair helped Elmer to his feet, steadying him before taking the bags in one hand and wrapping the other around his shoulders to guide him toward the doors leading out to the snow-covered tundra Eva had been banished to.

"You could have told me who you were."

Oh. Mister bodyguard didn't sound too happy with her.

Which definitely made her much more comfortable. She was used to men being unhappy with her.

She was frequently in charge of their downfall, after all.

Eva turned to face him.

Good lord what a face he had too.

Hopefully he was very unhappy with her, because there was only one thing she could think of that might make this situation a little less boring.

And that was not a good idea.

At all.

"What would the fun have been in that?"

19

His eyes narrowed.

She smiled. "You draw the short straw?"

"Something like that."

The man sent from Alaskan Security was huge. Taller than any man she'd met before, and broad in a way that said there was nothing but lean muscle hiding under the heavy coat that must have been custom made just for him.

But his size wasn't the most striking thing about—

"And you can't really be mad at me for not telling you who I am when you still haven't told me who you are."

His eyes barely widened. She'd surprised him. Again.

"Brock."

Eva took the opportunity to size him up a little, hiding the perusal under the guise of assessment.

But to be honest, she'd already assessed everything the man had.

Twice.

It was one of the things that made her so good at her job. She could spot a person a mile away. Break them down in a second, and figure out more than they would ever want her to know.

And this man stood out like a cactus in Alaska.

Eva snorted, tipping her head back as she laughed at her own idiom.

Brock watched her with an odd look on his face. More like an odd mixture of emotions on his face.

Confusion.

Interest.

And fear. The last one was the strange one.

Because for once Eva wasn't here to ruin this guy's life.

She was here so he could save hers.

At least that's what Mona believed was happening.

"You ready, Broccoli?" Eva grabbed the suitcase wrapped in her Gram-Gram's face and started toward the doors. "I've got things to do."

"Ms. Tatum."

Eva kept going. This guy was going to have to figure out who ran this show. Better he do that sooner rather than later.

"Eva." The sharpness in his tone put a little hitch in her stride.

She still didn't stop.

Not until a heavy hand clamped down on her shoulder, spinning her to face down a very angry-looking bodyguard.

His eyes raked down her body and he only seemed to get angrier. "Where the fuck is your coat?"

So Broccoli liked swears too.

That was good. Meant his ears weren't going to bleed when they had to be around each other.

"In my bag." She wobbled the case back and forth.

"Put it on."

Any ideas she might have had about digging out her winter coat stopped dead at the demand. "No."

One of Brock's dark brows lifted. "Is this how this is going to go?"

"Definitely."

Poor Broccoli clearly thought he was going to be getting a nice, agreeable lady to babysit. Hell, he was probably looking forward to it.

Instead he got her.

And was definitely going to be making some phone calls later. She'd probably have a newly-assigned replacement by morning.

Which was fine.

In the blink of an eye Brock shucked his coat and whipped it around her, completely ignoring the fact that she had upper limbs as he zipped her into the giant parka. "Come on." He grabbed one of the empty sleeves with one hand and her suitcase with the other, dragging both out the doors.

"Holy fuck." Eva's feet stopped moving and her lungs refused to accept the icy air, locking up as she tried to breathe.

"Yup." Brock didn't stop, just kept hauling her along as she tucked deeper into the warmth of his coat.

Her eyes burned from the air cutting across the lot, watering as they fought off the icy slice of the freezing wind.

She was dying. This was how she would end. Frozen solid because no one would let her do what she wanted.

Which was stay in Ohio and face down whoever was royally fucking up her life.

"This is why I didn't want to do this." Brock was mumbling under his breath now and it just kept coming.

"Pain in the ass."

"Make everything as fucking difficult as possible."

He yanked open the door on a bright red Land Rover. "Get in."

Eva tried to glare at him but her eyeballs were frozen in place.

"Jesus." Brock grabbed her by the waist and hefted her into the seat, grabbing her feet and spinning her into place before shutting the door.

He opened the back hatch and tossed in her luggage then rounded to the driver's door, folding his huge self into the seat beside her.

"You're a crab."

"I'm not." He started the SUV and switched the vents to high before flipping on the warmer in her seat. "You're just frustrating."

Eva tipped her head to one side. "Was that not in the file you have on me? I'm positive Mona would have made my temperament very clear."

"Who's Mona?"

"My business partner." Eva tried to work her arms into the sleeves of the coat Brock straight-jacketed her into. "And I'm supposed to text her so she knows I'm okay." Eva managed to fish her cell from the purse Brock zipped in with her and poked it out the top so she could power it up.

Brock immediately snatched it away.

"What are you doing?"

He tucked her lifeline into the side panel of his door. "You can't use your phone."

"What?" Eva wiggled around, fighting with the heavy fabric of the coat. The movement pushed the scent of pine and fresh air out around her no-longer-frozen nostrils.

Broccoli must smell as good as he looked. Too bad he was so damn cranky.

And definitely the fun police.

"Give me my phone, Broccoli." She managed to get the zipper down and shoved one arm out at him. "Don't make me call your boss."

His lips barely quirked.

But it was the glint in Brock's eye that gave his amusement away.

"Go ahead." He shifted into reverse then swung one long arm her way to grip the back of her seat as he turned to look out the rear window. "Call him."

Eva stared at the sizable bulge of a bicep his thick sweater couldn't even hide. "You work out a bunch, huh."

His eyes bounced to hers. "What?"

Eva pointed at his arm.

Then she took it a step further, poking at the spot. "How much can you curl?"

How much did she weigh? Probably well within the limits of those arms.

When her eyes lifted from the spot she was still jabbing, Brock's gaze was there, resting strong and steady on her face. "You're an odd woman, Eva."

"You'll have that." She shrugged his comment off.

It was old news.

Just because most people were scared to be who they were, didn't mean she was going to fall in line.

Conform.

It wasn't who she was or ever would be.

Which was the whole point.

"Hmm." He turned his attention back to exiting the parking garage, one hand braced on the top of the steering wheel, the other hanging off the edge of the armrest of his seat.

"Give me back my phone."

"I thought we'd moved on." Brock pressed the button to roll down his window and a blast of frigid air swept through the interior, sending Eva burrowing back in his coat.

She sniffed at the neck. Holy hell it smelled good.

No doubt the man beside her had led many women to make bad decisions based on attraction and hormones.

And she couldn't blame them even a little bit.

"Are you smelling my coat?"

Eva froze mid-huff. "No. I'm trying to stay warm because you rolled the freaking window down."

Brock shook his head. "You were definitely smelling my coat."

This was not how conversations normally went. She was the one calling people out on their actions.

Not the one going on the defensive.

And she never lied.

Eva straightened. "Fine. You are right. I was smelling your coat because I think you and my new friend Elmer wear the same cologne."

There. Put Broccoli back in his place.

He was not the one in charge here.

25

He might have her phone.

And his substantial form might be making her brain linger on ideas she would most certainly not be acting on.

But she was still in control.

One-hundred percent.

For sure.

The barely-there twitch of his lips was back. "Elmer has expensive taste."

Eva didn't even try to hide the next sniff. Like her perusal of him before, it would just seem like she was investigating.

That was her job after all.

Except it was a little more than a sniff.

It was a full-fledged, lung-filling breath. "Explains how he ended up with seven kids."

The twitch of Brock's lips moved to his left eye and his mouth flattened into a thin line.

He turned away, facing out the windshield, the hand on the wheel squeezing a little tighter than it did a second ago.

"I think I just hit a nerve, Broccoli." She should leave it alone, but holding back had never gotten her anywhere good.

Life worked better when everything was out in the open, spread for everyone to see.

No secrets.

No lies.

No deception.

Unfortunately that was not how 99.9 percent of the population lived their lives.

Brock ignored her.

Because it would seem he was a part of the majority.

Eva sighed, turning her attention to the contents of her purse. Thank God she printed out the address to her Airbnb. It meant she didn't have to reclaim her cell just yet, and considering Brock was getting less and less amused by her presence with each passing second, that was probably best.

Hopefully his replacement was more amiable.

She pulled out the printed paper and shook it open before shoving it Brock's way. "Here's the address for my place."

He frowned at the paper. "Your place?"

"Not *my* place, just the place I rented to stay in while I was here." She shook the paper, trying to get him to take it. "It's supposed to be close to the airport."

"You're not staying in Fairbanks."

"Uh. Yeah. I am." She waved the paper in front of his face.

Finally Brock grabbed it, scowling as he scanned the sheet. "Did you rent this in your name?"

What did he think she was? An idiot?

"No." Eva grabbed the paper back and went to work punching the address into the navigation system since Brock didn't seem like he was going to do it.

"I'm not taking you there." He pulled off the road and into the parking lot of a strip mall before retrieving the file that probably held all her secrets.

Not that she kept any.

Piles of snow stacked around the edges of the lot. Ohio could get a decent amount of snowfall, but this was insane. "How much snow do you guys get?"

"Do you ever stay on one conversation until it's finished before starting the next one?" Brock flipped through the pages.

"No." Eva leaned forward to punch at the navigation screen. After a few screen changes she found what she was looking for and tapped the green framed phone.

The sound of a ringing line filled the SUV.

Shawn picked up on the second ring. "I hope you're not calling to tell me something I don't want to hear."

"Hey, Shawn." Eva smiled sweetly at the irritation brewing in Brock's dark eyes. "I think we have a miscommunication here. Broccoli was unaware I was providing my own accommodations."

She could swear she heard Shawn laughing through the muffled line.

At least someone at Alaskan Security thought she was amusing.

A few seconds later the line cleared and Shawn's voice was back. "Ms. Tatum's contract with us states that she will be providing her own housing."

"You know damn well that's a terrible idea, Shawn. Anyone could find her rental agreement."

"I doubt that will be a problem." Shawn's voice was back to the all-business tone she was used to.

"Ms. Tatum understands the risk, and has assured me she's taken every precaution."

Well, maybe not every. But a few.

This whole thing was ridiculous anyway. If she was going to be in Alaska she was sure as hell going to be as comfortable as possible, and being holed up in some isolated cabin was not her idea of comfort.

Brock disconnected the line and turned to her, his scowl from earlier back and digging in deep enough to give her the tiniest glimpse of a dimple in one cheek.

"Do you only have one dimple?"

"No." Brock leaned closer. "I need you to listen to me and understand the words that are coming out of my mouth, are we clear?"

The deep, and a little threatening, tone of his voice was nowhere near as intimidating as it should be.

"Jesus Christ. Don't look at me like that."

Eva blinked. "Like…"

Brock shook his head. "Just—" He closed his eyes for a second and took a deep breath. When he opened them again his brow was less pinched, his jaw less clenched. "You are here because you weren't safe in Ohio, right?"

"Not exactly."

Brock's head tilted as he stared at her. "What in the hell does not exactly mean?"

"It means I don't share the same opinion as my partners." She fought the urge to pout.

She'd pouted for days.

Thrown a fit.

Offered to hire someone in Cincinnati to guard her.

Mona and Chandler wouldn't budge.

Acted like she'd made enemies over the years or something.

"Eva."

Ignoring Brock so he would say her name again was tempting as hell.

How long had it been since a man said her name without either disdain or fear?

Longer than she could remember. Because at the end of the day every man she met either hated her or feared her.

Rightfully so.

"Eva."

She jumped in her seat at how close his deep, rich voice was this time. "What? I'm right here. I can hear you."

Brock was leaned in so close it wasn't the coat's scent she was breathing in. Somehow he smelled even better. The heat of his skin warmed the notes of fresh water and wood, making them rounder.

Heavier.

"Shit." Brock suddenly leaned away, wiping one hand down his face. He threw the SUV into drive and pulled out onto the road, following the directions she put into the GPS.

He was completely silent except for the sound of his molars grinding together.

"You're going to break a tooth." Eva crossed her arms under the coat, craning her head to look out the window as they pulled up in front of the place she rented. It was a townhouse in a brand new complex, with big windows and high ceilings.

And a heated garage, praise the good lord.

Her hand was already on the handle when Brock stopped the Rover in the short driveway. "The opener is in the planter at the corner. I'll be right back."

"Nope." Brock's hand clamped around her arm, holding with a firm, but still gentle, grip. "You stay here. I'll get it."

"You don't even have a coat on." Eva grabbed for the handle again. "It will only take a second."

Brock pulled her close enough she could see the tiny ring of chocolate brown lining his iris. "No man is going to let the woman who flew across the country to be with him trot her ass out into the cold while he sits in the car."

Eva stared at him. "What are you talking about?"

The smile that she'd only seen bare hints of finally tugged its way onto Brock's mouth. "You wouldn't want anyone watching to get the wrong idea about us, would you?"

A second later Brock was out of the car, leaving her to process what he said.

He had to be kidding.

No way would they—

He was back before she could fully wrap her head around it, climbing into his seat, then pulling the SUV into the garage. Instead of closing the door Brock left it open as he jumped out and rounded to her side.

And opened the door.

Eva stared at him. "What are you doing?"

"Being a gentleman." He held one hand out to her. "Come on out."

"Uh. I can do it myself." What in the hell was going on? She leaned forward to peek out the car and through the still-open door. "Aren't you going to shut that?"

"In a second." Brock grabbed her hand and tugged her forward. She toppled out and into his waiting arms. One banded around her waist and the other slid up the center of her back to tangle in the hair at the nape of her neck.

Eva stared up into his eyes, unable to do anything else.

He was warm. Freaking cozy as shit, even without a coat in the freezing Alaska air.

The sound of the garage door going down barely registered.

"Good job." Brock released her so fast she almost lost her footing as his big body immediately stepped away. "That looked believable as hell." He glanced her way over one shoulder as he walked toward the back of the car. "You're a hell of an actress."

CHAPTER 3

SHE WAS A terrible actress.

And he was fucked.

Brock pulled Eva's grandma-covered suitcase from the back hatch and dropped it to the cement garage floor. "Go inside."

This woman definitely did not like being told what to do, and that might be his only saving grace. He glanced up at where she was still standing in the chilly garage, his coat pulled tight around her shivering body. "Now."

Instead of the irritation he was banking on inspiring, the woman who was proving to be a pain in his ass smirked. "I think I'll wait for you."

Of all the damn jobs for Shawn to give him, he had to dump this one out.

A month ago Brock would have had no problem with it. He would have charmed his way into Eva's good graces, keeping her safely where she belonged.

Out from under his skin.

But Bess and Parker came along and fucked all that up. Planted seeds he never intended to sow.

And he'd planned to dig them out while they were gone visiting Wade's mother in Florida. Clear his mind of any stupid ideas it might try to form about life and happiness and love.

He knew what love did to men.

What women like Bess and Harlow and Eva did to men.

They fucking ruined them.

Brock pointed to the door leading to the basement of the three-story townhouse. "Go."

He'd never been an asshole to a woman in his life. Not even close.

But this one was as dangerous as the other two fucking him up right now. It was written all over her in big bold letters.

Eva's smile widened. "Do I bother you, Broccoli?"

He slammed the hatch into place and walked her way, deciding maybe a little intimidation might be a viable option.

Most people in their right mind backed down when they faced him.

But if there was one thing he knew about Eva Tatum, it was that the woman most definitely was not in her right mind.

"As a matter of fact you do bother me." He stopped just in front of her, staring down into her wide eyes. "You're making this job a whole hell of a lot harder than it has to be."

He'd never said anything more true in his life.

Brock thought he had her when it became clear she didn't know the plan was to pretend to be lovers. He expected the revelation to knock her down long enough he could gain the upper hand.

But when he'd held her close, Eva looked anything but knocked down.

He was used to affecting women. Had seen desire and lust in more than a few gazes sent his way.

But the way Eva looked at him was different. Open.

Unabashed.

And he needed to put a stop to it.

"You said that already."

Brock blinked. "What?"

"You said I was difficult. And…" Her ringed eyes drifted to one side. Then the other. One finger popped out from the front of his coat. "A pain in the ass." She smiled at him. "If you want to offend me then you'll have to be more creative. I hear those two almost every day."

Who the fuck told her she was a pain in the ass every day?

Eva's eyes widened. "That was a mean look." She scanned him, forcing Brock to once again resist the urge to straighten. "I can see why you're a bodyguard. You probably scare the shit out of most people."

"Not you, though."

Eva shook her head a little. "No. Not me." She gave him an apologetic-looking smile. "Don't take it personally. I think it's a case of systematic desensitization."

The fuck did that mean?

Eva sighed, loud and long. "I'm hungry." She turned away, leaving him with a growing list of questions.

Ones he shouldn't give two shits about the answers for.

Didn't matter who told this woman she was a pain in the ass.

Or why she'd faced down enough angry men that she was no longer scared of anyone.

Brock scratched at his arm as he dragged the grandma bag to the door Eva left open in her wake.

It's what he was caught up in. The lingering ripples her presence caused.

And they were threatening to drag him under.

Already.

"Oh. This is nice." Eva was moving between the rooms on the bottom floor. She flipped a switch and her face lit up along with the room. She took a few fast steps in and jumped over the back of a large, black sectional, her body bouncing on the overstuffed cushions. "I was afraid this place was too good to be true."

Brock barely stepped into the black-painted room, eyeing the large screen taking up the wall opposite where Eva was laid out, her long dark hair falling over the side and reaching nearly to the floor. "I thought you were hungry."

"Are you going to frown at me every time I see you?"

"You mean all the time?"

Her brows came together. "No." Eva sat up slowly. "I mean when you come to take me out." Her long legs dropped to the floor and she stood.

Brock resisted the urge to smile. Not only was Eva Tatum unaware they were playing pretend, she also didn't realize they would be playing house.

"That's not how this works." Brock stepped closer, ready to make one more grab for control of the situation and the woman holding it tight in her grip. "This isn't a part time thing, Eva."

"But—" For the first time she deflated.

And he fucking hated it.

A woman who was so full of life should never be tamped down. Not by him or anyone else.

Which meant he was going to have to nut up. Find a way to keep her from making him cross lines that were more akin to cliffs.

One wrong step and he would never be able to hang on tight enough to avoid the eventual fall.

And the end that came with it.

The problem was he was already too close to that eventuality.

"I'm staying here." Brock said the next words like they weren't a potential death sentence. "With you."

She scoffed. "But that wasn't part of the deal."

"You'll have to take that up with your best friend Shawn." Brock backed out of the room. "You want me to find my own room?"

Eva's temporary unbalance was gone in an instant. She smiled. "That's fine."

"Fine." If she thought it was fine then he thought it was fine.

It was fine.

Brock made his way up the steps, each one away from her making him feel better and worse at the same time. He was going to lock himself in his room and stay there. The less he was around her the better.

Because Eva's presence could be addicting.

The main level was all open space, with a kitchen, living room, and eating area all looking out a huge, floor-to-ceiling window that faced downtown Fairbanks. The place was nice as hell. Contemporary and sleek.

Reminded him of the place he should be right now.

Straightening out his fucking life.

Brock kept moving, taking the last flight of stairs two at a time. He was dropping her bag off and then barricading himself in for a nice, long attitude adjustment.

Brock stopped as he hit the top of the steps. "You're fucking kidding me."

"What's wrong, Broccoli?" Eva stepped beside him, still wearing his coat. Her head tilted to one side. "Oh, shoot. That's right." She looked over the completely open top floor. "Only one bedroom."

He'd faced down men who killed for a living.

Hell, he was one.

He'd been shot at, hunted, tied up, and a whole list of other things most people wouldn't survive.

He was better than this. Stronger than this.

If he didn't want to let this woman rattle him, then she wouldn't.

"Looks like." Brock turned to face Eva, steeling himself against the feelings he thought didn't exist in him. "You're sleeping on the right side."

Then he turned his back on her.

Because Eva needed to realize this was not going to be her show to run. Brock shoved her wheeled suitcase toward her side of the bed and dropped his own on the side he claimed for himself.

"You can't sleep in bed with me." Eva moved in beside him.

"I can."

She was already shaking her head. "No."

"You say that a lot for a woman who doesn't know the meaning of the word." Brock unzipped his case and flipped it open.

"Oh, God." Eva stepped back, her eyes wide on the contents of his packed bag. "You cannot stay in this room." Her gaze was still locked onto the neatly folded line of clothes.

"Should of thought of that before you rented a one-bedroom place."

Her chin tucked in and her eyes snapped to his face. "I didn't know someone was going to have to stay with me the whole time."

Brock turned to fully face her. Eva was finally starting to lose her stronghold, and he wasn't letting up until she knew exactly who was in charge here. "Not someone." He stepped closer, forcing her to tip her head back if she wanted to see his face. "Me."

Eva was silent.

For the first time since she'd dropped a cup of fruit punch on his boots, the woman didn't say a word.

And he fucking wished she would.

Because instead of attacking him with a verbal spar, Eva assaulted him with something infinitely more deadly.

Her sweet scent drifted up between them, riding the soft breath easing between her parted lips. Her dark hair was messy and wild, a perfect parallel to its owner. Her cheeks were still flushed pink from the cold Alaska air.

Or something else.

"Don't look at me like that."

"I can't help it." The honest answer was immediate and unhindered.

Because Eva Tatum didn't pretend to be anything she wasn't. He'd known her all of two hours and there was no doubt in his mind she would take him to his knees, just like Bess did to Wade.

And he couldn't let that happen.

No matter how much the idea had tried to grow on him since Bess and Parker arrived in his life.

"You have to help it." Brock moved in closer. "Looking at me like that isn't going to do either of us any favors."

"Why not?" The innocence in her question caught him off guard.

"Because I'm not the guy you're looking for."

"Who said I was looking?" Eva eased closer to him.

"I don't do relationships. Not ever." He was confessing all his dirty sins. Laying out the life he'd led out of self-preservation and fear. "I'm a good time and that's all."

Her eyes dropped down to his chest, moving slowly over his shoulders before lifting back to his face. "Are you a fuckboy?"

"What? No." He loved women. Loved how they smelled. How they tasted. The way they softened under his touch.

And he respected them enough to make sure each one knew what he was capable of giving them.

Just sex.

"It sort of sounds like you're a fuckboy." She lifted her shoulders. "If you just screw women and then bounce, then that's a fuckboy."

"I don't just screw women and bounce." Her simplistic summary of his post pubescent life didn't sit well. "I don't hide what I am, Eva. They know and are happy to participate anyway."

"Of course they are because," one hand flapped around, motioning to his body, "of all this ridiculousness." She stepped closer, her chin lifting higher so her distinctive eyes could stay locked onto his. "But don't think for a second at least a few of them thought they would prove you wrong."

He shook his head and forced out the next words. "They wouldn't."

Eva needed to know. Needed to see him for what he was. That way she would stop looking at him the way she did.

"Well *I* know that, but most women believe they will be the reason a man changes." She stepped away, taking her almost palpable energy with her.

Robbing him of it.

"Most women believe a man like you just doesn't know what he's missing, and that they will be the one to show you." She shrugged out of his coat and draped it on a chair in the corner as she moved to her suitcase.

Brock stared at the shed coat.

He didn't like that she took it off.

It was keeping her warm.

"Aren't you still cold?"

Eva looked around like she could see how warm the air was. Hell, maybe she could.

"No. I think it's comfortable in here." She lifted her grandma bag, grunting as she hefted it up.

"I got it." Brock rounded the bed and grabbed the suitcase, taking it out of her hands and setting it next to his. "You should have told me you wanted it on the bed. I would have put it there for you."

Eva's brows came together. "You're a strange man, Broccoli."

"*I'm* strange?" He pointed to her bag. "You have your grandma on your suitcase and are wearing a shirt that's probably older than you are."

"At least I'm consistent." She raked her fingers through her hair, pushing it off her face and working it into a wad at the top of her head before wrapping a band around it. "You're all over the place."

"I'm not all over the place."

She snorted and started digging through her bag. "Okay."

He'd had enough. He needed to get away from this whole damn situation for a while. Unfortunately, his options were limited.

"I need a shower." Brock grabbed a pair of boxers and a shirt from his bag and slow turned in the room.

The upper floor was entirely open, with the exception of the toilet, which was tucked into a corner closet next to the glassed-in shower.

"What's a matter, Broccoli? You shy?" Eva grinned at him, her taunt was clearly meant to rile him.

And he was done playing with her for today.

Brock stomped down the stairs, all the way to the bathroom in the basement. The shower there was tiny as hell, but at least it was private.

And he needed some fucking privacy.

He locked the door and stepped under the scalding hot spray, scrubbing away the frustration of the day.

Of the month.

Of his life.

He could never have what other people took for granted.

Ignorance.

The blissful unawareness that let people believe happiness and love lasted forever.

That it wouldn't crush you in the blink of an eye.

It was a lesson he learned early and carried with him every day. A lesson he'd been reminded of not long ago.

He'd seen the pain love could cause. The way it could bring a strong man to his knees. Break him in an instant.

Brock closed his eyes and let the water burn into his skin.

Except when he closed his eyes all he could see was Eva's moon water eyes staring up into his, full of truth and life.

Her lips parted.

For him.

Waiting.

Brock shut the water off and bumped out the door, toweling off as he walked to the theater room.

No way could he be in the same bed as her.

Eva Tatum was going to get that big bed all to herself tonight and every night until he packed her belly laughing, boy-band-shirt wearing, old-man-helping ass up and shipped it back to Ohio.

Safely away from him.

CHAPTER 4

"WHAT IN THE hell are you doing?"

Eva ignored Brock, instead taking a deep breath and focusing on the stretching of her muscles. The air moving in and out of her body.

She'd heard him coming up the stairs, and the soft pad of Brock's bare feet up the risers was enough to take the Zen she'd been working on since five and throw it out the giant window beside her.

"Trying to find my calm." Eva didn't open her eyes.

No reason to look at him anymore.

Or any less.

Broccoli was a good-looking pile of man. One she hadn't seen the likes of before.

He was taller than any man she knew. Broad enough that his height didn't seem so staggering.

And those eyes. She could get lost in them. Had a few times already, which didn't seem to make him very happy. It would figure she would be stuck in a house with a man like him. This whole mess just got crappier and crappier.

"You're fucking it all up too." Eva opened her eyes, not looking his way until she took a jab at him. "I thought you were going to be my snuggle buddy last night?" When her eyes found him, the air rushed from her lungs.

Good thing she got the words out before the sight of Brock stole the functioning part of her brain and sent it sailing into the gutter.

He'd looked at her many ways in the few short hours they spent together yesterday.

Like she was crazy.

Like she was the biggest pain in the ass he'd ever met.

Like she was crazy again.

But the way he was looking at her now might be the most interesting of them all. Brock still looked like he thought she was crazy and the biggest pain in the ass he'd ever met, but now there was something more in his eyes.

Heat.

Until now she hadn't worried about her attraction to him. Figured it was a safe one since Brock clearly found her undesirable. She thought she could admire all he had to offer without ever having to put her money where her mouth was.

But the way he was looking at her made Eva think her money and her mouth might be fighting to get in the same place real soon.

"Why in the hell are you in your underwear?" Brock's voice was still a little rough from sleep and his dark hair stood up at the back of his head. He was fully dressed, but his feet were bare and his shirt was unbuttoned, revealing the tiniest peek at the wide plane of chest under it.

Brock caught her eyes as they drifted down the open placket. His hands immediately went to the buttons of the deep-blue flannel and started working them together.

It would figure he would be modest.

"It's not my underwear." Eva stood up and motioned to her hip area. "These are boy shorts." She pointed a finger at her chest. "And this is a sports bra. It's athletic wear."

"My ass." His eyes lingered on her a second longer before turning toward the kitchen. "For the love of God, put some damn clothes on."

"I can't meditate in clothes. They're too restricting."

"Is that what you call that?" His eyes barely flicked her way before he turned his back on her. "Looked a whole hell of a lot like you had gas."

"That is called the child's pose and it is fantastic for finding your inner peace." Eva propped her hands on her hips. "You should try it. Might improve your disposition."

"My disposition is just fine." He yanked the pot off the coffee maker with more force than necessary and snapped on the faucet.

"Clearly." She stepped in beside him, watching as he filled the glass carafe. "What are you doing?"

"What does it look like I'm doing?"

"I would say making coffee, except that doesn't make any sense." Eva moved in a little closer, stealing a little of the clean, masculine scent surrounding him.

Part of her wanted Brock to find her as appealing as she found him. Maybe simply to have a man see her as something besides a threat. A—what was it her last mark called her?

That's right. A nosy cunt.

And to be fair he wasn't wrong about half of that. She was nosy. Everyone had secrets they buried as deep as they could.

And she was a bloodhound, ready and able to find anything and everything, no matter how carefully it was hidden. It was the driving force behind her success.

It also made her a little less than interested in forming any sort of bond with the opposite sex. She'd seen what men kept from the women they supposedly loved and vice versa.

She saw how it ruined lives. Broke strong people down until they were nothing but dust.

Luckily it didn't seem like Brock had any interest in the sort of bad decisions a man like him made a girl more than happy to make.

That meant all she had to do was continue to be herself. Clearly Brock found her irritating, which was perfect. It meant she could continue to sneak peeks and sniffs while imagining all the ways she would never get to know him.

From a safe distance and without risk.

Or reward.

But whatever.

Unless…

"Didn't you say you were a no-strings-attached kinda guy, Broccoli?"

It might actually be the perfect thing to do while she was here, and the fact that Brock lived in Alaska and she lived in Ohio made everything so much more simple. A way to scratch an itch that she was having without worrying she might catch something terrible.

Like feelings.

Except Brock didn't seem to be on board. Not even a little.

His whole body went stiff beside her and the hand gripping the coffee pot's handle tightened until his knuckles turned white.

"So that's a no then." Eva made herself take a step back, but she couldn't stop a sigh of disappointment from slipping out. "I just thought since we were pretending, we might as well—"

Brock turned suddenly and whipped open the fridge, bending as he scanned the appliance from top to bottom.

Like he had to look closer to see it was empty.

"That's what I was saying earlier." Eva leaned back against the counter behind her, working to put a little more physical distance between them. "You ditched me last night before we went to the store."

Brock slammed the fridge shut and wiped one hand down his face. "Get dressed." He shoved the coffee pot back on the maker and turned away, heading for the stairs to the basement. "Dress warm." He turned his head to one side, barely looking at her over his shoulder. "I'm not watching you freeze."

Eva huffed out a breath. "I'm not stupid."

"Says the woman who tried to walk out of the airport without a coat." Brock was already down the stairs, forcing her to chase after him.

"That was before I knew how fucking cold Alaska was." Eva stopped at the top of the stairs, expecting him to turn around. Maybe pause to argue a little more.

Didn't happen.

"They don't really fill you in on the flight." She stomped down the stairs after him, an unexpected flare of aggravation spurring her on.

She might be a little mad he abandoned her last night. Just hid in the basement.

No explanation. No food in the place.

No keys to escape with.

Then again, maybe she was just hungry.

"And you could have maybe been nice to me about it. Said 'Oh, hey Eva. It's fucking cold outside. You might want to put on a coat or something'." She followed him into the theater room, catching up as the lingering frustration that started when she found out she was being shipped here flared to full-fledged anger.

Anger with Mona and Chandler. Anger with whoever was behind the bullshit that was happening back home.

Anger with herself for being upset that Brock found her irritating.

Who the fuck cared what this guy thought? It's not like he even knew her.

50

"But all you do is glower at me." Eva almost ran into his back as Brock stopped abruptly.

Then he turned and leaned in closer. "Glower? What the fuck is a glower?"

"It's a…" All thought left. Her brain was a void.

A word void. Images it was totally still good with.

Images of Broccoli brought on by his closeness.

The glower he was sporting.

Glower. That was it.

"It's a scowl." Her eyes fell to his lips and lingered. "You're always scowling at me because you don't like me."

"I never said I didn't like you." Brock's tone was softer than normal.

Lower.

"You didn't have to." It took everything in her to look him in the eye. "It's fine. I think there's a whole club of men who don't like me."

His eyes sharpened. "A club?"

"Not literally a club." Clearly there wouldn't be an actual organization dedicated to the dislike of her.

Brock stepped closer, his size suddenly feeling much larger than she remembered. "Who doesn't like you, Eva?"

Oh lord it was hard to breathe.

He should not say her name. Not like that anyway. Deep and a little dark.

Especially since Brock made it clear he was not interested in being anything more than a hired watchman.

"Lots of people." Her eyes fell back to his mouth.

How would a man like Broccoli kiss a woman?

Probably like he fucking owned them.

Eva shivered a little at the thought. She'd never been owned by a man. Didn't want to be.

Except maybe in the bedroom, and she would put all her money on the fact that Brock owned whoever he took to his bed.

"I need you to be more specific." Brock moved in a little more, bringing his body within inches of hers. "I want names."

"I don't think the who really matters." Eva's mouth moved on its own, her brain somehow managing to carry on a decently lucid conversation while it conjured up all sorts of coital possibilities involving the man in front of her. "Are you sure you're not up for a no-strings-attached sort of thing?"

Her eyes snapped to his as a low rumble moved through his chest. "You didn't have to fucking growl at me. It was an honest question." Eva's breath caught as Brock closed what was left of the space between them, his body barely ghosting against hers.

"Don't fucking ask me that again, understand?"

Was he mad? He looked a little mad.

But Brock also looked something else.

Something that made her whole body buzz with a warmth she hadn't felt since landing in this frozen tundra.

"But you didn't answer me." She could barely get any volume behind the words because her lungs weren't working just right.

She wanted to touch him. Prove what she saw in his eyes was true.

That he wanted her just as much as she wanted him.

Eva's fingers barely brushed the soft fabric of his shirt before Brock caught her by the wrist, holding her with a solid but gentle touch.

His eyes were dark as they stared into hers. His head barely shook. "Not with you."

Ouch.

That stung.

He used his hold to push her away, toward the stairs. "Go get dressed."

Eva sucked in a breath and straightened her spine before yanking her hand free of his hold. "Fine."

And then she turned and did something she never did.

She ran away, taking the steps two at a time, not slowing until her feet landed on the top floor.

This was stupid. All of it.

Being in Alaska.

Wanting to bed bounce with Broccoli.

Stupid.

Maybe she was just sexually deprived.

Eva snorted. There was no maybe about it.

She peeked down the stairs. Maybe she could sneak into the bathroom for a little one on one time. Take the edge off until Brock barricaded himself back in the basement rather than sleep anywhere close to her.

"Are you dressed yet?" His voice was loud and sharp.

And irritated. Because of course it was.

Her head dropped back and she stared up at the ceiling. "It's been like thirty seconds."

"I'll give you thirty more and then I'm leaving whether you're in the car or not."

"You've got to be—"

"One. Two. Three."

Was he seriously counting?

"Christ." Eva tore through her suitcase and grabbed the first articles of clothing she came across, pulling on a thick pair of fleece pants as she hopped toward the stairs. "You better not leave without me, Broccoli. I'll kill you."

"Fifteen."

Eva bounced down the steps as she tugged her socks on. "You are an ass, has anyone ever told you that?"

Brock's eyes barely sparkled. "You are the first."

"I find that difficult to believe." She dropped her boots to the wood floor and stomped her feet into their fur lining.

"Most people find me charming." Brock's tone carried something surprising.

Humor.

"Are you making a joke, Broccoli?" Eva fought her way into the heavy sweater she carried from upstairs.

"I'm actually being serious."

"Hm." Eva pushed past him. "Charming my ass." Her boots made heavy thumps on the stairs as she went to the basement. She opened the closet door and pulled out her coat.

Brock's eyes narrowed on the parka. "When did you bring that down here?"

"Last night after you ditched me." She smirked up at him.

"You came downstairs?"

Eva nodded.

And maybe peeked in on him sleeping in the theater room.

In his underwear.

Brock was definitely a proportionate man. Not that she'd be getting any personal tours of his proportions.

Which was fine. Better, probably.

"You're glowering at me again." Eva zipped her coat to her chin.

"It's not at you."

She turned to look behind her, which wasn't easy considering all the clothes she was wearing. "I'm the only one here."

Brock took a deep breath before blowing it out loud and long, like she was grinding on the last, tiny, shriveled bit of patience he had left. "You shouldn't have been able to come downstairs."

Son-of -a— "I'm the one paying for this freaking place. I can go wherever the hell I want to."

Brock pinched the bridge of his nose. "I mean, I should have heard you come down the stairs."

She straightened, a little proud she got one over on the bodyguard. "I was quiet."

55

"Doesn't matter." He eyed her. "Why were you so quiet?"

Eva lifted one shoulder and let it drop. She wasn't normally one to hold back on the truth.

Not ever, actually.

But admitting she was trying to see what he'd rather be doing than bothering her seemed a little...

Sneaky.

Which was technically her livelihood, but still.

"I guess I'm just a quiet person."

Brock's laugh caught her completely off guard, making her take a full step back.

"You are the least quiet person I know." He paused. "One of them."

The momentary reprieve from his perpetual frown was gone in an instant. "Come on. Let's go get some coffee before I lose my mind." He pressed one hand into the small of her back and directed her toward the door leading to the garage.

Why did they have to be in Alaska? Why not the Caribbean? Hawaii? Someplace where she would be able to feel where he was touching her.

Skin on skin.

Eva's cheeks heated instantly at the thought.

"Shit." His hand dropped and Brock stepped away, disappearing into the theater room.

Jesus. Was he getting his panties in a bunch over her thoughts now?

Brock was back in under a minute, a tiny plastic baggie in his hand. "I forgot to give this to you."

Eva eyed the small package. "What is it?"

"A ring." Brock pulled open the zipper and turned the contents out into his palm.

Sure enough, it was a damned ring. "What in the hell is that?"

Brock pinched the solitaire between his thumb and first finger and held it up between them. "I believe this is supposed to be your engagement ring."

"I don't think that's necessary." Eva tucked her hands under her armpits.

"I have a file that says it is." Brock held his hand out, palm up. "Come on. I'm hungry."

"I don't want that." Eva stepped away from him.

"I don't care what you want." Brock came closer, stealing back the space she gained. "It's what will keep you safe."

She shook her head. "That's the most ridiculous thing I've ever heard." She pulled one hand free to point at him. "*You're* supposed to be what will keep me safe." She snorted. "Not that it will be very difficult."

There was no one after her. Not really.

Being here was just a precaution.

"It's turning out to be very fucking difficult." Brock caught her outstretched hand and before Eva could stop him, he slipped the ring onto her finger.

They both stared at it.

Finally Eva lifted her hand up. Might as well look at the reminder staring her right in the face.

At least it was pretty.

She moved her hand from side to side, letting the familiar sadness move in and trample any happiness she might have been harboring into dust. "Never thought I'd see that again."

CHAPTER 5

HE SHOULD CALL Shawn. Tell him this wasn't going to work. That someone else would do a better job of keeping Eva safe.

It was probably true.

Because right now all he cared about was who in the hell put a ring on her finger.

"Again?"

"Hmmm?" Her eyes didn't meet his, instead they stayed locked on where he'd slipped the fake diamond in place.

And it grated on him. Eva was thinking of another man.

One who almost had her as his wife.

"You said again. Like you'd been engaged before."

It sounded like he was accusing her of something. Like he thought she'd done something wrong by letting a different man claim her as his.

"I was." Her lips twisted to one side in a half purse that carried an edge of sadness.

And this woman should never be sad. Not ever.

"What happened?"

Eva's eyes finally came to his. "Are you actually trying to have a conversation with me, Broccoli?"

"I just thought maybe it was why you were here. I thought it would be relevant information."

The lie was easy to give her. It was not as easy to digest.

So he chose to ignore it.

"Definitely not why I'm here." She fished a glove out of one pocket and pulled it over the ringed hand. "We just went in different directions. It was a friendly break-up."

A friendly break-up? With this woman?

"Are you positive he thought it was friendly?"

No way would a man walk away from her willingly. Definitely not happily.

Eva frowned at him. "Walter is happily married to another woman with a baby on the way."

"Doesn't mean shit."

"It means he is definitely not the reason I was shipped here to bother you." Eva wiggled the fingers of the other hand into their glove. "Are you ready to go? I haven't eaten since I got on the plane yesterday and I'm going to get real pissy soon."

Goddamnit. "Why didn't you say something?"

"I did. As soon as we got here." She lifted her brows. "And then you ran away and hid from me."

Brock braced one hand on her back and turned her toward the garage, pressing just enough to get her feet moving. "I wasn't hiding."

"You were definitely hiding." Eva resisted as he tried to direct her toward the passenger's side. "Can I drive?"

"No."

Her head barely dipped to one side. "Please? I've been thinking about getting one of these and it would be so nice to try it out in the snow." One hand pressed to her belly. "And it will distract me from how hungry I am."

Guilt. The woman was guilting him.

And it was going to fucking work.

"Fine." Brock pulled open the driver's door and held the keys up, yanking them back as she reached for them. "I will catch shit if someone finds out I let you drive, so be careful."

Her eyes were wide. "Of course I will be careful, Broccoli. I would never want you to get in trouble."

He dropped the keys into her cupped hands. "Don't make me regret trusting you, Tatum."

"Oh. I get a nickname now too." She smiled up at him. "If I didn't know better I would think you were warming up to me."

"You'd be wrong." Brock closed the door on her still-smiling face.

He gritted his teeth as he walked around the front of the Rover and got into his seat.

She faced him, watching his face as she pressed the opener on the garage remote clipped to the visor. "Did you pick the color of it?"

"Of what?"

"Of the car." She pointed out at the cherry red hood. "You don't seem like a red sort of man."

"What kind of man do I seem like?" Women were always very superficial with their descriptions of him.

Which was perfect. Kept things nice and simple.

Exactly how he needed to keep this.

Eva's lips barely curved into a soft smile. "The kind who doesn't really want me to answer that question."

Before he could ask what the hell that meant, Eva tapped the screen on the sound system and music filled the interior as she backed out of the bay, singing along loudly and without shame.

And she was not a good singer.

But it didn't seem to bother her at all as she belted out the lyrics to Mr. Brightside, her head bobbing along with the beat as she eased onto the road.

"Driving in Alaska isn't like driving in Ohio, Eva." Brock shifted in his seat as she accelerated a little faster than he expected.

"How do you know? Have you ever driven in Ohio?" Her fingers tapped against the wheel as the song hit its chorus.

"No." Brock looked up and down the street, checking for any other vehicles that might be in their path.

"Then how do you know it's not exactly like this?" She immediately turned into a small lot in front of a vacant building. It looked like it hadn't been plowed recently, and at least six inches of snow was piled over the pavement.

"What are you doing?"

"Nothing." Eva's eyes slowly slid his way and her lips pressed together. "Hold on tight, Broccoli."

"Eva, no—" He reached for the wheel just as her foot dropped to the floor and the SUV lurched forward, the all terrain tires and 4-wheel drive doing their job expertly.

Her laugh was louder than the music as Eva whipped the Rover around the lot, spinning it out before flooring it and starting all over again, squealing a little each time the SUV threw him in a different direction.

She managed to get out three passes before Brock braced himself against the door with one foot and grabbed the wheel from her. "Enough."

Eva's cheeks were pink and her eyes shined. "That was fantastic."

"That was not fantastic. You could have gotten hurt." He flipped the Rover into park and pressed the button to shut off the engine before taking the fab from the console, shoving open his door and jumping out. When he opened her door, Eva was smirking up at him.

"You weren't far enough away. I could have restarted the engine."

"Out."

"You're no fun." She stood, her eyes staying on his. "None. You are none fun."

She didn't have any clue how fun he could be. "I'm fun."

Eva shook her head slowly. "You're a fun faker." Her eyes slid up and down him. "You fake being fun to avoid being real." Her shoulder bumped his as she stepped around him on her way to the door he left open. She dropped into his vacated seat and belted up. "Come on, Broccoli. I'm hungry."

He didn't want to get in the car with her.

Didn't want to risk Eva seeing anymore than she clearly already had.

Somehow.

But the only other option was to call Shawn and tap out. Send someone else to come protect her.

And that wasn't fucking happening.

He fell into the seat and punched the ignition, shoving the seat back as far as it went before pulling out of the lot.

The Co-op Market was only a few blocks away, and for the first time since he'd met her Eva was completely silent.

Which bothered him.

"I'm sorry I yelled at you."

"No you're not." She didn't sound pouty or upset. Just said it like it was a simple fact.

"We could have rolled over and you could have gotten hurt." Brock stared down the light as he waited to turn into the lot.

He could feel her eyes on him and braced for whatever would come out of her mouth next.

"Why are you only worried about me getting hurt?" The question was soft. Hesitant.

Nothing like this woman.

But the question itself was enough to grab him by the throat and drag him back to reality.

To remind him why he was the way he was.

"Because it's my job to worry about you getting hurt."

That was the only reason her safety mattered to him. Had to be.

Otherwise he was fucked, and he'd worked too hard to let that happen.

Brock drove into the parking lot, easing past a dark sedan with tinted windows idling near the sidewalk, most likely waiting to retrieve someone inside. He pulled into a spot and got out of the SUV as fast as he could, hoping the cold air would stun his rational brain back into place.

Eva was out of the car and halfway to the store before he finally started walking. He needed to put distance between them. Literal and figurative.

But mostly literal, because this woman could close in on him without warning. Dig her way into his mind and under his skin with nothing but off-tune singing and a smile.

It was fucking terrifying.

She was already shopping when he walked inside, her cart full of the most random assortment of items he'd ever seen. Not that he would have expected any less from her.

"What kind of stuff do you like to eat, Broccoli?" She didn't even look his way. Not even a peek.

"None of what you have in that cart."

Her gaze went to the cart, skimming over the mish-mash of produce stacked inside. "Not even bananas?"

"No one should eat bananas. They're disgusting." He stepped closer, expecting the move to turn her attention his way.

"What did bananas ever do to you?" Her eyes skipped right past him on their way to the display of organic vegetables.

"Puked them up in third grade. Haven't eaten one since."

She finally looked his way. "So something wrongs you once and it's dead to you. Interesting."

"That's not what I—"

She pulled a crown of broccoli free from the stack and stuffed it into a plastic bag, holding it up, her brows lifted in question.

Brock shook his head.

"Didn't think so." She dropped it into the cart next to a clamshell of blueberries and a container of some sort of brown nuggety-looking things. "Cannibalism." She snorted before breaking into a full-on belly laugh.

"Glad you think you're funny."

"You think I'm funny too. You just won't admit it." She spun the cart around and pushed it away, leaving him once again lost in her wake.

Brock followed behind her, occasionally grabbing an item and tossing it into the cart. Eva leaned in to look at each one before going back to her own shopping.

"Stop it."

Once again she didn't even look his way, just squinted at the box of tea in her hand. "I'm not doing anything."

"You know damn well you are." He stepped closer. She should look at him when she talked to him.

At least pay a little attention to him.

"If you don't want me to look at what you're getting then you should get your own basket." She tossed the tea in and pushed the cart away.

This time he didn't stay behind.

Brock paced his steps with hers, sticking close enough she couldn't ignore him.

She did it anyway.

Ignored him all the way through the rest of the store and down the checkouts.

Eva smiled at the cashier and chatted up the bagger, giving them each one of her bright, honest smiles before going out into the lot.

Brock unlocked the SUV and moved in to take the cart from her. "Get in."

"I don't trust you to treat my bananas with the respect they deserve." Eva bumped him with her hip, knocking him out of the way as she reached to open the hatch.

Brock grabbed the bags four at a time and tossed them in the back. It was too cold out here. She wasn't used to it.

"See. I was right." Eva grabbed for the bag he was about to chuck in with the rest. Her hand wrapped around his, the cold tips of her fingers pressing tight into his skin as she tried to tug the bag away.

He didn't let go.

"Why don't you have your gloves on?"

"Because this should have only taken a second." She pulled at the bag again.

"It would have taken even less than that if you'd gotten in the car like I told you to." Brock yanked the bag, knowing she wouldn't let go.

Eva didn't disappoint him. Her grip stayed firm even as she fell toward him, thrown off balance.

Brock was ready to catch her before her body hit his.

He pulled her in close, pretending it was all to keep her steady.

But she wasn't the only one off-balance right now.

Whether he wanted to admit it or not, he was playing a dangerous game. One where winning could mean suffering a devastating loss.

"Why are you so damn difficult?" Brock stared down at her, letting himself soak in the flush of her cold-pinkened cheeks and the hint of desire in her unreal eyes. Just for a second.

Tires crunched through the lot around them.

An engine hummed in the distance.

Brock barely lifted his eyes to the spot just above Eva's head.

The same car that was parked in the lot when they arrived sat at one side of the store, barely visible from where they stood.

"Who are you hiding from, Eva?"

She barely edged closer to him, trying to turn her head to look the same way he was. "I'm not hiding from anyone."

Brock braced one hand on the back of her head, keeping her from giving them away. "Don't turn, Sunshine.

"Sunshi—"

"Shh." Brock pulled her tighter against him, fighting the urge to spin Eva away, block her body with his. "Just relax. Everything is okay."

"Everything is not okay if you're acting like this."

"I need you to be quiet right now." Brock moved his lips into a smile, making it seem like this was nothing more than a man holding the woman he cared about close while they shared a private conversation.

"What is happ—"

She wasn't going to be quiet. It was never going to happen.

And he was supposed to be her fiancé. The man she came to Alaska for.

"I'm sorry, Tatum, but you're going to have to roll with this." He fisted her hair, using the hold to tug her head back just enough to line her lips with his for a quick kiss. One that would make anyone who might be watching think this was all it was supposed to be.

But the second her mouth touched his, all plans for a quick peck fell around him like fresh snow. Silently drifting down to stack against every other plan he had since Eva landed in his life.

And then she sighed, her soft breath warm against his cheek as her body molded to his.

He was gone. Lost to something he'd sworn never to want.

Never to need.

A woman.

He turned her from the idling car, putting his back to whoever might be behind the tinted windows. They would have to go through him to get to her. Better they know it now.

And he would put up a hell of a fight. The world needed more women like Eva Tatum, and he'd be damned if he let anyone take her.

Her cool fingers speared into his hair, pulling him down as she pushed up, reaching for him as her mouth opened under his.

Brock held her tighter, breathed her in. She tasted like nothing he could describe and everything he didn't want to have. Sweet and soft and perfect.

But he couldn't enjoy it the way he wanted, because the rumble of the engine behind him was closer, joined by the gritty crunch of tires over pressed snow.

Brock tore his mouth from hers, fighting to keep his calm in spite of the barrage of emotions battering his insides. As the car slowly coasted past, he turned, blocking her from view as he directed Eva toward the passenger's side. "I need you to get in the car and stay there no matter what happens, okay?"

She nodded, the fingers of one hand coming to press against her kiss-swollen lips.

But damn he wanted to pull her close again. Replace her fingers with his mouth and pick back up where they left off.

He opened the door and tucked her into the car before quickly closing her in. He walked slowly to the other side as the car parked a few spaces down and two men got out. Their eyes met his.

He nodded. Gave them an easy grin. "Morning."

They both nodded back. Gave him the same calm smile he offered them. The driver rubbed his gloved hands together. "It's a cold one, isn't it?"

"They all are." Brock took in everything about them as they passed. Filed it all away. "Stay warm."

"Will do." The men walked at an even, measured pace toward the store, no pausing, no slowing.

They were barely inside when Brock started the engine and slowly pulled out of the lot.

"What in the hell was that?" Eva rubbed her lips together as she stared at him with wide eyes.

"We're supposed to be engaged, remember?"

"I was talking about you peacocking out there." She twisted in her seat to look back at the store. "Who were those two guys?"

Brock turned in the opposite direction of the house Eva rented, his mind running a mile a minute.

This whole game just changed.

In more ways than one.

Brock touched the screen of the SUV, moving through the options until he found what he was looking for. He tapped the icon before turning his attention to Eva.

"I'm guessing they were here for you."

CHAPTER 6

NO WAY.

"They were probably just guys." Eva craned her neck as the grocery store slipped out of sight. "Just normal guys grabbing lunch."

This was all just a stupid coincidence.

There wasn't ever any real threat.

"I'm sure it's nothing." She turned to face out the windshield, staring straight ahead as a line rang across the speakers of the Rover.

"Hey, man."

Eva glanced at the screen. "He has a nice voice."

The man labeled Dutch laughed low and deep across the line. "So do you."

"Shut up, Dutch." Brock's tone was sharper than she'd heard it before, even in the face of what he believed were two men looking for her. "I think we have two."

"At the house?" Dutch sounded as skeptical as Eva was sure she was.

"At the Co-op. They are definitely trained."

Trained. "What's that mean?"

Brock ignored her. "They're in a black Charger with tinted windows. I've got the plates for you to run."

"They following you?" The tone of Dutch's voice shifted in an instant.

"Not yet." Brock glanced in the rearview. "See if there are any cameras set up around the store. I want to see when they got there."

"You sure they didn't follow you there?"

Brock's hands tightened on the wheel. "That's why I want you to check for footage."

"Will do." Dutch's words were clipped. "You're not taking her back to the house until we're sure it's clear, right?"

"But we have all that food in the back." Eva leaned into the screen. "We have groceries. We have to go back to the house."

Was he laughing?

"Why don't you come to headquarters? Shawn and I are here for the foreseeable future." He paused. "And there's room in the fridge in the break room for whatever you need to store, Ms. Tatum."

"We're on our way." Brock tapped the screen, disconnecting the call.

"Headquarters?" Eva ignored the urge to look out the back window again.

No one was there. Thinking anything different was just silly.

Lightning didn't strike the same place twice. The chances of her having another crazy stalker were slim to none.

"It's the main campus for all of Alaskan Security." Brock glanced in the mirror again.

"I didn't expect bodyguards would have an office."

"First of all, we're a security company."

"And second?"

Brock's eyes came to hers and she could swear he almost smiled. "Second, why wouldn't we have an office?"

Eva shrugged. "I guess I just didn't think about it."

But now that she was thinking about it.

"How's the internet there?" Just because she wasn't in her own office didn't mean Eva planned to completely neglect her work duties. There were too many open jobs, and Mona and Chandler were already covered up trying to figure out who was behind the odd happenings that landed her here.

"I'm sure it's fine." Brock turned into an office park. The buildings lining the street were all similarly built. Clean, straight lines with warm brick exteriors that kept them from being too industrial-looking.

They were nice. Alaskan Security must be doing decently well.

Eva read the signs as they passed. Most were medical related. A few were services. Two lawyers.

And then the buildings ended, the last one butting right against a heavy tree line.

A large gate blocked the road in front of them. Brock pulled up to a small box and rolled down his window before flipping up the plexiglass lid and punching six numbers into the keypad underneath.

The heavy metal barrier slid to the right as Brock dropped the cover into place and rolled the window up.

"Where are we?" Eva leaned forward as they started moving again, passing through the gate and between the line of trees so thick it was impossible to see anything but the spot directly in front of them.

"Headquarters." He glanced her way as a row of buildings came into view. "Not what you expected?"

Eva didn't answer him. She was too busy looking out the windshield at the cluster of modern craftsman-style structures in front of them. One was larger than all the others, standing three stories tall with large windows that reflected the snowy landscape.

Two smaller versions flanked each side with a covered walkway connecting them to the main building.

She pushed open her door and stepped out to get a better look. "Christ!" Eva yanked her coat tighter. "It's so fucking cold here."

Brock was there a second later, stepping close, wrapping one arm around her. "Come on."

"What about the food?" Eva tried to drag her feet. "I don't want my berries to freeze. They'll taste like shit."

"I will take care of it." Brock kept her feet moving, picking up the pace as her teeth started to chatter.

Another keypad was beside the set of glass doors. Brock punched in a set of numbers and the locks clicked open. He held her close as they moved into the warm air of the building.

Eva sucked in a breath, trying to contain the running of her nose.

"Hey there."

A tiny dark-haired woman with glasses and a smirk was propped against the large desk dominating the space. A tall insulated cup was in her hands, held close to her chest.

"Shit." Brock barely whispered the curse under his breath.

"Who's your friend?" The woman pushed off the desk and walked their way.

Eva looked between the two of them. There was something happening and the woman clearly found it very amusing.

Brock, not so much.

"I'm Eva Tatum." She reached one hand out to the brunette. "I'm his current pain in the ass."

The woman's smile widened. "That is fantastic." She gripped Eva's hand, but instead of shaking it she pulled her in close, tugging her away from Brock. "I'm Harlow. You want some coffee?"

Eva glanced at Brock. "Um. I have some groceries that I should probably get out of the car."

Harlow waved her coffee around. "The boys'll get it." She looked to one of the open halls at each end of the room just as a group of men came in. "Hey." Harlow jerked her chin in the direction of the parking lot. "Go get Eva's food out of the red Rover."

"Always happy to help a lady out." One of the men shot her a grin and a wink as they passed.

"Pretty sure this one isn't for you, Tyson." Harlow sipped at her coffee and pulled Eva with the hand still holding hers. "Come on. Let's go find someplace comfortable."

When Eva glanced back Brock was watching her with a steady gaze, hands tucked in the pockets of his coat.

"He'll be fine. Dutch and Shawn are waiting for him. They have things they want to talk about."

Eva peeked into every open door they passed. "This place is huge."

"Right? Who knew there was any place like this in freaking Alaska?" Harlow pulled her through an open doorway into a huge room. A kitchen sat at one end with a table and chairs right beside it. A large sectional and a few armchairs sat in front of a line of windows overlooking a large body of water backed by distant mountains.

"Wow." Eva stared out at the beautiful scene. So far she'd seen very little of Fairbanks. "I didn't realize how pretty it was here."

"I hear ya." Harlow dropped her hand, leaving Eva at the windows while she went to the kitchen. "I was shocked as hell."

"You're not from here?" Eva struggled to tear her eyes from the view, eventually managing.

"Hell no." Harlow had a mug out and was pouring in coffee from a full pot. "How do you take this?"

"Black."

Harlow's brows went up as she nodded. "Nice. I'm impressed." She walked the cup to Eva. "I have to doctor the shit out of mine so I can drink it."

"Nothing wrong with that." Eva took a healthy gulp of the beverage.

"You hungry?" Harlow went back to the kitchen and started fishing around the commercial-grade fridge. "I think we got some pulled pork. Maybe lunch meat for a sandwich."

"I'm a vegetarian."

Harlow straightened, letting the door swing shut. "In that case we have to wait for the boys to bring in your stuff."

"Who are the boys?" Eva moved to sit at the island separating the kitchen from the rest of the room.

"The team." Harlow eyed her. "Brock hasn't told you about the team?"

Eva shook her head. "Brock's not a very chatty guy."

Harlow blinked a few times. "Brock?"

"Delivery." The men from earlier came in, each one carrying a bag.

"It took all of you to bring that in?" Harlow watched as they set the bags on the counter and went to work unpacking the refrigerated items.

"We didn't want to be rude." One of the men grinned Eva's way. "Brock wouldn't want us to ignore his new friend, would he?"

Harlow snorted. "I think that might be exactly what he wants you to do." She smiled. "Which is why I'm so glad you're not." She pointed to the tallest of the men. The one who thought she was a lady. "That's Tyson." Her finger moved down the line. "That's Reed, Nate and Abe." She lifted her brows at them. "And they're all supposed to be getting their physicals right now."

"Eli had to take an emergency." Tyson leaned against the counter. "Said he'd page us when he was finished."

"Shit." Harlow looked down the row of men. "Who's hurt?"

"Someone on Alpha Team." Tyson peeked in one of the bags. "I think it's minor."

Harlow snorted. "Your idea of minor and my idea of minor are two different things."

A low hum buzzed around them as each man slid a phone from his pocket.

"And it sounds like Eli is ready for you." Harlow pointed at the door. "Go. Leave me and my friend alone."

Eva stared at the small woman.

Harlow watched as they left, waiting until they were out of sight before turning back to Eva. "Let's get some food and take it back to my office. I've gotta try to find those cameras Brock's all wound up about." She pulled out all the fruit smiling wider at each container. "Thank God. I was worried with Bess gone I would be stuck with all these carnivores and only fed steak and sausage." Her eyes snapped to Eva's. "I didn't mean that the way it sounded." She let out a long sigh. "It's been a long damn time since I've had good sausage."

"Same." Eva stood from her stool and helped fill one of the bags with some of the easier to eat foods.

"Really?" Harlow glanced at the door. "How long is a long time to you?"

Eva thought back. "Ugh. Like a year."

Harlow lifted a finger. "So, you've been alone in a house with Brock Cassidy and you still haven't had sex in a year?"

"What's going on?"

They both looked Brock's way.

"I'm finally getting fed." Eva shoved a tray of hummus into the sack along with a bag of pita chips.

Brock studied Eva for a second before turning to Harlow. "Dutch wants to know if you found those feeds yet."

Harlow's head dropped back and she groaned. "Maybe Dutch should find the damn feeds himself."

Another man stepped into the room behind Brock. He wasn't short, but standing next to Brock made him look that way. His brown hair was slicked to one side and his short beard was neatly lined and trimmed close. "We hired you to help Dutch, Mowry. If you're not going to do it then I'm going to have to find the second best hacker." The man's voice sounded familiar. "And I really don't want to do that."

"Whatever." Harlow rolled her eyes at him before turning to Eva. "Come to my office before you leave." She grinned. "Maybe you can come back and hang out tomorrow."

"Not happening." Brock's answer came before Harlow was even finished talking.

She didn't even glance his way. "Not talking to you, Cassidy." Harlow grabbed her in a quick hug. "We girls gotta stick together with all this testosterone trying to choke us to death."

Brock grabbed the bag of food with one hand and pressed the other to the small of Eva's back, easing her out of the room and into the long hall before turning the opposite way that she came in.

"Who's the team?" Eva peeked into what looked to be a board room.

"We can talk about it later." Brock directed her into the next door on her right.

"What if I want to talk about it now?"

"We have other things to discuss right now." The man with the short beard came into the room right behind them. He offered his hand. "I'm Shawn. We spoke on the phone."

Eva took his hand. "Eva."

"I ran those plates, Brock."

She spun just as yet another man appeared. "You're the guy with the nice voice."

He shot her a devastatingly handsome grin. "I am."

"Shut it." Brock stepped between them, blocking her view of Dutch with his broad body. "We need to talk."

"We?" Eva looked around the room. "Who is we?"

"All of us." Shawn answered her question as he sat beside Dutch and motioned to the chair across the long conference table from them.

"So it's me against you guys?" Eva grabbed the chair and pulled it out, sitting down before Shawn could answer.

If he thought she was the kind of woman intimidated by facing down three men, then Shawn was about to find out he was real fucking wrong.

She set her elbows on the table edge and folded her hands.

This was her arena. Her strength.

"What is it you would like to discuss?"

Dutch and Shawn exchanged glances.

"Told you." Brock yanked out the chair next to hers and dropped into it, scooting it in close at her side.

Eva watched him get situated. "You told them what?"

Brock draped one arm across the back of her seat as his lips pulled into a barely-there smile. "I told them they better bring their A-game in here." He leaned in close enough she was the only one who could hear his next words. "Make me proud, Tatum."

Of all the things he could have said, somehow he came up with the one that would fluster her.

Why would he ever be proud of her?

Why should she care if he was?

"The information we were given on your case seems to be pretty bare bones." Shawn flipped open a file and scanned the pages inside. "No specifics about the threats you received. No police records associated with them. No potential culprit." He closed the file and slapped his hand on top. "Nothing."

"Because it's completely irrelevant information." Eva leaned back in her seat, but bumped into Brock's arm which sent her sitting straight up again. "You were hired to make sure I was safe from whatever."

"We need to know what that is." Brock's tone was significantly softer than Shawn's. "What happened that made you come here?"

"Nothing serious." Eva looked around the faces of the men at the table with her. "I didn't even need to come here. I would have been just fine." She grabbed the bag Brock brought in and pulled out the hummus.

"Why are you here then?" Shawn watched as she shoveled in pita chips piled with dip.

"Because my business partners made me." Eva blocked her chewing with one hand. If they wanted to talk now they were just going to have to watch her eat while they did it. "They are blowing shit way out of proportion."

"Does this have to do with that guy who stalked you in college?" Harlow's voice sent her spinning toward the doorway. The other woman shot her a grin. "You didn't think I'd leave you in here all by yourself, did you?" She flopped down in the seat at Eva's other side, sliding her laptop onto the table in front of her. "He was pretty freaking crazy."

"He was confused." Eva corrected the assumption. "He believed I wanted a relationship with him and I didn't." She lifted her shoulders. "That's all."

"It doesn't usually require a protective order to convince a man you're not interested, though." Harlow tapped on her keyboard. "It looks like it just expired too." She turned her computer around for Shawn and Dutch to look at.

"Got it." Dutch was staring at his own screen.

Eva shifted in her seat. "Stop." She stood and reached for Dutch's computer. "That's none of your business."

"You paid a lot of money for this to be our business, Ms. Tatum." Shawn's expression was impassive. He was sitting there like this was all perfectly above-board.

"I paid a lot of money for you to make sure nothing weird happened, not for you to go digging through my past." She leaned forward and made another grab for Dutch's laptop.

He scooted it away. "Looks like the guy was convicted of menacing, stalking, breaking and entering, and theft."

"Stop it." Eva shoved her chair back, planning to go around the table.

"Throw this at him." Harlow slid the container of hummus closer.

"What? No. I want that." Eva grabbed her food and held it close to her chest.

"Hmm." Harlow eyed her. "I pegged you as a thrower." She went back to her own computer. "Don't worry. I won't hold it against you."

"A thrower?" Eva thought this was going to be her game to play, but these people were nothing like the ones she was used to dealing with.

"Sometimes you just gotta throw something to get your point across." Harlow glanced up. "Are you gonna go fight them or are you going to sit your ass back down so we can figure this out?"

Eva glanced at Dutch and Shawn.

Harlow started cackling beside her. "You actually had to think about it." She wiped at one of her eyes. "I love it."

"Sit down, Eva." Brock was standing beside her. When did he get up?

He gently took the container of hummus from her and set it back on the table. "I know this feels invasive, but we have to know what we're dealing with." His eyes rested on hers. "I need to know who I'm protecting you from."

Eva's belly flipped at the thought of Brock as her protector, which was silly.

There was nothing to protect her from. It was all ridiculous.

"Fine."

She flopped back into her seat.

"When I was in college a guy at school broke into my apartment and stole all my panties."

CHAPTER 7

HARLOW'S HEAD SNAPPED to Eva. "Holy shit. Were they expensive?"

Brock stared at her. "That's what you're worried about?"

Harlow lifted one hand, palm up. "Do you have any idea how much panties cost?"

"They were nice ones." Eva held up her thumb and finger about an inch apart. "The kind with the lace band around the top."

"Thongs?"

Eva looked like Harlow slapped her. "I don't hate myself."

Harlow wrapped one arm around Eva's shoulders. "You are my favorite person right now."

"Did you get them back?"

Harlow's eyes snapped to Shawn. "First, don't pretend you're part of this conversation. Second, ew. He probably whacked all over them."

Shawn pinched the bridge of his nose. "I wasn't asking out of concern. I was asking to find out if she knew what he did with them."

"He whacked all over them." Eva's head bobbed in a nod. "I didn't want them back."

Brock grabbed Eva's chair and pulled it closer to his. Hearing what had gone on when she was younger made him edgy.

Harlow leaned to look at him around Eva. "Just because you sucked her face in a parking lot doesn't make her yours."

Eva's body stiffened. "That was because of those guys."

Harlow snorted. "I saw it. It was definitely not because of those guys."

"Can we get back to the guy from college?" Shawn leaned into the table, eyes on Eva. "How did you know him?"

"I didn't."

"You didn't?"

Eva shook her head. "No. He was just some guy who'd seen me around I guess. Decided I should want to date him."

Shawn's eyes met Brock's.

"Do you think he knows where you are now?"

"Like now, now?" Eva tapped one finger on the table with each word.

"Like in Cincinnati. Do you think he knows where you are in Ohio?"

"I don't know. Maybe. I'm listed on the website for Investigative Resources." She shook her head. "There's no way what happened was him."

Shawn didn't miss a beat. "What happened?"

Eva sighed. "I was getting things left on my porch."

"Things?" Brock scooted his chair even closer to hers, glaring at Harlow as he did, daring her to say anything.

"Nothing big. Like flowers. Sometimes food and clothes and stuff."

"Panties?" Harlow sounded almost hopeful and it was impossible to tell if it was because she was hoping to confirm it was the same guy, or because she was hoping everything was right in the world of missing panties.

"Like a shirt, or something." Eva's answer sounded off.

"What kind of shirt?" Brock tipped his head, trying to catch her moving gaze.

"It was a shirt for a music group I like."

She was being purposefully evasive.

"What group?" He already knew the answer. Felt it to his bones.

"New Kids on the Block."

Brock dropped back, wiping one hand down his face. "Christ."

"Don't give her shit for liking them." Harlow's eyes narrowed on him. "They were huge."

"I don't care that she fucking likes them." Brock leaned in close. "For the love of God, tell me it wasn't the shirt you were wearing when I picked you up at the airport."

Eva's eyes moved over his face. "How do you remember what I was wearing?"

"Shit." He wanted to drag her away, hide her somewhere she would be safe from herself. "Someone left a shirt on your porch and you've been wearing it around?"

"Not around. Just at home." Her brows lifted. "I washed it a bunch of times first."

"I don't care how many times you washed it." He was burning that fucking shirt the second they got back to the house. "You can't use gifts from stalkers."

"It's vintage!"

"So you potentially accepted a gift from the man who stalked you five years ago?" At least Shawn was struggling just as much as he was with this.

"No." Eva looked from Shawn to Brock. "It's clearly not the same guy. One took my shit, one brings me shit. Two totally different things."

Harlow was watching the whole interaction with her pen braced between her teeth. Finally she tossed it onto the table. "So I feel really bad right now, but I gotta side with them on this." She shook her head. "This is probably the same guy." Her head tipped to one side. "But your ability to rationalize this shit away is impressive as hell."

"It's not rationalizing. I'm just looking at it all objectively." Eva touched both hands to the table gently, bouncing them as she spoke. "When I got a protection order Howard backed off immediately. He got the point. He realized I wasn't interested in him, and I'm sure the same thing will happen with this."

"Howard didn't want to go to fucking jail is what happened." Harlow blew out a breath. "Let's see where good old Howard is living now."

"It's not Howard." Eva's eyes moved to Brock. "It's not Howard." Her assertion sounded more like a plea now.

"It's probably Howard." Harlow didn't look away from her computer. "But that's good news. He went away once, he'll probably go away again."

Suddenly Eva straightened in her seat. "If it's Howard, then who were those guys at the store?" She smiled wide.

Like somehow this revelation was a better option.

"Maybe they're not involved at all." Harlow looked up at Dutch. "Did you run the plates on the Charger?"

"Stolen."

Eva's attention fixed on Dutch. "They were stolen?"

He nodded. "Reported this morning."

Shawn and Dutch shared a knowing look.

"That would definitely make this more interesting." Harlow tapped her pen as she rocked back in her seat.

Eva's smile slipped. "What would?"

"Those guys might not have been after you at all." Harlow closed her computer and stood up.

"That's good." Eva let out a breath and went in for another pita chip.

"Not really." Harlow scooted behind Eva's seat.

"Why, not really?" Eva dragged her chip through the hummus she refused to throw at Dutch.

"Because it means they were probably after Brock."

****

"I DON'T UNDERSTAND why someone would be after you." Eva hadn't stopped staring at him since they got in the Rover.

"It's complicated." Brock forced his attention to stay on the road. He couldn't look at her. Not right now.

"Do they know where we're staying?"

We're. He didn't miss the way she put them on the same team. He also couldn't miss the way it sat in his gut. Warm and solid. Grounding

"Probably."

"So why in the hell would we go back there?"

"Because we have to." He knew Eva was as smart as she was quirky, but until this afternoon Brock hadn't realized just how similar her skills were to Harlow's.

Eva was the digger of dirt. The revealer of scandal.

And didn't like having the tables turned on her one bit.

She leaned in closer. "Are these people dangerous?"

"Very."

If Harlow was right, it was going to be nearly impossible to tease out one issue from the other.

"And we're just supposed to go back and sit there like ducks?"

"We're supposed to go back and act like we think everything is connected to you." Brock passed the beat-up van parked a few houses down the street.

Tyson and Nate were already in place, eyes and ears on the townhouse. As they coasted by, his phone started to ring over the speakers. He connected the call. "All good?"

"Everything's clear. We did a sweep. If anyone's been inside they didn't leave a trace."

"Good." Brock turned into the small drive and punched the button on the opener, pulling in and shutting off the engine as he sent the door back into place.

Eva sat perfectly still, staring out the windshield at the blank cement wall.

"Everything is going to be okay. I promise."

She nodded. "I know."

He wanted to reach for her. Find a way to calm her fears. Help her understand he would never let anything happen to her.

Before he could, she was out of the car and at the back, opening the hatch and grabbing the groceries they bought what felt like forever ago.

Eva was silent as they went inside and put everything away.

Didn't say a word as she lined a few ingredients down the counter and pulled out a pan.

"Talk to me, Eva. Tell me what you're thinking." The mind was a powerful thing, and hers was running wild right now. Brock could see it in her eyes. Probably coming up with all sorts of scary scenarios and dangerous possibilities.

He didn't want her to be scared.

She stood very still, one hand on the knob to the gas cooktop, her socked foot tapping silently on the floor. Finally she turned to him.

"Was Harlow right?"

"I don't know. She and Dutch will do everything they can to figure out who those men were." Brock stepped a little closer, the need to comfort her growing stronger with each passing second.

Eva was away from home. Away from her friends and family.

Thought she was alone.

She barely shook her head as he reached her side. "That's not what I was talking about."

"Wha—"

"When you kissed me. Was it because of those men?" There was no hesitation in the question. None.

He shouldn't give her the truth. So much was already on the line, dragged there by a stalker-shirt-wearing, off-key-singing, bringer of metaphorical death. "Partly."

"What was the other reason?" Her lips rolled in, sliding against each other, reminding him of how they felt against his. Soft and warm and—

Fucking right.

"Because I had to." He'd kissed many, many women.

Always because he wanted to.

None of them were like this one.

None of them made him *need*.

"That's the same thing." She turned back to the stove, clicking on the flame before putting her pan over the heat.

Dismissing him.

"It's not even close to the same thing." Brock moved closer, craving her attention. Wanting it.

Maybe needing it.

"You had to kiss me so those guys thought we were together. I get it. It's fine." She drizzled a little olive oil into the pan.

"Is it fine?" Brock caught a bit of dark hair falling over one of her eyes and tucked it behind one ear.

"Of course it's fine." She grabbed a handful of pale white cubes of something or other and tossed it into the hot pan. "Why wouldn't it be fine?"

"Because you want me to kiss you again." He traced the shell of her ear with one finger. "Don't you, Eva?"

"I have no opinion on that." Her eyes stayed locked on the pan of food, never veering his way.

He continued the touch, dragging the tip of his pointer to the soft skin just behind her ear. Sliding over the dip just below her lobe. Down the line of her neck. "Tell me you want me to kiss you, Eva."

"No." She aggressively stirred the contents of the pan.

"Say it." Brock grabbed the handle of the pan and slid it off the heat, catching her wrist as she reached for it and dragging her closer.

He'd listened to all the fucking stupid ways she'd put herself in danger. The threats Eva minimized until they were small enough she could handle them.

Heard her rationalize everything away.

And all it made him think of was all the times she could have been hurt. Maybe worse.

The thought of anything bad happening to her sat hard and heavy in his belly, burning for more reasons than Brock was ready to deal with right now.

He looped her arm around his neck and laced his fingers into her hair, the soft strands sliding over his skin like silk.

"I don't like being kissed out of obligation, Brock." Her face was twisted into a scowl. "I understand why you did it, but I think it's best it doesn't happen again."

"I disagree." Brock lined her body against his.

Her ringed eyes stared up at him. "Why are you doing this?"

She was giving him every opportunity to come to his senses, and that's exactly what he should do. Back away from the woman changing the fabric of his life with every breath she took. Do what it took to keep her safe and then let her go before it would be an impossible task.

But it might already be too late for that.

"I think you know exactly why I'm doing this."

Eva's eyes narrowed. "You don't have any idea what I know."

He reached out to trace a line that started at the center of her forehead and ended at the tip of her nose. No woman ever looked at him like she did. She could be considering him naked one second and contemplating punching him the next. "Why did you ask me if I was interested in a casual fuck?"

Her lips pursed. "I don't know."

"Liar." He twisted the knob on the stove, killing the flame. "You thought we could have a little fun while you were here, and then you could go right back to business as usual and never give me a second thought."

Isn't that what he'd done for so many years? What he claimed to want to continue to do?

And would be doing if Bess and Parker hadn't come along and fucked him all up.

Made him want what he knew would kill him.

And Eva was only making it worse.

"A few months ago I would have taken you up on it, you know that? I would have had you under me before you took your next breath." Brock pushed against her body, pressing Eva away from the cooktop and toward the corner where two lines of cabinets met, boxing her in. "But now I can't." He braced her body, careful not to press her into the edge of the counter. "And it's driving me fucking crazy."

The whole damn thing was making him crazy.

She was making him lose his mind.

"Why couldn't you just be like everyone else? Why couldn't you have just been another woman?" He spread his hands across her back, sliding one up and one down, groaning as more of her body pressed into his. "Why did it have to be you?"

"What are you talking about?" She sounded genuinely confused. Like she really didn't know how irresistible she was.

How addicting.

One damn day. It was all it took for her to make him question everything.

Make him consider if the risk was worth the reward.

Because Eva Tatum might be one hell of a reward.

His hand fisted into the heavy mass of her long hair, holding on. "Let me kiss you again."

Her head barely shook. "I don't think it's a good idea."

Brock was positive it was a bad idea.

Maybe the worst he'd ever had.

Because the more he got of her, the more he wanted.

The more he needed.

And needing a woman could kill him. Leave him a dead man walking.

But for the first time in his life Brock didn't care.

"I didn't ask if you thought it was a good idea, I asked for permission to do it again."

Her eyes dropped to his lips. "You didn't ask last time."

"Last time I did what had to be done to keep you safe." Brock traced the line of her jaw with one finger. "Let me kiss you, Eva."

"Does this mean you want to have a friends with benefits sort of thing after all?"

He shook his head. "We're not friends."

She deflated a little. "Oh. So just the benefits, then?"

He couldn't help but smile at her. He'd been so worried about his own lines he hadn't noticed Eva was trying to lay down a few between them herself. "If you want benefits then I'd be happy to give them to you."

Her breath caught just a little as his fingers trailed down her neck and over her collarbone, sliding along the neckline of her sweater. "What kind of benefits are we talking about?"

"No fucking." He didn't mean for it to sound so abrupt, but fucking this woman right out of the gate just seemed wrong.

Too fast.

And he'd lived a life of being fast. Always skipping straight to the act, moving fast enough there was nothing to feel.

Nothing to want.

But Eva made him want to slow down. Savor every bit of his time with her.

Memorize the curve of her shoulder. The soft slip of her hair through his hands.

"It doesn't sound very beneficial of an arrangement then." Her hands stayed clasped between them, fingers laced tightly together. "I think I'll pass."

Brock froze. "You think you'll pass?"

Eva nodded. "Probably not worth it if there's no penetration."

CHAPTER 8

BROCK HADN'T SAID a word in a very long time.

Just stared at her.

The vein in the side of his head throbbing a little more with each passing second.

Eva stood tall. She learned a long time ago most people didn't appreciate her straightforward tendencies, and Brock appeared to fall into that category.

Oh, motherfreaking well.

"What's a matter, Broccoli? You look a little upset."

"Not upset, Sunshine. Just working real hard to find a way to give you what you're asking for." He inhaled long and loud before leaning down, eye to eye, hands holding onto the counter at her sides. "Define penetration."

"If you don't know what penetration is then I'm not interested at all anymore."

"Why do you keep lying to me?"

"I don't lie." She snapped it out at him. It was the reason she was like she was.

Because everyone lied, and saying exactly what she meant made her different.

The sins she saw and bathed in every day were never her own.

Eva pushed off the counter, crowding him. "If you don't know how to properly fuck a woman then I take my offer back."

Brock didn't back down. Didn't look the least bit intimidated by a move that had made countless men shrivel over the years. A strong woman could be a terrifying thing. Especially one who knew what she was and owned it.

"Define penetration, Eva."

She pointed in his face. "If you think you can finger bang me and I'll be satisfied then you are very wrong, Brock Cassidy." She stabbed at him. "I'm not some little girl dying for a boy's attention. I can get anyone I want, anytime I want." She barely smiled at him. "Maybe I'll go across the street. See what Tyson's up to."

Brock's whole body went completely still. "Do you want to watch me kill a man?"

She laughed. "That's awfully dramatic."

Brock didn't look amused. He actually looked something else.

Something that made her pause. "Have you ever killed anyone?"

He stared at her silently.

Holy shit.

"Um." Eva scooted out from the corner he had her backed into. Brock stepped away, his eyes following her as she moved. "I think I'm a little tired."

She made it to the base of the stairs leading to the top floor before his voice stopped her.

"Eight."

Eight. There was no mistaking the meaning behind the number, and it left her staring at the steps as reality sank in.

The man behind her was a killer.

Eight times over.

She slowly turned to face him. "Who were they?"

"Men who didn't deserve to live."

It was a simple answer.

One she understood more than most people.

She knew men like that. Every day she found their demons, lined them up, and displayed them for the world to see.

But knowing the world would be better off without someone in it and actually making that happen were two different things. "Does it bother you?"

He barely nodded. "Sometimes."

For the first time Brock seemed small. Vulnerable.

Eva walked toward him. The thought of him suffering now because of her questions dug into her belly with an uncomfortable ache. "I didn't mean to upset you."

"I know." He didn't reach for her like she thought he might.

He'd just spent the past ten minutes nearly pressed against her and now she felt a little empty.

Sad. For him. For having to live with the things he'd done.

"So, is Alaskan Security..." Finding a way to finish the question was difficult. "Are you all mercenaries?"

Chandler found them. Said this was the best company in the country. That it was the only possible way to deal with what was happening. Eva never looked for herself. Didn't think it mattered.

Didn't really want to come here in the first place.

Now she was wondering why in the hell Chandler would have chosen them.

"I don't set out to kill men, Eva." His hand barely lifted toward her before falling back into place. "But I will do whatever it takes to keep the person I'm guarding safe. We all will."

"What about me?" What would have happened if the two men at the store had really been after her?

Had tried something.

Brock's jaw clenched tight and she could swear his eye twitched. "I would do anything to keep you safe."

She chewed her lip. "You don't have to kill anyone for me."

"I'll take that under consideration." He tipped his head toward the kitchen. "Go finish your dinner."

She pressed her palm to her belly, stifling the growl brought on by the reminder of the tofu sauté she started. "Okay."

Eva clicked on the stove. When she turned, Brock was on his way to the lower stairs. "Where are you going?" She fully faced him. "Aren't you hungry?"

His eyes drifted to the fridge.

"Have dinner with me." She opened the refrigerator door and scanned the items Brock bought at the store. "You might have to make it yourself though, I don't eat any of," she waved her hand around the stack of packages taking up the entire middle shelf, "that."

The man bought an entire cow from the looks of it.

"You don't eat beef?" Brock was beside her, his voice low and soft.

Eva shook her head. "I don't eat anything with a face."

He leaned in close, gaze staying on her as he reached for one of the foam trays. "Vegetarian or vegan?"

"Vegetarian." She wrinkled her nose. "I just can't stomach the idea of eating flesh."

He glanced down at the steak in his hand. "Will it bother you if I eat it?"

"No. It's fine." It was mostly true. She tried really hard not to be bothered by the sight of people eating charred tissue.

He slid the tray back into place. "What are you eating?"

"Tofu."

"Which is?"

"Curd made from soybeans." It probably sounded as appetizing to Brock as his dinner sounded to her. "It's like a sponge. It soaks up whatever flavors you put with it."

"Really?" Brock stepped to the stove where she abandoned her dinner. He picked up the pan and sniffed at the cubes before turning to her, one eyebrow lifted. "May I?"

"You want to try tofu?" Most people were not extremely open-minded when it came to tofu.

Brock shook his head. "I want to cook it for you."

She took the pan of half-cooked curd cubes from his hand and set it back on the stove. "Forgive me for not trusting your ability to make a quality dish out of something you've never eaten before."

"Then teach me."

She eyed him. "Why would you want to learn how to cook tofu?"

"Why wouldn't I?" Brock opened the cabinet where Eva stowed a handful of sauces she picked up at the store. "Teriyaki?"

She swiped the bottle from his hand. "Thanks."

"What do you put in your gravy?" His voice was deep and dangerous in her ear.

Eva kept her eyes on the pan in front of her. "I don't think I understand what you're asking."

"Biscuits and gravy." Brock turned his back to the stove and leaned against it, close enough the outside of his thigh rested against hers. "What do you put in your gravy instead of sausage?"

She shrugged. "I don't make that."

"That's tragic."

"Why is that tragic?" She stepped away from his closeness and went to work chopping a stack of peppers, mushrooms, and broccoli, trying to ignore the way he moved into her vacated spot, stealing back the space she was trying to put between them.

"Because biscuits and gravy is the best breakfast food there is." He picked up the spoon and gently moved the cubes of tofu around in the hot pan. "Let me guess. You only eat oatmeal for breakfast."

She gagged.

Almost retched.

It was a very sexy reaction no doubt.

"No. No oatmeal. Ever."

Brock laughed softly. "I will keep that in mind."

Eva tossed the vegetables into the pan with the tofu. Brock spread them evenly with the spoon, making no move to give her the spot of dinner cook back.

Somehow he'd demoted her to sous-chef.

"Where are the bags of rice you bought today?" Brock started opening the cabinets around him until he found one of the already-cooked, microwave packages of ready rice. "You a convenience cooker, Tatum?"

Was he digging at her for using premade rice? "I live alone. Why would I go to all the trouble to make a pot of rice for just me?"

"Because it's better." Brock tossed the pack in the microwave and set it to cook.

"Not thirty minutes of my life gone, better." Eva grabbed the bottle of sauce and tried to twist the cap off, but before she could wrestle it free, Brock gently took it from her.

"Go sit down. I'll finish up."

"You don't have to do that." Eva tried to grab the bottle back from him. "I am perfectly capable of making my own dinner. I've done it since I was a kid."

Brock's gaze sharpened. "You made dinner as a kid?"

Eva froze.

Knowing other people's business was her business.

Sharing hers was something completely different.

"It doesn't matter." She made another grab for the sauce, this time managing to take it out of Brock's hand before immediately turning her back to him and pouring it over the vegetables and tofu.

Hopefully he would lose interest and move on. Go down to his lair and hide for the rest of the night.

"Obviously it does." He came close at her back, his body barely ghosting hers. He reached around her to stir the contents of the pan with the spoon still in his hand. "I've never cooked dinner for a woman before."

The admission was so low she had to strain to hear it. Once she had, a thousand questions cluttered her brain.

And she wouldn't ask any of them.

Because she didn't want Brock asking her any.

"Breakfast is a different story."

Her eyes widened as she stared down into the pan, watching Brock stir. And thank God he was, because right now she would have absolutely let everything burn.

Because some teeny tiny, but highly active, part of her was very unhappy at the thought of Broccoli cooking breakfast for the women he'd taken to bed.

Women who were not her. Because Brock didn't want her in his bed.

"I'm not hungry anymore." Eva bumped his big body with her back, knocking him away so she could do what she should have done earlier.

Escape.

Get away from this man before she got stupid.

Stupider.

But Brock caught her around the waist, stopping her before she could get anywhere. "Hold up, Sunshine."

"Let me go." Eva fought against his grip. Partly because she wanted away from him.

Mostly because she didn't.

And that was not a good thing.

Yesterday it seemed like having a little fun with Broccoli and then going on her merry way was the best idea she'd had all year. Hell, this morning it still sounded like a great plan.

But somehow something shifted in the last few hours.

And now being with Brock did not seem like a good idea at all.

In spite of how good it still sounded.

"Nope. Not until you tell me what just happened." His arm was solid and warm around her body. Grounding.

Eva shook her head. "No, thank you."

Lying wasn't her style. Telling him nothing happened would be just that.

He leaned down until his breath warmed the edge of her ear. "Please?"

Where was the Brock who hid from her in the basement last night? What happened to the man who looked at her like she was the biggest pain his ass had ever seen?

Because she liked him better. He was safer. Less likely to cause any sort of attachment.

Fuck. That wasn't true. She liked him then too.

"God." Eva pushed at his arm and this time he let her go. "I can't be around you right now." She stomped her way across the room to the stairs. This night was over.

She needed to go to sleep and start fresh.

The bed caught her as she fell face first into the blankets, burying her head under the pillows.

Blocking it all out.

Most of it anyway.

She couldn't seem to block out the fact that the teeny tiny part of her that was full of bad ideas was currently pouting because Brock let her go.

Which is what she wanted him to do.

She had to do something. Drastic. Now.

Eva grabbed her bag and fished out the information from Shawn, picking up the cordless phone on the nightstand and punching in his number.

He answered on the second ring. "Eva Tatum. To what do I owe the pleasure?"

"How'd you know it was me?" She looked around the room. Tyson said he'd cleared the house. They wouldn't have put cameras in it, would they?

"This is the number for the house you rented. I'm a little offended you didn't think I would know that."

"Oh." They weren't watching her every move. That was good.

Because what if she had to fart?

Scratch her ass.

Pick her nose.

Eva peered around the room, her eyes scanning all the nooks and crannies where a camera could be tucked. She slowly crawled off the bed.

"Is there something I can help you with, Ms. Tatum?" Shawn sounded a little too accommodating. Not that he was an ass to her before, but he certainly was all business any time they spoke.

"There is, actually." She crouched down, slow-walking toward a fake plant in a large pot sitting in one corner of the room. She leaned around it, moving from side to side as she peered into the leaves. "I would like a new bodyguard."

"Are you unsatisfied with Brock?"

That was a whole can of worms she had no intention of exploring. "He is perfectly fine. I just think we have conflicting personalities."

"Do you believe that will prohibit him from being able to keep you safe, Ms. Tatum?"

There.

111

Eva zeroed in on a tiny black device clipped to one of the hundreds of leaves on the giant plant, grabbing it and pulling it free.

"Ms. Tatum?"

"I think it's just best if you send someone else." She turned the thing around, looking until she found the small lens.

Just as Eva pointed it at her face for a smile the phone was ripped from her hand.

"Why the fuck is there a camera in her room, Shawn?"

The vein was back in Brock's forehead, protruding a little more with each passing second. His eyes were sharp and narrow, the flare of his nostrils making him look like a different man.

"Where else are they?"

He marched to the bed, depositing a tray she hadn't noticed him holding on the mattress before going to the curtains, pulling them back and skimming his hands down the fabric. "If I find anything anywhere I shouldn't I swear to God—"

His mouth clamped shut as his fingers clenched the phone tight. "Goodnight, Shawn." He disconnected the phone and turned to face her. "You want someone else here with you?"

No. She didn't.

But she also didn't want to want him with her.

Which she did.

"You don't seem very happy with your assignment." It was a cowardly thing to do. Deflecting the blame to him.

One she would have called anyone else out on.

"Fine." Eva rubbed her face. "No. I don't want someone else." She dropped her arms to her sides and sucked in a steadying breath.

Honesty was always the best policy. Always.

"I do not get in relationships, Brock." She wiggled her fingers, fighting for the truth she prided herself on always giving. "I just don't do them, and I offered you a stringless opportunity and you turned me down, which is fine, but—"

"You don't seem fine with it."

"Shut up." She continued on, riding the momentum because it might be the only thing to carry her through this. "Everyone lies. I see it every day and it has changed me."

That wasn't completely true. She came into it already damaged.

Went into her profession because of that damage. Used it as a way to seek a vengeance she would never have.

"I don't trust anyone, and if I can't have something simple with a man then I don't want to have it at all."

"So unless I'm willing to fuck you and walk away, you don't want anything to do with me?"

Initially that was her plan.

But then he started growing on her. Like fungus.

"I don't think we should fuck at all, actually."

Brock's lips barely twitched. "I'm glad we're on the same page."

CHAPTER 9

BROCK STEPPED IN close beside her, barely brushing Eva's body with his as he reached for the tray of food he brought upstairs. "There's no more cameras up here."

"Why was there one up here in the first place?" Eva glared at him. "I don't appreciate being spied on. What if I was walking around up here naked?"

"It was aimed at the stairs." The reminder was more for his own sanity than to make her feel better. The idea of anyone watching Eva made his blood pressure skyrocket.

Eva's eyes moved to the stairs. "No one is coming up them." Her chin barely lifted. "I'm sure those guys weren't looking for me today."

"So am I." Brock pulled the towel he'd draped over their dinner off the plates of vegetables and rice.

And fucking tofu.

"I'm serious. They weren't—" She blinked at him, clearly surprised by his agreement. "Oh. Why do *you* think they weren't here for me?"

"Stalkers don't normally hire outside help." He nodded to the blanket-covered mattress. "Get comfortable."

Eva looked at the bed, then at the plate of food balanced on his palm. "You want me to eat in bed?"

"Are you against eating in bed?"

"No. I eat in bed all the time." She eyed the food.

"So do I."

Her gaze immediately jumped to his, eyes wide, cheeks pinking up instantly. Her dark hair was still a little wild from the wind. It fell long and loose around her shoulders, a thick mass of almost chaos that was a perfect fit for the woman wearing it.

Calling Eva beautiful felt wrong. Not that she wasn't.

She was just so much more than that.

And now that she claimed to no longer want to fuck him, it felt safe to admit to himself how fucking attractive he found her.

And maybe be a little bit of the man he really was around her.

Eva cleared her throat, eyes falling to the food in his hand. "Do you know who those men were?" She slowly eased onto the bed, propping up against the headboard.

"Not yet." Brock handed her the plate before picking up the other one. "Dutch and Harlow are working on it."

"I like her." Eva stabbed her fork into the pile of food.

"I knew you would." Introducing Eva to Harlow was not something he intended to do. The two of them together would be dangerous. There was no telling the trouble they could cause.

"I could help them."

The offer caught him by surprise. He'd only imagined the havoc the two of them could unleash just for fun. It never occurred to him they could also be a hell of a team professionally speaking.

Eva didn't seem to notice. "I mean, I was thinking about having you take me to headquarters so I could get some work done tomorrow anyway."

"Why can't you work here?" Taking Eva to headquarters today had been a necessity. Going back tomorrow would mean she would spend the whole day with Harlow.

It was what he should want. The less time he spent with Eva the easier it would be to keep from thinking of her as anything more than his current assignment. And with Eva's skills added to Dutch and Harlow's they would no doubt be on the fast track to finding out who in the hell those men were.

Not that he didn't already have a good idea.

"I could." Eva shrugged. "But the internet is kind of spotty."

"Maybe for a few hours." Brock took a bite of tofu. "It's spongy."

"But in a good way." Eva grinned at him as he struggled to get the bite down.

"There's a good spongy?" Brock nearly choked as he swallowed.

"Cake is spongy." Eva forked in a chunk of broccoli. "So's bread."

He wanted to feed her cake and bread. Show her he wasn't really what he led her to believe.

"You eat cake and bread?"

Eva's brows lifted. "Uh. Yeah. They are the best part of life." She shoveled in more of her dinner.

"What about biscuits?"

She nodded without looking up at him, all her attention staying on the pile of food diminishing by the second. "I guess."

"You guess? Breakfast is the best meal of the day."

Her eyes slowly lifted to his. "You just think that because it's the only meal you don't eat alone."

Brock stared at her for a second. "That's not why." He shifted a little on the edge of the bed. "It's because it has the best food options."

"Mm-hmm." She was back to being focused on her food.

"It is." Brock stabbed at a few vegetables and stuffed them in his mouth.

"Whatever you say." Eva scraped the last of her rice to the edge of her plate and tipped it up, shoveling it into her open mouth before standing up. "Thanks for dinner, Broccoli." She reached out one hand. "You finished pretending to eat tofu?"

Instead of handing her his plate he took hers and headed for the stairs. "I ate some."

Eva's belly laugh slowed his steps. Made him drag out his departure.

"You wanna watch a movie?"

He turned to find her sprawled across the blankets, remote in hand as she switched on the large television across from the bed.

She gave him a smile that barely faltered as her eyes found the plant in the corner. "Or are you going back to hide in the basement?"

"No one will get to you, Eva. I promise."

She huffed out a little breath. "I know that. I'm not worried."

"What movie are you watching?"

"Probably something you will hate." Her eyes narrowed on the television. "How about *John Wick*?"

"Never seen it."

Eva wiggled her eyebrows at him. "There's lots of violence and murder." Her smile was back, wide and real. "It's about a guy who gets vengeance when someone kills his dog."

"Why are you smiling about that?"

"Because he totally gets it." She pressed a button on the remote and dropped it to the bed at her side. "Better hurry if you want to watch."

His gaze drifted to the big empty spot on the bed beside her.

"I won't bite, Broccoli." Eva held up one hand and pressed the other over her heart. "Promise."

The thought of Eva biting was probably the most appealing thing he could imagine.

Her teeth sinking into his shoulder while he—

"You okay?" Eva's head dropped to one side. "You looked like you zoned out there for a minute." Her spine straightened as she stared down the stairs, lips pressed tightly together.

She might claim to be positive those men weren't after her, but Eva was scared. Probably wouldn't sleep at all if he left her up here alone.

"I think I'm just tired." He nodded to the stairs. "I'll be right back."

He hurried to load their plates into the dishwasher and get it running before changing into a pair of flannel pants and a t-shirt. After a quick brush of his teeth, Brock was on his way back up the stairs, grabbing a couple bottles of water before shutting off all the lights on the main floor and going up to the bedroom where Eva was already tucked in with an iPad in her hands.

"Better not be telling anyone where you are."

"Do you think I'm stupid, Broccoli?" She peeked at him over the top of her tablet, eyes scanning him from head to toe. "Huh."

"What's that mean?"

"I didn't picture you as being a pajama sort of guy."

"Did you think I was going to come up here in my underwear?"

"I didn't think you were going to come up here at all." She switched the iPad off and closed the cover, sliding it onto the bedside table. "Are you going to watch from there?"

"No."

She lifted her brows.

Never in his life had he hesitated to get in bed with a woman.

He walked to the side of the bed nearest the stairs. The same side Eva was currently occupying. "Scoot over, Tatum."

She didn't budge. "This is the side I like." She snuggled deeper into the covers. "Maybe if you hadn't been such a chicken shit last night you could have claimed it first."

"This isn't up for debate." He pointed to the other side of the bed. "Go."

"Do most women just go along with whatever you say?"

"Yes." He smiled. "And to be fair, it usually works out well for them."

Eva's eyes flew open wide and her cheeks pinked up instantly.

He was finally gaining the upper hand with her. No more knee jerk reactions to her. No more living in constant fear that the next thing she said would only make him like her more.

"Well since I'm not interested in fucking you anymore I guess I'll just have to take your word for it." She scooted down, resting her head against the pillow.

He was happy she didn't want to fuck him. Delighted Eva planned to keep their relationship to nothing more than it was.

Didn't bother him at all that she only considered what it would be like to fuck him for less than two seconds.

That's why he leaned down and grabbed her, blankets and all, and tossed her across the bed to the side she belonged on. Brock barely made it onto his side before she had the covers flipped back and was coming for him.

"You ass." Her whole body lunged at him, hair flying, fingers gripping his shirt as she landed against him. "Get on your fucking side of the bed." She pulled at the fabric of his t-shirt, one leg hooking around his as she fought to put him where she believed he belonged.

The spot in her life she was comfortable having him occupy.

"That looks like your side of the bed, Tatum. Might as well get comf—" The word broke off in a yelp as her fingers locked onto a healthy-sized clump of chest hair through his shirt.

"You just thought you could come in here and take my side of the bed like you owned it." She started to pull.

He locked onto her wrist with one hand, keeping her from taking out anymore hair. "If I wanted to own any part of your bed I would." He caught her other hand as it came his way, catching it before he ended up looking like he had mange when his shirt was off. "Stop it."

"No." Her wrists twisted in his grip. "You aren't as charming as you think you are, Brock Cassidy."

"The number of women who would argue with you is shocking."

She glared at him. "They just expected you to have a big dick." Eva suddenly shifted tactics, pulling her hands back instead of pushing toward him. The change took him by surprise and she broke free.

A second later he had her again, but this time she was even more wild. More angry.

And probably going to take out one of his eyeballs.

A knee bounced off his thigh, indicating her sights were on a lower set of balls. Before she could hurt either one of them, he rolled, pinning her to the mattress with his weight.

"Get off me."

"Not until you calm down." He held her wrists tight, being as careful as he could not to hurt her. "I'm not losing a nut because you're pissed at me over something."

"I'm pissed because you don't know where you belong."

"Don't I?" Brock took a deep breath, trying to find the calm he needed. "Because you've made it very clear where I'm supposed to be."

"Then why in the hell won't you just go there?" Her words didn't carry the same anger as before. Eva shook her head. "Please just go."

Brock stared down at her.

Leaving now would give him everything he wanted when Shawn dropped Eva's file into his life.

He could go to his cabin. Take the time he needed to right his mind. Get back to himself.

Then when Eva was gone he could come back and life would be back to normal.

Only it wouldn't.

His life would never be normal again.

Because whether Eva left or not, he would never again be safe. His happiness already hung in the balance.

His sanity.

Even if Eva Tatum hadn't shown up, he would have still been staring down potential devastation every damn day.

"Is that what you really want? Me to go?" He loosened his hold on her wrists. If she wanted to wail on him she could.

He deserved it.

All he'd been feeding her were the same lies he tried to tell himself.

That he didn't want her.

That he could send her back home without a second thought.

In just under two days this woman had gnawed her way into places he'd sworn to never let anyone.

Especially a woman.

She stared up at him. Silent.

"Tell me to go. Tell me you don't want me here." It was a dare. One he hoped she wouldn't take.

Brock waited, chest tight.

He'd never cared if a woman wanted him before. If one didn't, there were three more behind her who would.

But there was no one behind Eva. No one he cared to see anyway.

"I don't want to want you here."

"I know." He skimmed his hand down her arm, the tips of his fingers brushing over the softest skin he'd ever touched. "I don't want to want to be here."

She chewed her lower lip. "Why?"

"Lots of reasons." Telling her the truth of how he came to be like he was might not ever happen. It felt too much like tempting fate.

"Give me one." She was no longer fighting him and it made it easy to see how well she fit him.

He was not a small man. Most women made him feel like he had to be careful with every move he made or risk being too heavy. Too rough.

But Eva was tall and solid, with curves filling out everywhere they should. She was the perfect combination of strong and soft.

In every sense of the words.

"You scare the shit out of me." She was everything he avoided. For years he chased the women he knew would never make him think twice. Women who, as beautiful and sweet as they were, would never make him risk it all.

Eva wasn't like those women.

"I get that a lot."

"I bet." Brock smiled, the pressure he'd been carrying since Bess and Parker left easing a little as her lips barely curved into a whisper of a smile. "You probably scare the shit out of every man you meet."

And they would still come back for more because she was like a drug.

"Something like that." Eva's eyes dropped from his.

Brock eased off her. "I'm sorry I've been—"

"An ass?" Eva didn't scoot away as he stretched out beside her.

"Among other things." He wanted to touch her again. Feel the softness of her skin under his palm.

But for the first time in his life he didn't know how to act around a woman.

Because for the first time he didn't just want to fuck her and walk away.

"I'm sorry I'm difficult."

"I like that you're difficult." Brock reached for the covers he'd completely displaced in his effort to prove he chose his place in her bed.

In her life.

"I should go downstairs." He pulled the covers around her, tucking them between her body and his as he eased off the mattress.

"Why?" The question sounded honest. Real.

It made him give her an honest and real answer. "I don't know what to do with you."

She watched him for a minute.

"Same." Eva chewed her lower lip. "I don't trust anyone, Brock. I never have."

"No one?"

She shook her head. "And as you can imagine that has caused some pretty big issues for me in the romance department."

"I would believe it." He sat on the edge of the bed. No part of him wanted to leave her, even before he knew she faced everything alone.

That's what happened when there was no one you trusted to have your back. It would make you hard and cynical.

But this woman wasn't that.

"What about your parents? Not even them?"

Eva's gaze hardened a second before it left his, shifting to the television. "Are we watching a movie or not, Broccoli?"

He should go to the basement. Spend the night finding a way to want to be apart from the woman inviting him into her bed.

But he didn't want to. He didn't want to be away from her.

Especially since her eyes kept finding their way to the top of the stairs.

He'd be damned if she spent the night alone.

Afraid.

Not that she'd ever admit it.

"Pick a comedy." He laid down on top of the covers. "I need something to laugh at."

CHAPTER 10

WHAT IN THE fresh hell was going on?

Eva dropped down the last step leading from the bedroom and stared into the kitchen. "What are you doing?"

Brock grinned at her from his spot in front of the stove. "Making breakfast."

"In your underwear?"

She'd seen it before.

Sneakily.

But now here it all was. On full display. A giant man in a pair of boxer-briefs, grinning at her like the cat that swallowed the canary.

The same man who'd been scowling at her for the past two days.

"Are you hungry, Eva?"

Her eyes bounced up from where they'd gotten stuck. "Probably."

"You're probably hungry?" His eyes crinkled at the corners. "That doesn't sound very convincing."

"Okay."

She wasn't making any sense, which fit perfectly in this whole situation.

It made no fucking sense.

"I'm making you biscuits and gravy." Brock's attention turned back to the pot on the stove in front of him.

Thank God, because she was back to staring at everything he was putting out there.

He was fucking glorious.

Which was terrible.

Knowing that body was on top of hers last night made her want to pick a fight with him again.

Also terrible.

"I don't eat sausage."

Brock turned her way just in time to catch her staring at his—

She snapped her eyes shut. "I'm a vegetarian, remember?"

"Of course I remember." Even his voice seemed different this morning. Smoother. Deeper. "I worked very hard to make sure this was sausage you'd be happy to try."

Was he flirting with her?

Eva opened one eye and jumped back, losing her balance over the wall of bare chest staring her down.

Brock caught her with both hands. "Didn't mean to scare you."

"You don't scare me."

He did.

"I think I do." Instead of letting her go, Brock pulled her close. "I think I scare you as much as you scare me."

"Nuh-uh."

Shit. Of all the times to lose every bit of brain power she had.

Eva cleared her throat. "You do not scare me."

"Good then." His arms tightened around her a little more, pulling her body closer to the hard lines of his. "Because I've been thinking about your offer."

Oh God.

"I think I rescinded that."

"Did you?" Brock leaned in close to her ear, the barely-there stubble across his jaw scraping her skin in the most deliciously masculine way. "Why don't you at least try my sausage before you make any final decisions."

This was the most ridiculously corny, innuendo-filled conversation she'd ever been a part of.

And lord help her, she absolutely wanted to sample his sausage.

Because she was as corny and ridiculous as he was.

"Is it very meaty?"

Brock barked out a laugh that made her jump. He didn't laugh often, and it took her by surprised every time it happened.

"I guess you'll have to tell me." He stepped away, but instead of releasing her, Brock kept one arm wrapped around her waist, using it to direct Eva to a chair at the table. "How many biscuits do you want?"

"Three."

His attention focused on her, one dark brow lifting. "Three?"

"I'm feeling optimistic about your skills."

"You should." Brock's voice was soft as he once again leaned close. "I pride myself on them."

Why did that make her thighs clench?

Because she was fucked. That's why.

He straightened, backing away. His eyes stayed on her, lips lifted at the corners in a way that made it clear she wasn't the only one who knew she was fucked.

"How long do you need to work today?" Brock stood at the counter, breaking open what looked like homemade biscuits onto a plate.

"I'm not sure. I need to go through my emails and check in with Mona and Chandler. See how things are going." She watched as he poured a heavy-handed serving of gravy over the biscuits.

"We'll just play it by ear then." Brock came back toward her, plate in one hand, cup in the other. "I made you tea."

"Thank you?"

"Was that a question?" He set both in front of her but didn't walk away.

"Not for you." Eva leaned to peek into the mug.

Who in the hell was this man? Was he the sexy but crabby one that picked her up from the airport?

Or was he whatever this was?

"I think we got off on the wrong foot." Brock picked up the fork next to her plate and held it out. "You seem to think I'm something I'm not."

Eva took the fork. "I'm not sure what I think you are."

He pointed to her plate. "I'm one hell of a cook for starters."

"Humble too." She waited for him to go back and get his own plate.

"I want to watch you take the first bite."

"Why?"

"Because I don't want you lying to me and telling me it's not the best biscuits and gravy you've ever had."

"I don't lie." It came out harsher than she intended.

No it didn't.

Lying was the basis for every life she'd ever been hired to investigate. It was always the rot that led to a person's downfall.

One they created themselves.

"Not ever?"

She shook her head.

A slow smile worked its way onto Brock's lips. "Good to know."

Eva pointed her fork at him. "Don't even think about using it against me, Broccoli."

"Do you think I would do something like that?"

"Yes." She nodded along with the answer.

"Smart girl." He finally turned away, giving her a full look at his backside.

And glutton that she was Eva took full advantage.

"Stop staring at my ass and eat your breakfast, Eva." He peeked at her over one wide, well-muscled shoulder. "Unless you want to tell me you weren't staring at my ass."

"Fuck you, Broccoli." She shoved in a bite of biscuit and gravy.

Shit.

"Who's made you the best breakfast you've ever had, Eva?"

How did he get so close? A second ago Brock was across the room, calling out her inappropriate gawking, and now he was right beside her, leaning in until she could smell the ruggedly manly scent of his skin.

"Tell me."

His voice sent a shiver down her spine.

And fuck it all he wouldn't shut up.

"Tell me I'm the best you've had."

This man should be weaponized. He could topple women into bed with nothing more than a few suggestive phrases.

The only way to win a war with him was to fight back in kind.

Eva straightened in her seat, leaning a little closer as she licked her lips. "You are the best I've ever had, Brock."

It seemed like a good idea.

Like she might be able to poke at him the same way he was poking at her.

In hindsight it might not have been her smartest move.

Or maybe it was.

It could go either way honestly, because a second after it was out of her mouth, Brock had her out of her seat and pulled tight against his almost naked body, one hand spread across her back and the other shoved into her hair.

"You make me absolutely fucking crazy, you know that?" His lips grazed hers as he spoke. "I feel like I'm losing my grip and I don't know how to fix it."

"I'm sorry." Apologizing wasn't something she made a habit of doing. Apologies were like lies. A tool people used against others so they could continue to do what they wanted.

But nine times out of ten they didn't mean it.

"Are you sorry, Eva?"

She almost nodded.

But it would have been a half-truth.

"Sort of."

He smiled, the hand on her back pressing higher, holding her closer. "What are you sorry for?"

"That I'm making you crazy." Her hands were caught between their bodies, palms pressed into the warm skin of his chest. It was so darn tempting to move her fingertips until they found the patch of dark hair covering his sternum and pecs.

"What *aren't* you sorry for?"

She bit her lip, trying to find a way to avoid the honesty she was so proud of always offering. If she gave it to him everything would change.

And nothing would change.

Because at the end of the day none of this mattered. It couldn't.

She was damaged. Unable to give the thing every relationship had to be built on. It was the reason she was alone.

The reason her engagement fell apart.

Eva took a breath. Brock deserved the truth of what she was and would never be, and better to get it out now before either of them wished she was different.

Before Eva tried to believe she was.

"Brock, I—"

The sound of the doorbell cut her off and sent Brock spinning with her tucked tight against him, his body blocking her view of the door and windows leading to the walk-up porch as he all but carried her to the short hall that ran behind the kitchen to the half bath on the main floor.

"Who the fuck is that?" Brock's voice was a low growl.

"I don't know? How in the hell would I know?"

One hand clamped over her mouth while the other pressed against his earpiece.

"I swear to God if you're wrong and you put her in danger I will—"

His eyes narrowed.

"Fuck you, Reed."

Brock's gaze moved to hers as his hand eased away. "Stay here. Don't move until I come back to get you."

Eva started to lean toward the doorway as he stepped away. Brock moved back in close, his body pushing her backward as the bell rang again. He didn't stop until she was in the bathroom. "Lock the door and don't come out for anyone but me or Reed, understand?"

"But—"

He shook his head. "No buts. I need you to listen to me. Please."

She huffed out a breath. "Fine."

Brock smiled. "That's my girl." He locked one hand around her neck and pulled her in, pressing his lips to hers in a fast kiss.

And then he was gone, closing the door silently. "Lock it, Eva."

His voice was already far away.

Too far away.

He was going to answer the door in nothing but his underwear. No weapons.

Not even any freaking socks.

What if it was those men? What if they really were after Brock and came here to grab him and drag him off to God knows where?

He would freeze to death.

Eva leaned against the door, pressing her ear to the smooth wood. She held her breath and listened.

Brock's voice was there. Low and calm.

And it was joined by another voice.

A woman's voice.

And didn't she sound happy as shit at her current situation.

"You must be cold." The words dripped with suggestion.

Before she could think through the ramifications of her actions, Eva was out the door and down the hall. Marching into the living room ready to—

"Hey."

That was the extent of her plan, which meant she was now facing down a less-than-happy looking Brock and a beautiful flower delivery woman.

No sense trying to run away now. The damage was done. Her only option was to power through.

Luckily the woman at the door immediately threw her a bone. "Oh my gosh. These must be for you." She smiled wide at Eva and held out a huge vase of roses. "They are so pretty." She winked. "Someone must love you a lot."

"Someone must." Eva stepped in and took the flowers, feeling guilty about her earlier feelings toward the woman.

Blaming someone for appreciating a mostly-naked Brock was about the most hypocritical thing she'd ever done.

He gave the woman a tight smile. "Thank you. Have a nice day."

"You too." She held one hand to the side of her mouth and leaned toward Eva. "Keep him warm."

"Okay." Eva managed to smile even as Brock's eyes found her and stayed.

The woman turned and hustled down the long flight of shoveled and salted stairs to a white florist van parked against the curb.

Brock closed the door, his gaze never leaving Eva.

She stared at the flowers.

Because they seemed safer than he did right now.

And they were probably sent by someone who might be crazier than she thought.

"You were supposed to stay in the bathroom until I came for you." Brock took the large vase from her, removing the barricade giving her some sense of security. He set it on the long table running behind the plaid sofa in the living room. "I can't keep you safe if you don't listen to me, Eva."

She had no argument. None she wanted to share with him.

Because her reasons for rushing out of the bathroom were impulsive and fueled by unfounded jealousy.

Brock stalked closer. "Why did you come out?"

"It was an accident."

She could swear it looked like he might smile. "You accidentally came out of the bathroom when a pretty woman was flirting with me?"

Shit.

Shit.

Double shit.

"I didn't know she was pretty."

He chuckled at that. "So the thought of *any* woman flirting with me had you running into potential danger."

"That's not what happened."

"Then enlighten me." Brock was almost against her, his closeness forcing her head back so she could look him in the eye.

"I don't want to." She pressed her lips together. Lying wasn't an option.

But neither was the truth.

Because the truth made everything seem very complicated.

Not nearly as complicated as everything seemed when his hands came to rest on each side of her face. "You were jealous."

All Eva could say was nothing. She shouldn't give two shits if a woman flirted with Brock. Hell, she shouldn't blame them at all. He was beautiful and charming and thoughtful and funny and—

Shit.

Brock's lips pulled into a smile as they came toward hers. "You like me, Tatum."

"I don't want to talk about it." He knew her weakness. She'd served it to him on a silver platter.

"I would imagine not." His hands moved down until they rested on her hips. "You don't seem thrilled about it."

"I said I don't want to talk about it." She gasped a little when he pulled her against him.

"Fair enough." His lips brushed hers. "Then maybe you should consider letting me occupy your mouth another way."

Brock occupying her mouth was a dangerous thing to consider. She'd offered him no-strings fun and he'd turned her down flatly.

More than once.

And the longer she was around him, the more clear it became she might not be capable of giving him that anyway.

Who could blame her?

"I don't think that's a good idea."

"I'm sure it's probably not." He made another pass across her lips. "I think we should do it anyway."

The air in her lungs slid free on a soft sigh. One of resignation.

She leaned into him, relaxing into the heat of his body, letting him hold her tight.

No one had ever watched out for her. That must be what this was. She was just finally feeling like she had someone in her corner. Someone whose sole purpose was to make sure she was okay.

Because she'd paid him to.

Shit. She couldn't even convince herself of that anymore.

"Why are you doing this?"

"Because I want to." Instead of finding hers, his lips moved to the line of her jaw, skimming their way toward her ear. "I wish I didn't." He nipped at the skin just below her earlobe. "Tried not to." The nip turned to a gentle suck. "But you are fucking irresistible."

Before Eva could argue with his assessment of her, Brock's mouth finally covered hers.

He'd kissed her before, but that was under duress. To prove a point.

This was completely different.

This was real.

It could be overwhelming if she let it. If Eva thought about what might be happening.

What the fallout would be because of it.

"Stop worrying." His lips moved against hers, soft and sweet as his hand moved from her hips to her back, one sliding up to press between her shoulder blades and the other sliding down to cup her ass.

How long had it been since she'd given in to something like this?

It had been never.

Giving in wasn't something she did. Being with a man was all about control. Emotional management.

Keeping things nice and neat and detached so when the lies came they didn't hurt.

But controlling this man would never be an option. Brock wasn't the kind she could reign in. Push into place.

He made that very clear last night.

"This is crazy." She didn't mean to say it. Didn't even mean to think it.

Because admitting the insanity of it was also admitting the existence of this thing between them.

The thing that had been there since the first time she laid eyes on him.

When she tried to casually meander past him at the airport and ended up tripping over her own feet at the sight of him up close.

The way he took care of her in ways he didn't have to.

He could have let her freeze. It wasn't his job to keep her warm or fed. Only to keep her from being victimized by a non-threatening pseudo-stalker.

Who might have just sent her flowers.

To a place he shouldn't have been able to find her.

CHAPTER 11

THE FRONT DOOR bounced open behind him.

"Who sent the fl—"

Reed came to a dead stop in the center of the living room. Brock didn't turn to face him.

He didn't give a shit about Reed right now.

All he cared about was the woman in front of him.

"Go downstairs and start packing my shit up." Brock didn't look away from Eva and he sure as hell wasn't letting her go.

Reed silently hurried down the stairs.

Eva's eyes moved to where the large arrangement sat on the table. Without a word she stepped away, pushing out of his embrace to grab the card from its tiny plastic pitchfork.

She ripped the envelope open and pulled out the small rectangular card, her face unreadable as she stared at it.

"What does it say?"

Instead of answering she simply turned the card around.

Found you

"Go pack." He tapped his earpiece. "You there, Tyson?"

"I'm here. Harlow's looking for the florist's system now trying to find who sent them."

"How's it look out there?" Brock followed Eva up the stairs to the bedroom and started collecting her toiletries from the bathroom.

He needed her the fuck out of here.

"Nothing. Street's quiet."

"Good. We're packing and will be out in ten."

Eva was stuffing clothes into her suitcase when he came in. "Don't miss anything. I don't want that motherfucker sniffing your panties while he jacks off."

"That's a visual I didn't need." Eva slammed her case shut and zipped it closed before dropping it to the ground at her feet. "Ready."

"Good." Brock grabbed her bag with one hand and used the other to hold one of hers. "Come on. I want you out of here."

She followed him down the stairs but slowed as they passed the kitchen, her eyes dragging across the table. "I didn't even get to eat my biscuits and gravy."

"I will make you all the biscuits and gravy you can eat as soon as I know you're safe." He kept moving, pulling her along as he rushed down the stairs toward the theater room where Reed was just finishing up. He tossed a stack of clothes at Brock.

"Everything else is packed."

Brock caught the pile, reluctantly dropping Eva's hand as he pulled on the jeans and thermal shirt. "I need someone to get everything out of the kitchen and bring it to headquarters."

"Done." Reed was already on his way back up the stairs.

"Why are we going to headquarters?"

"I need to touch base with Harlow and Dutch before we leave."

"Leave?" Eva sounded a little panicked for the first time. "Where are we going?"

"Somewhere no one will find you." Brock shoved his feet into the boots beside the door.

"Can I still check in with Mona and Chandler?"

He grabbed his bags and stacked them in the hall next to Eva's. "Only if Harlow is there with you to make sure you don't say anything you shouldn't."

"What does that mean?"

He grabbed her, pulling Eva close. "It means I love how honest you are, but right now that could be a huge fucking problem." He kissed her, intending for it to be nothing more than a peck.

But this woman made him forget everything he'd ever known. Made it seem like it didn't matter.

And now the person who brought her into his life was flexing his muscle. Proving he could find her if he wanted.

Flaunting his ability to hunt a woman who was nowhere near as scared as she should be.

All of it put him on edge.

She was the only thing that cleared his head. Helped him find the focus he needed right now.

Brock pulled her closer, holding her body tight to his. His breath came easier as her body softened, her lips parted.

The woman was sex incarnate, and if she attacked the act with half the enthusiasm she went after everything else with, he was a dead man walking.

Reed cleared his throat from the doorway, waiting until Brock finally managed to pull away from Eva long enough to glance his way. "Time to go."

"Come on, Sunshine." He kept one hand on her at all times, letting Reed help load the bags into the back of the Rover while he got Eva situated in the front seat. "You ready?"

She nodded.

He closed her in before jogging to the driver's side and climbing in as Reed got into the back seat.

Eva turned to give Reed a smile. "Do you want to ride in the front?"

"Nope." Brock rested one hand on her thigh as he waited for the garage door to lift. He tapped his earpiece and waited for Tyson.

"You're clear as far as I can see."

"You have backup coming for you?"

"Nate and Abe are ten minutes out."

Taking Reed with them meant Tyson would be alone in the van until Nate and Abe arrived, but it had to happen.

Because there was a worst case scenario digging into the back of his brain. One that was worse than a panty-sniffing stalker.

Those flowers might not have been meant for Eva.

Brock backed out of the garage and immediately pulled away, driving in the opposite direction of the van where Reed and Tyson had been camped out.

"This isn't the way to headquarters." Eva spun to look out the back window. "Where are we going?"

"We are just being extra careful." He squeezed her knee. "Just relax. Everything will be fine."

Eva might not think lying was ever the right thing to do, but he disagreed. Sometimes it was the best option available.

Like now.

Because the second the townhouse was out of sight, a dark sedan pulled out of an unmarked drive.

In a different situation Brock would have told Tyson immediately, but Eva was the most important thing right now, and no way would he scare her. Not unless he absolutely had to.

Reed's eyes caught his in the mirror before dropping to his cell where he was punching out a message.

The sedan stayed far enough behind to make it an obvious tail. One that had his hold on Eva pressing tighter with each passing second. Each matched turn.

"They're following us, aren't they?" Her eyes slid to the side mirror on her door.

"Yes."

"Who is it?"

Brock looked to Reed.

"Dutch is working on it." Reed shifted in his seat, pulling the gun strapped to his leg from its holster. "No front plates so he's trying to tap into the city's traffic cameras to see if he can catch the rear plates."

"They'll be stolen." Eva leaned back in her seat and closed her eyes.

Brock's attention snagged on her, resting long enough to make him miss the changing of a light. He sailed right through the red, never even tapping the breaks.

Making it seem like he was trying to get away.

"They're speeding up." Reed tapped at the screen of his phone and pressed it to his ear.

"Damn it." Brock punched the gas. "Hold on, Sunshine."

Eva's hand pressed onto his, her fingers holding tight as the Rover sped along roads most people would struggle to maneuver at a normal speed.

Brock took the next side street, fighting to keep the Rover on the snowy pavement as its wheels fought for purchase. The second they grabbed he floored it, hoping to be out of sight before the sedan caught up. Another turn and he was out of view, racing along a less-populated part of Fairbanks.

"You see anything?"

"No." Reed watched out the back window, scanning the road behind them as Brock took another turn.

And put the brake to the floor.

"Holy shit." Eva barely had the words out of her mouth before his hand was at the back of her head, shoving it down as the two men standing in front of the car blocking the road in front of them lifted their arms and took aim.

Brock threw the Rover into reverse as Reed rolled down a back window. He held Eva in place as he steered the SUV back the way they came, spinning out at the end of the road just as their tail caught up. The Rover bounced off the sedan, knocking the tail back a few feet as bullets started to ping against the doors. Reed held tight to the back seat with one hand as he returned fire with the arm he had shoved out the window.

"Got the tires on the sedan. Get the fuck outta here." Reed ducked down as a bullet came in through the back window and out Eva's side. "Go!"

Brock shifted into drive and took off, fighting the urge to floor the gas until the tires grabbed the sandy roadway. "You okay, Sunshine?"

"This is fucking crazy. You know this is crazy, right?"

He smiled. "Not enjoying your Alaskan adventure?"

"Ask me again when we're safe."

"You're always safe." Brock glanced in the mirror, checking for any sign the men they left behind were considering another game of chase. "I promise."

"Those men were not after me, were they?"

"Technically, no."

"What does that mean?" Eva popped up, her hair and eyes wild as she looked around the vehicle.

"It means technically they were probably more interested in me and Reed." Brock kept his eyes out the front of the SUV as he tapped through screens on the console. A second later Dutch was on the line, interrupting the string of questions Brock wasn't excited about answering.

"Was that the same guys from the store?"

"That would be an affirmative." Brock headed straight for headquarters, moving as fast as possible through the light traffic, darting in and out of lanes, hoping to force anyone who might be trying to follow them to show their hand early in the game.

"Is Eva okay?"

"Harlow?" Eva leaned down close to the system, like she could have a private conversation over the speakers of a vehicle. "They shot at us."

"Seriously?"

Eva nodded.

She might be in shock.

"Did they hit anything?" Harlow sounded way more excited than she should.

"They hit the car." Eva's head barely turned toward the bullet hole pierced in her window. "A few times."

"Holy shit. Were you scared?"

"I didn't really know it was happening. My head was in Brock's lap." Eva reached up to smooth down a matted clump of her hair.

149

"You're getting to have all the fun today, aren't you?"

Eva turned to look toward the back of the Rover. "I didn't even get to eat my breakfast." She started to crawl between the seats.

"What are you doing?" Brock tried to grab at her.

"If those bastards shot my stuff I'm going to kill someone." She landed on Reed, knocking him back in the seat. "Sorry. Didn't mean to knee your nuts."

Harlow was laughing in the background as Dutch came back on the line. "Are you coming to main campus?"

"Headed there now. We're about ten minutes out."

"We'll be ready."

Brock ended the call, glancing in the mirror as Eva's butt lifted in the air over the seat behind him. "Can you stop her? She's a fucking perfect target with her ass up like that."

Reed tapped Eva on the hip. "If someone starts shooting at us again you're probably going to get hit if you don't move."

"Son of a mother fucker." She fell to her bottom on the seat beside Reed. "Those dick wads shot my Gram-Gram right between the eyes."

"I will get you a new Gram-Gram." Brock cut across two lanes to take the turn into the business park that bordered the property owned by Alaskan Security.

"Ugh." Her head fell to the back of the seat. "This is stupid."

Reed stared at him in the mirror, eyes wide.

He understood completely. "Everything is going to be fine. We're almost there. Just relax."

"Relax?" She sat up straight and leaned forward. "I was fine before I came here."

"That's not true, Eva. You know that." He squeezed the wheel, hating that she was at least a little right.

"It is true. The person following me left me cool shirts and brownies. The dicks after you shot my Gram-Gram."

Reed leaned back to peek over the seat.

"Brownies?" Brock shot her a quick look. "You ate them, didn't you?"

"They were frosted." She said it like that made it perfectly normal to eat something left on your porch by a crazy person.

"I can't believe you are still alive, you know that?"

"Do you actually hear what you're saying to me?" Eva pointed to the back of the SUV. "You can't believe I'm still alive because I ate stalker brownies? I can't believe I'm still alive because someone just fucking shot up our car."

"I swear to God if you're laughing I'm going to kill you, Reed." Brock tried to find him in the mirror, but Reed was leaning out of view.

He didn't have time to throw out any more empty threats anyway. Brock rolled down the window and punched in the code to open the gates leading them into one of only two places he could be positive Eva would be safe.

The minute they were parked she was out of the car and at the back hatch, cussing at the top of her lungs about the cold and the bullet hole through her suitcase grandma.

"I bet they got my favorite pair of jeans too." She stuck her finger in the hole and twisted it around. "You better fucking kill them."

"You want me to kill someone because they shot your pants?" Reed blinked at her.

"Not only because of that." Eva grabbed her giant leopard-print bag and slung it over her shoulder. "But you should add it to your list." She grabbed the handle of her suitcase. "Do you have any idea how hard it is for women to find jeans that fit?"

"Eva!" Harlow came running out of the main building, arms out. She grabbed Eva in a hug. "I'm so glad you're okay." She pushed her out at arm's length. "And I'm fucking jealous as hell that you got to be in a gun fight."

"It wasn't a gun fight." Brock stepped in close to Eva, intending to put his arm around her, but Harlow beat him to the punch, wrapping Eva up and pulling her toward the glass doors.

"Tell me everything." She punched the keypad and shoved Eva inside, not even bothering to hold the door open for him and Reed.

"You might be fucked." Reed punched his code into the pad and held the door open for Brock to pass through carrying his own luggage.

"Seems like." He dropped it all beside the door. "She's been a handful from the beginning."

"I can imagine." Reed gave him a grin. "I'm a little jealous you're the one who got to her first."

"Kicking your ass is still on the table, Reed." Brock walked in the direction of where Harlow led Eva, following their feminine voices down the hall.

"Brock." Dutch stood from his desk as Brock passed his office. "I need to go over what happened with you."

"Later." He kept going but Dutch didn't give up, following him down the hall. "Not later. Now. Shawn's already in the big conference room with Pierce."

Brock stopped. "Pierce?"

The head of Alaskan Security being in a meeting was not a good sign.

Dutch nodded. "This isn't good, man."

"Fuck." He started walking again. "Fuck, fuck, fuck."

Years he'd successfully kept any woman from getting to him. From getting close.

And now, the first time one did, she instantly had a target strapped to her back.

"Brock?" Eva's voice was soft behind him. When he turned her eyes were on him as she took slow steps his way. "What's wrong?" She lifted a finger as he started to speak. "Please don't lie to me."

"What just happened was bad." He closed the distance left between them. "Very bad."

Her brows came together. "I'd already mathed that out." She rested one hand on the center of his chest, smoothing down the fabric. "I didn't think they were trying to invite us to a party."

Telling her the truth of what might be happening wasn't something he wanted to do.

But lying to this woman wasn't an option.

"Come with me." He caught her hand in his. "We have a meeting to go to."

CHAPTER 12

"SO YOU DICKS brought me here knowing this was happening?"

She stared at the man at the end of the table. A dozen eyeballs burned into her from around the room. "And you didn't think that was a bad idea? Drag an innocent person into your fucking mess?"

Eva stood, knocking her chair back as she leaned forward, pressing her hands on the table so she could lean closer to the man watching her with a mild amount of amusement.

Which only pissed her off more.

"This is bullshit and you know it. I could have stayed home and been perfectly fine. Now I'm a freaking target in a turf war?"

"You weren't perfectly fine or you wouldn't have been willing to fly across the country to come here, Ms. Tatum." His words were calm and measured.

And condescending as hell.

"I didn't want to come here at all." If this prick thought she was the kind of girl who backed down from someone like him then he was about to be surprised as shit.

She ate men like him for fucking breakfast.

"I came here so my partners would shut up about it." And what a freaking mistake that was.

"Then that would be your mistake."

"My mist—" Eva straightened. "You arrogant, gas-lighting, son of a bitch."

The man leaned to look around her, lifting his black brows at Brock.

Brock leaned into her side.

Eva braced herself for what was coming. No doubt he was going to tell her to calm down.

To shut up.

"You forgot to tell him about how they shot Gram-Gram."

Her eyes snapped his way.

"What?" Finally the guy at the head of the table sounded something besides cool and indifferent.

Eva nodded, turning back to face him. "Right between the eyes."

Harlow pointed at him with the tip of the pen always in her hand. "Gram-Gram got a kill shot because of you, Pierce."

He fucking looked like a Pierce. Like David Gandy without an accent.

And with a few almost-hidden weapons stashed under the impeccable cut of his suit.

Pierce turned his gaze to Harlow. "How in the hell did her Gram-Gram get involved in this?"

"She was in the trunk of the Rover." Eva glanced to Harlow.

She'd never had a partner in crime before. No one who could handle the same shit she could.

Mona was great, but at the end of the day she intimidated way too easily.

And Chandler was the type who would have told her to calm down.

To reign herself in.

Not Harlow. She was right there beside her, taking Pierce where he deserved to go.

And doing it with a straight face.

"She was in the fucking trunk?" Pierce slammed one hand down on the table, his eyes hard on Brock. "Why in the hell was her Gram-Gram in the trunk?"

Eva tried to breathe slowly. If Pierce said Gram-Gram one more time she was going to lose it.

Harlow coughed.

They were going to have to practice this.

"I put her in the trunk." Eva stepped in front of Brock, blocking him from Pierce's penetrating glare. "It seemed like the best place for her."

Pierce stared at her and for a second she saw a familiar flicker.

Apprehension.

Not fear. This man didn't seem like the type to fear anything.

"Where is she now?" His tone was a little softer, but the apprehension was quickly being replaced by something else.

Suspicion.

Pierce might be smarter than most people she was used to dealing with.

"In Harlow's office."

"Go get her." He leaned back in his seat, slipping back to the man from a few minutes ago.

"Fine." Eva spun and marched out.

He was going to be pissed. She smiled.

A minute later she was walking back into the room, wheeling her suitcase along beside her.

Pierce stared at it for a few seconds longer than she expected before his eyes lifted to hers. "What do you do for a living, Ms. Tatum?"

"I hunt lies."

He didn't look the least bit confused by her broad explanation.

"Do you usually find them?"

"I do."

He took a long, deep breath, dark gaze studying her in a way that probably made most people uncomfortable.

Made grown men shift on their feet.

She stood taller, straighter. Pierce didn't pay her bills and he sure as hell didn't fuck her.

That meant he could suck it.

"What is it *you* do for a living, Pierce?"

"I own this company."

"Makes sense." Eva scanned his expensive suit. Hell, his watch alone cost more than her first car.

Not her current car, though. "If you're trying to intimidate me it won't work."

"Is that what you think I'm doing? Trying to intimidate you?"

"Did your mother ever tell you it was rude to answer a question with a question?"

"My mother died when I was two."

"My mother couldn't have cared less about my existence." She tipped her head to one side. "And I still have manners."

"Enough." Brock stood beside her. "If you need anything else you can call me." He held Pierce's gaze longer than necessary as one hand rested on her hip, gently squeezing. "Come on. It's time for us to go."

Eva kept her glare on Pierce until she cleared the doorway. "I don't like him."

"I'll be sure he knows." Brock led her back down the hall to Harlow's office. "Get your stuff."

"I didn't even get to check my emails." She backed into the room. "And I told Mona and Chandler I would be calling to check in today."

"I'm sure they'll forgive you." Brock picked up her bag.

"They are already worried about me. I had like, five hundred texts from them."

Brock stopped. "How did you get texts from them?"

Shit.

"I meant I *probably* have five hundred texts from them."

"Uh-huh." He came closer. "How did you let them know you would be calling to check in today?"

"Is that what I said?"

He smiled, slow and easy as one finger came up to trace the line of her jaw. "I think you might have just lied to me, Eva."

Goddammit.

"It's your fault." She smacked at his hand. "You make me discombobulated."

His smile didn't waver as Brock moved closer, knocking the door closed with his foot. "Good."

"It's not good. It's terrible." She poked at him with one finger.

"I understand completely." He pressed against her, backing her against the door. "It's fucking awful." His body was big and warm as it blocked out everything else around them. "But something is there and I'm tired of pretending it's not." His nose slid along hers as his lips hovered just out of reach.

"I don't know if I can—" She choked a little on the last part, swallowing down the feelings daring to claw their way free.

"Just try." His voice was so soft. So deep.

"What if I'm bad at it?"

His smile was back. "I'm positive you're going to be bad at it." One hand curled against the side of her neck. "I think that's part of why I can't seem to make myself let you go."

"You should have let someone else take care of me." Eva closed her eyes, fighting to stay in control. Fighting to keep from feeling what he made her want to feel.

"That might be true." The pad of his thumb stroked across her lower lip. "But it's too late now."

A second later he tugged her away from the door. "Come on, Sunshine. It's time to go."

Eva blinked at the sudden shift. Two seconds ago she was pretty sure he was going to kiss her again.

And now Brock was grabbing her bag and swinging open the door, his big hand holding hers as he led her down the hall toward the front of the giant building. "Where are we going?"

"Someplace no one will find you." He stopped at the front door where her Gram-Gram suitcase was already waiting with Harlow leaned against the wall beside it, tapping her foot as she scrolled through her phone. She glanced up and grinned.

"You are my new hero."

"Don't act like you haven't ripped Pierce a new asshole more times than you can count." Brock grabbed a few bags and walked outside to a black Range Rover.

"It's exhausting being the only one not scared of him, though." Harlow went back to the phone in her hand. "Be ready. He's probably going to offer you a job."

"Who? That Pierce guy?" Eva pulled on her coat and zipped it up to her chin before tugging on the hat her Gram-Gram knit for her last year. "I doubt he's interested in ever seeing me again. Definitely not in a professional capacity."

"I wouldn't be so sure. He must like it or he would have fired me the first time I met him." Harlow held out the phone. "Here's a satellite phone. You should be able to get reception no matter what."

Eva stared at the cell. "What's that for?"

"For you to use while you guys are holed up." She pushed it closer until Eva took it. "I don't want you to be stuck there with no way to call if you need help." She glanced out the door where Reed and Dutch were helping Brock load up the SUV. "They have a bad habit of doing shit they shouldn't when things get crazy." Her eyes snapped back to Eva's. "How are your first aid skills?"

"What?" Eva pressed her temples. "This is not what was supposed to happen." She squeezed her eyes shut. "What did I do to deserve this?"

"Something amazing." Harlow leaned back against the wall. "You must be a way better person than I am, because I still haven't gotten any action." She wiggled her brows. "Of the danger or the dick variety."

A group of men passed, all tall and fit and good-looking as hell. "How is that possible? This place is literally crawling with it."

"Right?" Harlow groaned as she straightened, stretching her arms over her head. "None of them will even give me the time of day." She glared as Dutch came in. "It's probably his fucking fault."

"What's my fault now, Mowry?"

"My vaginal dry spell."

Dutch's jaw twitched. "How is that my fault?"

"I don't know." She waved one hand his way. "But I'm sure it is somehow."

Brock wrapped one arm around Eva's waist and pulled her in close. "Time to go."

"Where are we going?"

"Somewhere no one will be able to get to you."

"You keep saying that." Eva tried to slow down, but Brock kept moving, his long strides forcing her to almost run to keep up with him. "Why did Harlow give me a phone that works anywhere?"

"Did she?" Brock glanced down at the cell clutched in her hand. "She's a smart woman. I didn't think of that."

"You aren't answering me." Eva grabbed the front of his coat and yanked as hard as she could, pulling him in close. "Where are you taking me?"

He smiled and kissed her on the tip of the nose. "My house." Brock opened the passenger door on the already-running Rover. "Get comfy. It's a long drive."

Two hours later Eva was staring at a two-car garage stuck out in the middle of nowhere at the end of what some people might call a road.

Some people was Brock.

"You live in that?"

"What did you expect?" He grinned before climbing out to unlock the handle in the center of the door, pulling it open to reveal an empty bay.

Mostly empty. A large snowmobile sat to one side.

Brock's cheeks were pink from the cold when he climbed back into the Rover. "You look terrified, Tatum."

Her eyes stayed on the sled as Brock pulled the SUV into the garage and parked. He climbed out and opened the back hatch before starting to unload their luggage and the groceries Tyson and Reed brought from her Airbnb.

Her beautiful, heated, Airbnb.

"You can't sit in there forever." Brock gave her a wink as she looked back through the SUV at him. "Might as well get out and start suiting up."

"Suiting up?"

He nodded to where a pair of white pants and a coat hung on the wall beside the snowmobile. "Those go on over your clothes."

This was crazy. She lived in a condo on the river. One she could walk to from almost anywhere she had to go.

There was a freaking grocery store within five minutes.

"This is where you live?" She shoved out of the SUV, her breath catching as a cold gust of wind whipped through the open door.

"When I'm not working." Brock loaded the last of their bags onto a small enclosed trailer and closed the lid. He glanced up at her. "The rest of the time I stay with whoever I'm working for." Brock grabbed the pants and coat and walked her way. "Arms out."

She did as he asked, mostly because what the hell else was she going to do?

Brock zipped her into the coat before working the thick canvas pants on over her jeans.

"I don't think they're going to stay up." She wiggled in the too-big pants, trying to keep them in place.

"You're going to be sitting the whole time. They just have to stay on." Brock turned to push the sled out into the snow before hooking the tiny trailer up to the back. "Come on. We need to get going before the sun goes down."

Eva leaned out, peeking at the landscape around them. "What happens after the sun goes down?"

He smiled, reaching one gloved hand out to her. "It gets cold."

This wasn't cold?

Eva braced for the smack of the wind as she took Brock's hand and stepped out of the garage. She felt the pressure as it hit her, but the extra layer kept it from being any more than that.

Everywhere except her face.

"I forgot." Brock reached into the pocket of her coat and pulled out a knit hat.

Nope. Not a hat.

He pushed back her hood and tugged the mask over her head and face before pulling the hood back into place.

She watched as he slid the garage door back into place and locked the handle. "What about you? Aren't you going to freeze?"

Brock was still only in his parka and jeans. Nowhere near as protected from the elements as she was.

"I'll be just fine." He wrapped one arm around her back and hefted her body against his. "But I like that you're worried about me." He kissed her through the opening of the mask. "It's go time, Tatum." He grabbed her around the waist and picked her up off the ground, dropping her butt onto the long seat of the sled before climbing on in front of her. "Hold on tight."

The engine fired to life and a second later they were moving, the sound of the wind and the roar of the sled drowning out her scream as they flew over the snow.

The cold air made her eyes water and her nose run. She pressed her face into Brock's back and closed her eyes, holding onto him for dear life.

She was going to die. All this work to shut Mona and Chandler up was going to kill her.

No one would find her until spring.

Was there even spring in Alaska?

"Almost there, Sunshine." Brock's voice was barely audible between the layers covering her ears and the wind battering her head.

She nodded against his back.

A few minutes later the sled slowed enough that she was willing to risk taking a peek.

"Holy shit, Broccoli."

"That a good holy shit?" He pulled to a stop in front of a modern-lined building made of wood and concrete. The roof was covered with solar panels as was a large portion of the ground beside it.

"This is your house?" It was bigger than she expected and definitely nicer.

"It is." He climbed off the snowmobile and reached out a hand. "Come on. Let's get you inside where it's warm."

Eva kept her eyes on the house as she stood on one leg and bounced her way off the seat, letting Brock support her weight as she did. "Why do you live somewhere you can only get to by snowmobile?"

"That's only in the winter." He gave her a wink. "I can drive all the way to the front door in the summer."

"Which is like two months." She peeked around as they walked to the small covered porch. "The steps are shoveled." Eva leaned back to look up at the solar panels. They should be covered in snow, but each one was clear and snow-free.

"One of my neighbors comes over once every few days when I'm out of town." Brock shoved a key in the door and unlocked the deadbolt before stepping back. "Go on in. I'll bring in our bags."

Eva peeked inside.

"You're letting all the warm air out, Sunshine."

"Sorry." She stepped in and Brock immediately closed the door, leaving her in his space.

All alone.

The inside of the place was just as surprising as the outside. Thick rugs covered the rugged wood floors and large leather sofas and chairs dominated the open living room. Everything was dark and sleek, but still cozy-feeling.

But that wasn't the surprising part.

Eva fought her boots off, leaving them on the rug just inside the door before making her way across the room to a wall off shelves. A good number of books lined a few, but discovering Brock was a reader didn't even make her blink.

It was the rest of the items that had her mind spinning. She reached for one, carefully picking the priceless object up for a closer look.

"Eva?"

She spun to face him, tucking the small sculpture safely against her chest as she did.

Brock's eyes dropped to where she held it over her heart. He took a deep breath.

"You probably have some questions."

CHAPTER 13

"WHO ARE ALL these kids?"

Eva still held the clay pot his oldest nephew made when he was six, both hands wrapped protectively around the brightly painted item as if she understood its value.

"My nieces and nephews." Brock moved toward her. He thought this moment would be a hurdle.

That explaining his life would be difficult.

"I'm the youngest of four brothers." He reached around her to pick up one of the photos lining the shelves. "This is us when we were kids."

She smiled at the shot of him and his brothers piled up in an open tent at one of their many family camping trips. "That's a lot of testosterone your mother had to wrangle."

"She's amazing." Brock pointed to the most recent picture of his mother, flanked by two of her grandsons.

Eva grabbed the photo. "She's beautiful."

"I'll tell her you said so."

He had no intention of doing that. He fully intended for Eva to tell his mother herself.

"Good. Most women like to hear that." She replaced the photo along with the pot.

"Not you, though."

Eva's eyes met his. "No. Not me."

"Why?"

"Because being beautiful isn't always a good thing." She looked down at the heavy coat still zipped on her body. "Thank you for letting me wear this." Her lips pressed into a frown. "You were probably freezing."

"I'm used to it." His acclimation to the frigid weather was not why he still felt warm even after a bitingly cold trip to the cabin. "Is it warm enough for you in here?" He reached out to work down the heavy metal zipper of the coat.

"It is." Her eyes moved around the cabin. "How do you heat this place?"

"Depends." He'd never shared this place with a woman. Never wanted to, but seeing Eva in his private space settled a part of him that was forever on edge. "I use solar for as much as I can, but I have a propane tank for back-up." He nodded to the buck stove set between the kitchen and living room. "When I'm here I can pretty much heat the whole place with that."

"Wow." Her brows lifted. "I kind of doubted you when you said we were going where no one could find me."

He pulled off the coat and tossed it over the back of the large leather sofa. "I'm sorry you've been dragged into this."

"Is it fixable?" She watched as he unfastened the pants and worked them down her jean-covered legs. "Would I be safer to just go home? Hire someone there?"

He wanted to be able to tell her there was no place she would be safer than here. It was true.

But it was also not possible to keep her here forever. She had a company to run. Bad men to investigate.

"Is that what you want? To go home?" The thought made his chest ache.

"Well." Eva chewed her bottom lip the way she did when the desire to lie made it hard to tell the truth she prided herself on always giving. "I have to go home sometime."

It wasn't the open honest answer he was hoping for. Eva might not lie, but she sure as hell skirted the truth.

And he was tired of it. "I don't want you to go."

Her eyes barely widened.

He wanted her to be honest. Wanted her to tell him all the reasons she was trying to pretend there was nothing real happening between them.

So he would give her his reasons for being like he was. Hopefully she would return the favor.

"All my brothers got married young." He laid the pants on top of the coat before grabbing Eva's hand and pulling her toward the couch. "Had kids young." He sat, tugging her down beside him. "They were husbands and dads before I finished high school."

Eva smiled. "Uncle Broccoli."

He laughed in spite of the truth he was about to offer her. The honesty he'd never given another person. "Believe it or not, none of them have ever come up with that one." He reached out to smooth down the side of her hair. "I'm sure they'll be thrilled when they hear it." He didn't give her time to think too much into the comment. "My oldest brother married the girl he dated all through school. They'd been together since eighth grade."

"That's sweet." Eva rested one elbow on the back of the couch and leaned into her palm.

"They had four boys back to back. She wanted a big family." He chuckled a little. "Said she wanted a basketball team."

"Because you're all so tall." Eva followed along perfectly.

He nodded. "You would have really liked her."

The soft smile she'd been wearing slipped. "Would have?"

"She died a few days after their youngest was born. A blood clot from the c-section."

A line of tears edged each of Eva's ringed eyes. "Oh my gosh." One hand covered her mouth as her gaze moved to the shelves where dozens of photos of his family sat. "That's—" She shook her head. "I don't even have a word for it."

"My brother was devastated." Brock reached for her other hand and held it in his. He swallowed around the lump of pain clogging his throat. "He couldn't live without her."

Eva shook her head. "No." The pain in her eyes almost stopped him. Almost made him keep the rest to himself.

173

But he couldn't hold back. Not with her.

"He shot himself on the first anniversary of her death."

A tear slid down her cheek and she let it fall. Didn't try to wipe it away as another followed behind it. "Who has their boys?"

"My parents." He brushed his thumb across her cheek, stopping the slide of another tear.

She sniffed in a long breath. "Are they okay?"

He lifted one shoulder. "As okay as they can ever be. I'm not sure that's something you can completely come back from."

Eva's head barely tipped to one side, her eyes moving over his face.

She was connecting all the dots he'd given her. Putting together the pieces of his life like the puzzle they were.

"But you're not okay."

He shook his head. "No."

He'd never given any woman this much of himself. Not even close.

Never planned to. In a life filled with lethal men and constant threats, this was the most dangerous thing he'd ever done.

Letting Eva Tatum in.

Her hand slowly reached out, the move more tentative than anything he'd seen from her.

The Eva Tatum he'd seen was strong and sure and confident. Unwilling to be anything besides what she was.

Now she was giving him the smallest glimpse of the part she kept hidden. Held close.

Her palm finally rested against his cheek, warm and soft.

She didn't tell him any of the things most people did in situations like this one. She didn't apologize. Didn't talk about what a tragedy it was.

Her eyes just rested on his, a war of understanding and indecision fighting in their rippled depths.

Her chest lifted and fell on a long, deep breath.

And then she was on him, straddling his lap, hands shoving into his hair, full lips finding his. She held him tight, fingers pressing into his scalp as her body rolled against him, trying to get closer.

Brock never wanted to want this. Was never willing to admit to himself or anyone else how empty his life was.

How fucking empty he was.

He tried to pretend it wasn't there. Did his best to stifle the loneliness with companionship. Meaningless sex with women who deserved better.

But that would never happen with Eva. He knew it the second he saw her helping that old man in the airport. The way laughter erupted from her lips. The way she refused to hide who she was. The full honesty in every breath she took.

She didn't hide behind a wall, waiting to see if he would like her. Because she didn't care.

It cut him off at the knees. He couldn't avoid seeing *her*.

All of her.

And every bit of it was fucking perfect.

"You ruined everything, you know that, Sunshine?"

"I'm not the problem here, Broccoli. You're the problem." She grabbed at his shirt. "You just couldn't be shallow, could you?" Eva shoved the fabric up his chest, yanking when it got caught on his armpits. "What man doesn't want to have casual sex?" Her hands were on his skin, not an ounce of hesitation in the way she touched him. "It's freaking ridiculous." She went back to his shirt, nearly strangling him with it in the fight to get it off. "This could have been so simple."

He raised his arms and she whipped the garment off and threw it over her head before grabbing the hem of her sweater and shucking it in one quick move.

"Stop." He grabbed at her hands as they went to work on the button of his pants, catching her by the wrists just as she flipped it free. "Stop."

"I don't want to stop." She twisted in his grip. "I want to keep going." Her eyes locked onto his. "And so do you."

"Not if you're still going to pretend this is just fucking."

Her shoulders dropped and her hands went limp in his. Eva pressed her lips tight together, but not before he saw the tiny quiver of her chin.

"I have had a lot of meaningless sex."

Her lips curved into a frown. "Are you trying to make me jealous? Because it won't work."

"It would work, but I wouldn't do something like that to you." He leaned forward, straightening so their eyes were in line. "I want you to know I've never had meaningful sex. Never wanted to." He wrapped both arms around her back. "Not until you. You fucked me up, Sunshine." He skimmed his fingers down the soft skin over her spine. "And if this isn't going to mean something to you then I'm not doing it."

"I don't want it to mean anything to you." Her voice was soft.

Scared.

But Eva wasn't scared for herself.

She was scared for him.

"I didn't either." He caught one of her hands and lifted it to his shoulder. "But it does." He found her other hand and rested it on his other shoulder. "I couldn't stop it from happening. And I fucking tried."

"You were so crabby. Like an old man."

He smiled. This is why he couldn't keep her in the same place he'd managed to put every other woman. She could make him smile even now. When the one thing he never wanted to risk was pressing down on him, unrelenting and unavoidable. "You love old men, though. Remember your friend Elmer?"

"He was way more charming than you are." Her lips barely lifted before she pressed them flat again. "But you are a clear winner in the body department." One finger traced a line down the center of his bare chest.

"I'm glad you find me physically more appealing than an eighty-year-old man."

"Less charming, though."

"Charm isn't real, Eva." He shook his head at her. "Not ever."

She nodded. "I know." Her mouth twisted to one side in an off-kilter pout. "I wish you were more charming."

"I wish you were less—" He tried to come up with a single word to sum up all the reasons he couldn't help what was happening. "Everything."

Eva shrugged. "I am what I am."

"And that's why you have to deal with this." He pushed up from the couch. "Because I like what you are." Her arms tightened around his neck as he stood. "I like that you drink fruit punch and help old men and do yoga in your underwear."

Her eyes narrowed on his. "Athletic wear."

"Call it whatever you want, Sunshine." Brock walked down the short hall. "That was the moment I knew I was fucked."

"Because I looked so hot?" Her tone dripped with judgment.

She was still trying desperately to box him in.

"Because I would have been doing my best to talk that athletic wear off anyone else." He stepped into the bigger of the cabin's two bedrooms, crossing the room to go straight to the bed. "And the thought of you being naked in my bed scared the shit out of me." He slowly lowered her to the mattress.

Her head barely turned to one side, eyes sliding over the quilt beneath her. "Does that mean I'm not going to be naked soon?"

"It means I'm willing to face it if you are."

"Oh." Her arms were still wrapped tight around his neck, keeping him close. "What if I'm not ready to do that?"

"Then I'm happy to ask again tomorrow."

Eva's fingers combed through the hair at his nape. "Kay."

He leaned in close nosing the line of her neck, breathing deep. "I can be patient as hell, so don't think for a second you can wait me out. If you don't want this you're going to have to say it."

"What if I say I don't want it?"

"Then I will call Shawn. You can have your pick of who steps in."

"You would pass me off?" The fear edging her voice said more than she was willing to.

"You can't have it both ways, Eva. Not with me." He leaned up, pressing his forehead to hers. "You might be able to look at me every day and pretend you don't feel anything. I can't do that." He skimmed his hands up her bare arms. "I will let you go if that's what you want, but if that's what you're going to ask me to do, then ask now. For my sake."

She shook her head. "You don't understand what could happen."

"Don't I?" He cradled her face between his palms. "My brother died because he lost the woman he loved. Her death is what killed him. Their kids lost both parents because he couldn't live without her."

"You could live without me."

"I could." Brock waited until her eyes met his. "That's why I'm asking you to walk away now if it's not what you want."

Eva blinked, working a line of tears back into place. "I'm so scared."

"I know." He pressed a kiss to her forehead. This woman had seen so much of what happened when relationships went bad. When men lied. When trust was broken.

He'd only seen the opposite. Men who loved women with everything they had. Treasured them.

Protected them.

"Don't be scared of me, Eva."

Her head barely shook. "I'm not scared of you."

He smiled. "Good."

He'd let her lie this time. Soon it wouldn't be a lie.

"This might not be what you think it is, Brock." Her eyes moved over his face before coming back to his. "It might not work out."

"I know that." The thought actually gave him comfort. Made it possible to take this step. If it didn't work out then he wouldn't ever be where his brother was.

She was quiet for a minute as her hands smoothed over his shoulders. "We might fight over everything."

"We might."

She was talking herself through the same possibilities he had. Working them into a life raft of sorts. Something to keep her afloat in deep and treacherous waters.

"We might not get along at all."

"Might not."

Her touch moved down his arms, sliding over his biceps and forearms. "We might end up just being friends."

They wouldn't. There's no way he could be just Eva's friend. "It's possible."

The tips of her fingers moved across his stomach, her soft touch progressing along with her thoughts. If it took the expectation of failing to get her to take this step then so be it. Whatever she needed, he would let her have.

"I like you, Broccoli." Her eyes followed the path of her hands. "I like that you're crabby and bossy and no fun."

"I told you. I am fun." He relaxed a little giving her more of his weight. "But I will never think you putting yourself in danger is fun."

One brow lifted. "You just put me on the back of a snow motorcycle. How is that any different?" The other brow went up to meet the first. "It's not."

"You're a pain in the ass, Tatum."

"Does that mean you changed your mind about," her hand pushed down into his pants, "oh."

"Does it seem like I've changed my mind?" He gritted his teeth as her fingers skimmed the side of his dick.

"I don't know." She smiled, slow and sweet. "I might need to take a closer look."

CHAPTER 14

WAS HIS EYE twitching?

"What's wrong?"

She wasn't the kind of chick who laid back and thought of England, so if Brock was expecting a woman who was fine with putting her satisfaction in someone else's hands then he was going to be disappointed in this interaction.

"Nothing is wrong." His eyes shut as she managed to get her hand a little farther into the open fly of his jeans. "I'm fine."

"You don't look fine." Between the tight fit of his boxer briefs and the unforgiving cut of his jeans she was barely able to get her hand around him. "You look unhappy."

"I'm not unhappy." His lids pressed tight together as she eased down the length of his cock. "I'm focused."

"On what?"

"Not making an ass of myself." He tried to pull away but she caught him by the belt loop with her free hand.

"Where are you going?" She used her hold on his pants to work them down a little, trying to find more working room. "Can you take your pants off?"

His eyes opened at the request.

"Please?" She gave him a smile, wiggling her brows. "If you take yours off, I'll take mine off."

"How about you just take yours off and we see where that takes us?"

"That seems like less fun than both our pants coming off." Eva tried to shimmy his jeans further down his hips, but the damn things were stuck. She lifted her head to peek down at the situation. "You ass."

Brock's legs were apart, one knee resting on the mattress at either side of her thighs, the position preventing her from progressing in her quest to get him more naked.

He grinned down at her. "No one's ever called me an ass in bed before."

"That's shocking." Eva pushed at his chest. "Are you going to be like this the whole time?"

"Probably." Brock's fingers worked the fly of her jeans open. "Maybe worse."

"Worse?" She scoffed as he snagged her hand and pulled it out of his pants. "Hey."

"You can have it back later." He pushed upright, hovering over her on his knees. "When I'm done."

"Done with what?" She pushed up on her elbows as Brock peeled down her jeans, only struggling a little with the skinny fit, and that was mostly around her ankles.

He frowned down at her underwear.

She looked at the prettiest pair of panties she owned. They were black satin with a pink floral design. Her bra even matched. "What's wrong?"

"I thought I knew you better than this." Brock reached out to trace the dipping cut of the underpants with one finger.

"What were you expecting?"

"I kind of expected your underwear to be the ones with the days of the week on it." His finger dragged across her skin to follow the line of the cup of her bra, tracing over the swell of her breast.

He seemed so disappointed in himself. Upset he didn't see her as clearly as he thought.

But he did.

"I have those." Eva considered not telling him the full truth, but he just looked so dejected. "Yesterday I wore Monday."

Yesterday wasn't Monday.

Brock's finger kept moving, following the dip into her cleavage. "Why aren't you wearing them now?" His gaze slowly lifted to hers and her stomach slipped.

"Because I wore them yesterday." Hopefully the explanation would appease him. Just in case she slipped one hand behind her back and unhooked the expensive bra she saved for special occasions.

Sexy special occasions.

His eyes didn't leave hers as she pulled it free and tossed it over the side of the bed.

"Why aren't you wearing your normal panties, Eva?"

"Reasons." She took a deep breath, purposefully pushing her breasts higher, hoping to distract him. "Touch me, Brock. Please?"

He shook his head. "Not until you tell me what I want to know."

Damn him. Why couldn't he be like every other man in the world and go half stupid over boobs? "You're an ass."

"I plan to reward your honesty." He dropped back to his hands and knees, his body hovering just over hers. "Tell me."

"What are you going to give me if I do?"

His lips slid over the skin of her neck. "First my fingers." He nipped at her skin. "Then my tongue." The wet heat of his mouth closed around the lobe of her ear, his tongue circling in a way that had her thighs pressing tight together. His teeth barely raked over her skin as he pulled away. "And then my cock."

She literally whimpered. Like some sort of inexperienced woman who trembled when a man touched her.

That was not her. Not ever.

"Why are you wearing these panties, Eva?" His fingers barely dipped under the elastic banding her waist.

He already knew.

"You are an ass." She wiggled a little, trying to work his hand closer to where she wanted it.

"You keep saying that but you're not going anywhere, so I'm not convinced you believe it." His touch skimmed over the top of her pubic bone. "Just say it. Give me the truth."

"Are you going to use that against me forever?"

"I hope so." His fingers moved an inch lower.

Almost there.

"I wanted to be prepared."

"You said you weren't going to sleep with me." His tone held a smile.

Gloating.

"I wasn't."

"But you changed your mind."

"Ugh." She stared up at the ceiling. "Maybe."

He pushed lower, barely skimming her labia. "You're so close to getting what you want, Tatum."

"Yes. Fine. I changed my mind."

A low rumble moved through Brock's chest. "I knew you could do it."

His fingers immediately found her clit, stroking with a steady, purposeful touch. One that was unrelenting. There was no teasing. No hesitation.

None of the normal trial and error that normally happened the first time. Probably because this man had more experience than most of the ones in her past.

Thank God.

She was coming in what felt like seconds. The slide of his fingers slowed, dragging out the climax with expert precision.

She should have been at least a little satisfied. Partially placated.

"You are so fucking sexy." Brock's voice was a little ragged. A little rough.

"I know."

He smiled. "Good."

"You're a little sexy too."

"A little?" He hooked a finger from each hand under the waistband of her panties and dragged them down her legs. "I just got you off and I'm only a little sexy?"

She lifted one shoulder. "If getting me off is how we're going to measure sexiness, then I definitely have you beat."

He growled low in his chest. "You are fucking dangerous, you know that?" Brock tossed her panties over the side of the bed. "Hazardous to my sanity."

"I question your sanity anyway, Broccoli." She reached up to grab him by the hair, pulling him down until his body pressed against hers. "You kill people for a living. That's not sane."

"I kill bad people." He groaned when her legs wrapped around his waist, seating him where she most wanted him to be.

Her eyes moved over his face. "There are a lot of bad people in this world. People you would never expect to be as awful as they are." She traced a path across his cheekbones and down the slightly-rough stubble covering his cheeks. "I see it every day. They lie. Cheat. Steal. And they always blame someone else. No one ever owns what they do."

"Why do you do it?"

The answer to that question was complicated and convoluted, but still painfully simple.

And it was something Eva didn't want to think about right now. If she did this wouldn't happen.

She would push him away. Convince herself it was for the best.

But it would be a lie.

"Lots of reasons." She lifted her hips, hoping to shift the emotional closeness he was hoping for to a more physical one. "I feel like you made me certain promises, Broccoli. Something about mouths and cocks, and I've seen none of that."

Brock leaned in so close his nose almost touched hers. "You act like we aren't snowed into a cabin in the middle of nowhere." His hand skimmed up the side of her body, coming to cradle her face in his palm. "If you think for a second I have any intention of rushing this then you have lost your damn mind."

"Does that mean you can only go once?"

He stared at her.

"I'm just asking. So I know what to expect. Because so far there's been a lot of talking and not very much doing."

The world was not kind to demanding women, and she was no exception.

But it was who she was. Who she'd learned to be proud to be.

Because hiding who you are does no one any good. Not ever.

But Brock didn't look frustrated with her. He actually looked amused.

"Where did you come from?" His thumb traced her lower lip. "Just when I think I've seen the best you have to offer, you go and give me more." His lips took his thumb's place, moving against hers as he kept talking. "Now I'm going to have to ask you to shut up for a while."

"How long is a while?" She pressed her lips together.

"Long enough." His hand trailed down her body, fingers finding a nipple and rolling it between them. "Don't want you to wake up tomorrow disappointed."

"I guess we'll see." She arched into his touch.

"You'll see. I already know." Brock shifted, moving down until his mouth replaced his fingers, teeth and tongue working her nipple until she was writhing under him. When he released it she thought he would move lower. Instead he found her other breast, nipping and sucking at that nipple like he had all the time in the world.

And it was driving her crazy.

"What's wrong, Tatum? You seem impatient." He sucked her tightened tip deep into his mouth, tongue swirling before flipping back and forth.

"You're teasing me."

"You just came. Remember?"

"And I would like to do it again."

Brock laughed but it sounded more like a growl. "The first one was for you." He moved lower again, kissing his way down her belly. "This one is mine."

"Why would you want—" The lap of his tongue over her clit stole the rest of her words.

"I'm laying a foundation, Eva." Another swipe of his tongue. "One I plan to build on."

The next lick made her whimper again. It made her sound needy. Out of control. "Stop making me do that."

"No." His thumbs parted her, pulling her open so he could torture her with nothing in his way.

And that's what he fucking did.

Brock would give her just enough to have her climbing toward release, and then he would take it away. Steal it right out from under her.

Then the asshole would do it again.

Sometimes he would lick and suck relentlessly until she was right there.

Then the next time he would give her clit slow, teasing rubs with the tip of his tongue, just enough to push her along.

It was too much and not enough. Over and over until she was begging. "I can't do this anymore, Brock. Please."

"You can. And you will." His thumb made slow passes over her as he kissed the inside of her thigh.

Her head rolled from side to side as the orgasm once again tried to get traction. "I can't." She reached for him, grabbing his hair, trying to force him to end it now.

Brock pulled her hands free, holding her wrists tight at her sides as he used his shoulders to shove her legs higher, wider. "This one is mine, Eva. I will take it when I'm ready for it and not a second before that, you understand me?"

How was that the most awful, but single hottest thing a man had ever said to her?

She was stuck, held in place while he gave her only what he wanted her to have.

190

And it was as unbearable as it was arousing.

"I will always give you what you need, Eva." His mouth was everywhere that wasn't useful. Brock sucked her labia. Slid his tongue along her slit. Carefully avoided the thing that could send her over the edge.

At this point it wouldn't take more than a single touch.

"But sometimes you will have to be patient. Trust me to take you where you deserve to go." One thumb stroked the inside of her wrist as he blew a warm stream of air across her clit.

Trust was something she didn't have to offer. Not him or anyone else.

She didn't even give it to herself.

"I can't, Brock."

"Just this. Just trust me in this." His voice was softer than before. Like he knew how much he was asking of her.

Like he understood.

Eva squeezed her eyes shut. Tried to close out the way he made her feel.

"Only this. Only here." His mouth was against her again. "Trust me."

He didn't give her the chance to answer, because the second the words were out his tongue was on her, stroking with relentless efficiency, shoving her back up the same path he'd taken her countless times.

But this time he didn't stop.

The second before she tumbled over the edge his lips closed around her, sucking with the same rhythm Brock set with his tongue, sending her body

191

curling up and around his, holding onto anything she could find as she came apart.

Out of control.

Out of her mind.

Out of her body.

Lost to something that terrified her.

But then he was there. Warm and solid.

Strong.

Real.

His arms held her tight, his weight held her down. Kept her safe from the demons threatening to steal this moment.

Make it theirs.

Eva clung to him as the world spun out of control.

Her world spun out of control.

This was never supposed to happen. It wasn't fair.

Wasn't right.

Except there was no stopping it. Not now.

Probably not ever.

"I'm so sorry." She shook her head, eyes squeezed tightly shut. "I didn't mean for this to—"

"Shh." His lips were soft as they moved over her skin, skimming the line of her collarbone before working up her neck. "Relax and just be with me."

It sounded so simple.

But Brock didn't know. Didn't understand the truth of how things usually went. He thought he knew the worst of it, and to some extent he did.

But there was another, completely different sort of worse.

One that was just as devastating.

"But—"

His thumb pressed to her lips. "No. No buts." The thumb moved, making way for his mouth.

He held her close, his body a steady weight that grounded her at a time where all she wanted to do was flee.

Protect him from what could be hiding in the shadowy parts of her. What she never wanted to risk setting free.

"It will be okay, Eva." His hands cradled her face, tipping it toward his.

She made herself look at him. Made herself show him the truth she couldn't say.

But the fear clawing at her didn't scare him.

Didn't make him pull away.

Because Brock was stronger than she was. Braver.

He smiled down at her, thumbs skimming her cheeks. "It's okay to be scared."

Not true.

Brock thought love killed and he was still here. Still trying.

She thought the same thing.

And wanted to run from this man with everything she had. Get away before she could prove them both right.

"Say you still want this." He shifted over her, the movement of his body making Eva notice something she missed.

He was naked.

Eva looked between their bodies, eyes locking on his condom-wrapped dick, long and thick and straining.

And he was still asking for permission. Giving her the choice to do what she wanted and run.

Or be brave and stay.

Because this wasn't a casual fuck. Not even close.

This would change everything. Push her over a line there was no coming back from.

And maybe it was already behind her.

Eva looked back into his eyes, dark and warm and so full of promise.

The line was definitely already behind her.

She nodded. "I want this."

"Thank God." The air left his body, dragging out with a low groan as he pressed into her, long and slow.

She'd never been so full. Physically. Emotionally. Her dams were at the point of breaking. Swelling with a flood they might not be able to control.

So she held onto him, relying on someone else for the first time in her life.

Praying she wouldn't let him down. Wouldn't make him regret every second of this.

Wouldn't hurt him.

Brock's body rocked into hers, that same perfect rhythm he had before lifting her up again, carrying her with him. Taking them both to places she'd already been.

Only because he took her there.

He held her so tight she could barely breathe. His body was hard, muscles flexing and bunching beneath the heat of his skin as his movement became less controlled. Less careful.

"Eva. I can't—" His voice broke as his forehead dropped to hers. "What do you need?"

Brock thought something physical was holding her back. That a simple touch here or there could finish what he started.

But it wouldn't.

She pulled him closer, trying to find the same strength he had as she pressed one palm against his cheek. His eyes locked onto hers and held, giving her nowhere to hide.

No way to pretend.

"I think I might just need you."

The truth wasn't always easy. Sometimes it hurt. Sometimes it made things worse.

But it was always best.

And it was the only way she could keep him safe from the demons she inherited.

She would always have to give him the truth, no matter how much she didn't want to.

And this was one of those times.

Brock's gaze didn't budge as he moved faster, hips jerking as his body pushed into hers. "Come with me then."

Joint climaxes were a fantasy. Something made up by someone who thought orgasms could be timed.

Commanded into happening.

"Now, Eva. It's time to come now."

The sharpness of his voice. The swell of his cock. The slap of his hips.

Somehow it all worked.

Brock made her come on demand.

"That's my girl." His voice was a low growl in her ear as he ground into her, the friction of his body taking a perfectly great climax and making it almost unbearable.

Unbelievable.

His movements slowed as his body pressed hers deeper into the mattress. His breathing was ragged in her ear, choppy and rough. "You okay, Tatum?"

"No." She pushed at his chest. "What in the hell was that?"

His big body didn't budge from hers.

"That," he leaned up to press a kiss to the tip of her nose, "was more than fucking."

CHAPTER 15

"WHY ARE YOU already awake?"

Brock turned as Eva stumbled her way into the kitchen, one of his shirts hanging almost down to her knees. "I'm an early riser, Tatum."

"Ew." She peeked into the coffee cup sitting on the counter beside the maker. "Can I use this?"

"Didn't think you were a big coffee drinker." He poured a slow stream of milk into the pan in front of him.

"I'm not." She filled the cup and blew across the top. "Normally."

Her cheeks barely flushed.

"Are you saying I shouldn't have kept you up so late?" He stirred their breakfast, grinning at her.

"I'm saying I didn't realize you were a freaking machine."

"If I remember correctly, you were the one concerned that I might only be able to go for one round." He watched as she walked to go sit at the table set between the small kitchen and living room.

"I didn't realize you were going to take that as a challenge." Eva leaned back in the chair, tucking her knees close to her chest, sock-covered toes hanging over the edge of the seat.

"You sure about that?" He turned the burner down to low and went to where she was, leaning in close. "Because I'm pretty sure you knew damn well I would take it as a challenge."

Eva smiled up at him, a devilish sparkle in her eyes. "Maybe I knew."

Brock leaned down to catch her smiling lips. "Does that mean you worked up an appetite?"

"As a matter of fact, I am feeling rather famished." Her smile stayed, warm and soft.

He'd made more women breakfast than he should admit. It was a parting gift of sorts.

Not Eva. This was a carrot. One he planned to keep dangling in front of her, teasing her along with him.

"Good." He kissed her again, careful not to let it snowball out of control.

Because that's what she did to him. Eva looked innocent and harmless, but the second she opened her mouth there was no denying the threat she was.

And he couldn't stop himself from standing right in her path.

"What's on the menu this morning?" Her eyes followed him back to the stove, watching over the rim of her coffee cup.

"Biscuits and gravy."

"Does this mean you're a one-trick pony in the kitchen?"

He was used to women stroking his ego. Telling him he was handsome. Charming.

The best they'd ever had.

"You are a skeptical woman, Tatum." He shot her a grin before leaning down to pull the biscuits from the oven. "But for the record, my kitchen game is as on-point as my bedroom game."

"Interesting."

"What's that mean?" He set the hot sheet pan on the butcher-block counter between them.

Eva shrugged. "It just means I'll believe it when I see it."

He stared her down. "You're doing it again."

Her eyes opened wide. "Doing what?"

Brock leaned against the counter, hands braced on the smooth surface. "And you know what? It's probably going to work."

"I have no idea what you're talking about."

Like hell she didn't. "If you want something from me, all you have to do is ask." He rounded the counter and prowled back toward her. "I will give you anything you want, no taunting required."

"Anything?" Her feet dropped to the floor and she sat up straight.

"Anything."

Eva's knees separated, legs spreading wide as she skimmed up the hem of his shirt. "I'm not wearing any panties."

He couldn't look away as the shirt slid higher, exposing more and more of the soft skin of her thighs. His dick was hard before the fabric cleared her pussy.

She pushed her legs wider, skimming two fingers over the dark hair covering her pubic bone.

He was on his knees as they slid lower, stroking over the line where her labia met. Brock slid one hand behind each of her knees, pulling her feet off the floor, rocking her back in the chair, watching as she continued to tease herself.

Finally her hand moved, abandoning her pussy to wrap around the back of his head, pulling him close, putting his mouth where she wanted it.

She was as honest in her desire as she was in everything else.

Almost everything else.

He licked along her slit, teasing her swollen clit with the tip of his tongue as he slid two fingers into her, matching the strokes of each, building her up fast and hard.

Letting her immediately fall.

Because she had breakfast to eat.

He carefully set her feet back on the floor and pulled down the hem of his shirt, kissing down the inside of her thighs as he went.

"It's stupid how good you are at that." Eva's head was back, face pointed toward the ceiling.

"Glad you are happy with the services I provide." He stood, scooting her chair around to face the table.

Her laughter filled the cabin.

He'd been up here countless times. Always to be alone. Reset after a hard job.

It was where he planned to go when Wade left with Bess and Parker. Their arrival shifted more than just his friend's life. Bess opened the door he tried to keep locked.

He always thought falling in love with a woman was the risk. That as long as he didn't get close enough to care, he would be safe.

But he wasn't in love with Bess.

And he still felt the pain when she was shot. The deep, void of desperation when he saw his friend holding her bleeding body.

In that second Brock knew he wasn't safe anymore.

That falling in love wasn't the only way a woman could break him.

It was the reason he let Eva in. Because the risk was already there. And he never saw it coming.

Brock broke open a biscuit and covered it in gravy. It was in his hand when he heard a sound.

Eva straightened in her chair, eyes locked on the front door. "Brock?"

He dropped the plate to the counter and ran to grab her, pulling her body in close as he dragged Eva away from the windows and into the hall. His hand clamped over her mouth as she started to speak. Her eyes locked onto his.

She barely nodded.

He pulled his hand away and leaned out of the protected space. Eva grabbed his shoulders, pulling him back, fingers digging into his skin. Brock carefully pulled her hands free and held up one finger as the sound of the sled engine came closer. This time she stayed put as he leaned out to pull his handgun from on top of the fridge.

Brock tucked against the corner of the hall, watching around the break in the wall, Eva's body shielded by his.

The snowmobile engine cut off and a second later boots stomped up the stairs.

"Brock. Let me in. It's fucking cold out here."

"Is that Shawn?" Eva peeked around the corner. "What in the hell is Shawn doing here?"

"I don't know." Brock switched on the safety to his pistol and went to open the door, stepping back when Shawn came in along with a rush of frigid air.

The team's coordinator was bundled up in all white, pants, coat, mask. Brock peeked out the narrow window beside the door at the all-white sled parked in front of his cabin. "What's going on?"

"I'm starting to think about building my own place like this." He peeled off his coat. "You got any coffee?" As soon as his boots were off, Shawn was heading into the kitchen and grabbing a cup from the cabinet.

Brock glanced to where Eva was still tucked into the hall, watching Shawn make himself at home.

"What are you doing here, Shawn?" Brock tried again. No one ever came out here. It was too far. Too isolated.

"I needed out of the fucking office." He downed half his coffee before setting the mug on the counter in front of him. "Did you know Harlow changed all Dutch's passwords?"

"What?" Harlow was a lot of things, but she didn't seem like the kind to put the whole team's safety at risk just to prove a point. "Did you fire her?"

Shawn's brow wrinkled in confusion. "Why? Because Dutch couldn't sign into his Netflix?"

"She changed his *personal* passwords?"

"Every damn one of them." Shawn shook his head as he polished off the rest of his screaming hot beverage. "Credit cards, banks, Amazon." He snorted. "Poor guy couldn't even listen to his fuckin' Spotify." Shawn pointed at him. "Then when he finally got it all straightened out, he saw she'd deleted all his saved songs and replaced them with gospel." His eyes lifted to the ceiling. "Not that there's anything wrong with gospel, but it's not the kind of shit that gets you pumped up for a work out." He poured the rest of the coffee into his cup. "I can't handle their shit, Brock. The two of them are going to make me lose my mind."

"You should probably bake her brownies." When Shawn looked her way Eva shrugged. "Girls like brownies."

Brock pointed at her. "No more porch brownies. You understand me?"

Eva scoffed. "I know."

"What the fuck are porch brownies?" Shawn's gaze moved between the two of them.

"I don't want to talk about it." Brock rested his hands on the counter. "So you came all the way out here to tell me Dutch and Harlow are being a pain in your ass?"

He liked Shawn. The guy was calm and smart and organized as hell.

But right now he deserved an ass-kicking.

"No." Shawn went to take a drink of his coffee, stopping just as it reached his lips. "I came because you guys have to come back to Fairbanks."

"What?" Eva stepped in beside Shawn. "Why?" Her gaze darted to Brock.

She didn't want to leave. Eva was enjoying their time together just as much as he was.

Shawn leaned one arm on the counter, turning to fully face Eva.

"Because Mona and Chandler are there, and apparently they have something to discuss with you."

****

"I CAN'T BELIEVE they wouldn't just tell Shawn what they wanted." Eva hadn't stopped frowning since they left the cabin. He couldn't see her face on the sled, but he could feel her irritation the whole trip back to the garage.

And she was still frowning in the passenger's seat of the Rover.

"I can't believe they wouldn't tell you over the phone." Brock thought the satellite phone Harlow sent with Eva would solve all their problems. Keep them from having to leave the one place where he could feel relaxed right now.

No luck.

She'd managed to get Mona on the phone, but her partner had been unwilling to give her anything beyond saying *something happened*.

And it appeared to be pissing Eva off significantly.

"They're just being dramatic." She slunk lower in her seat, kicking her socked feet up onto the dash. "I swear to God if they drag me all the way back there and this is stupid I'm going to lose it."

"Careful, Tatum. I'll think you like being around me."

Her eyes stayed out the windshield. For a minute Brock thought she didn't hear him.

"I do like being around you." The words were quiet. Like it almost caused her pain to admit it to him and she made herself do it anyway.

He reached across the center console to lace her fingers with his. "I like being around you too." He pulled her hand to his mouth, pressing her knuckles to his lips. "You know you're the only woman I've made breakfast for twice?"

Eva let out a little grumpy-sounding grunt. "I didn't get to eat it the second time either."

Once Shawn got a little coffee in his system he was ready to go.

Or just ready to have someone else to run interference with Dutch and Harlow.

Brock glanced her way. "I packed it all up and put it in the fridge. It can be breakfast round three."

She nodded, her eyes still on the snowy landscape outside of the Rover.

"What's wrong?"

She shrugged.

He wanted her to tell him everything, but Eva wasn't like most of the women he'd known.

Sometimes that was a great thing. Sometimes it meant he had to be patient. Careful.

Because as scared as he was when Eva came strutting into his life, fruit punch in hand, Gram-Gram suitcase rolling behind her, he had at least a little warm up before all the pieces of his life came crashing down.

She didn't.

Eva blew out a long, loud breath. "Ugh." She waved her hands around a little before pressing the heels of her palms against her forehead. "I need to tell you something."

"Okay."

She was still facing forward, eyes out the front of the SUV, head barely nodding as one leg bounced.

Another quick exhale and she turned to face him.

"My mom cheated on my dad all the time and he became an alcoholic and then died from a heart attack." The words tumbled out of her mouth in quick succession. Not a single pause between them.

Brock nodded. "I figured it was something like that."

Eva blinked at him. Lips pursing. "Oh." She scratched at the top of her head. "Okay then."

"Are you disappointed I was paying attention?"

"No." It came fast. "That would be ridiculous."

He lifted one shoulder. "Not if you're the kind of person who likes to keep their personal life private."

Eva moved her lips from side to side. "Is that why your cabin is so far away?"

Brock smiled. "Obviously Shawn didn't get the message."

She laughed, filling the car with the rich, slightly raspy sound. "I'll make sure he gets it."

"Just don't have Harlow hack into his email to do it." Brock glanced into the rear view mirror where Shawn was following behind them in another of Alaskan Security's Land Rovers. "Apparently even mercenaries have limits."

"Shawn is a," her voice lowered as she looked side to side, "one of those?"

"Technically—"

Eva lifted a finger. "I know. Technically you're not mercenaries because you aren't hired specifically to kill people."

"That's right." It was the loophole they all clung to.

They weren't hired hit men.

And they didn't kill anyone who didn't deserve it.

Ever.

"Do you think we'll be able to go back to the cabin tonight?"

"That depends on your friends." He didn't want to admit chances were good they would be spending the night in one of the rooms at Alaskan Security. Not to her and definitely not to himself.

Having Eva in a place that had always been only for him was nothing like Brock expected. If anyone ever came to the cabin it felt invasive. Like Shawn's visit today.

Unwanted.

But having Eva there was anything but. Seeing her curled under the blankets in his bed, gently touching the pictures of his nieces and nephews, the sound of her voice singing off-key in the shower.

The cabin would never feel the same without her.

After one, damn day.

Her head dropped back to the head-rest of her seat. "They are probably just being dramatic and overreacting."

"Says the woman who ate porch brownies and wears around a stalker shirt." He reached for her again, this time resting his hand on her knee. "You do recognize they were not overreacting on that, right?"

She pointed one finger right at his face. "If you go into this on their side I will cut you off, Broccoli." Her head slowly moved from side to side. "No more sexing me up."

"Don't make me prove you're a liar, Tatum." He pulled the Rover up to the gate at Alaskan Security's headquarters and lowered the window to punch in his code. "I will do it specifically to prove I can."

"Nope. You can't." She crossed her arms over her chest. "I have way more willpower than you think. I have all of it. All of the willpower."

Brock parked in front of the largest building, leaving the engine idling as he unbuckled and leaned in close, barely letting his lips touch her ear. "You're wrong."

A soft almost whimper slipped from her lips. Of all the sounds he pulled from her last night that was his favorite.

A barely-there cry of complete want and surrender.

She shoved at him, palms pressed against his chest. "You're an ass."

He pulled her close, one hand cradling the back of her head. "I love when you call me that."

She was still laughing when his mouth covered hers.

A second later the passenger door whipped open, sending a rush of freezing air into the Rover. "Come on. You can do whatever this is later."

"Has it been that long, Shawn? You don't even know what it is anymore?"

Shawn leaned to glare at him around Eva. "Ms. Tatum has people waiting on her."

"Eva?" A woman with short, white-blonde hair came rushing out of the front doors of the building. She made it three steps. "Fucking fuck!" Shoving her hands into her armpits she spun on one heel and ran back into the building.

"Christ." Eva shoved one foot out the door. "You couldn't even give her a damn coat, Shawn?"

Shawn shoved one hand toward where the blonde was standing behind one of the glass doors. "I wasn't here, Eva. How in the hell am I supposed to get her outerwear when I'm busy dragging your ass back from the love shack?"

Eva snorted, throwing her head back as she laughed. "The love shack."

She pushed Shawn out of her way before heading toward the building, singing Love Shack and doing some sort of dancy walk.

Shawn slammed the door to the SUV closed. "Shit."

Brock didn't look away from Eva as she wiggled her way up the sidewalk. Couldn't. "What?"

"Now I've gotta deal with that one too." He grabbed a handful of snow and chucked it at Brock. "And she might be worse than the other two."

Brock grinned as he dodged the snowball. "She definitely is."

CHAPTER 16

"THIS PLACE IS huge." Mona's head moved from side to side as she and Chandler followed behind Eva.

"It's ridiculous." Chandler's unwavering frown dug in deeper as they passed the break area. "Is that a full kitchen?"

Eva ignored him.

"I think it's kind of nice." Mona slowed at the open doorway, staring into the space.

"Nice for what? This is where they work. Not where they live."

"I think some of them live here." Eva didn't normally acknowledge Chandler's occasional pissiness, but this time it felt personal.

Chandler snorted. "I'm sure their parents are proud."

Eva stopped, spinning to face her business partners. "What the fuck is your problem, Chandler?"

Mona waved his way. "He doesn't feel good. Got sick on the way here."

She'd been giving their third an awful lot of excuses lately. At first it was fine. Chandler was great at what he did. Made it simple for her and Mona to do what they enjoyed without worrying about the actual business end of things. No payroll to deal with. No taxes to worry about. Chandler handled all of that so she and Mona could focus on finding fresh talent to help juggle the constant stream of new clients clamoring to gain a standing spot on their list.

"That doesn't mean he gets to be a dick." Eva crossed her arms over her chest. "You need to check yourself. I'm tired of your bullshit, Chandler."

His head bobbed back. "My bullshit?" He pointed back toward the lobby where she left Brock with Shawn and Dutch. "You've been holed up in a cabin with some guy, while Mona and I are left trying to hold down the fort by ourselves."

"Uhh." Eva stepped closer to Chandler. "First of all, you're the one who made me come here. Second, I made damn sure my team could hold up without me, so there should be nothing for you to do."

Mona handled the corporate side of what they did. New employee checks. Existing employee reviews. Embezzlement.

Eva and her team dealt with their domestic cases. Cheating spouses. Theft between family members. Will manipulation. Anything bad one family or friend could do to another, she and the people that worked under her would dig into.

Find the truth hidden in court records, bank statements, and now frequently Facebook pages.

"Your team quit."

Surely she didn't hear that right. "What?"

It had taken her five years to build the team she had. Weeding through the ones who would never have the inherent skill required to know when something didn't add up.

When someone was lying.

She eyed Chandler. "They wouldn't do that."

"They would if their own personal security was compromised and their fearless leader wasn't there to convince them otherwise." He pushed past her into the meeting room Shawn set aside for them to use.

Eva stood in the hall, breathing deep.

Dealing with her partners had always involved a careful balance of brutal honesty and careful language. Chandler didn't listen to anything that wasn't at least half a yell, and Mona was more sensitive than most people realized.

Her best friend might be able to hold her own with an agitated client, but when it was over Mona couldn't leave it behind like Eva could.

She carried that shit around. Wallowed in it.

Upsetting Mona was the last thing Eva wanted to do, but someone needed to hand Chandler his ass, and right now she was the only one available.

"We don't have all day, Eva."

She might even slice it up before she served it to him.

Eva turned. "I'm sorry. I didn't know you had somewhere else to be."

"I need to be in my fucking bed." Chandler blew his nose, tossing the used tissue into the corner trash can before dropping into the chair right beside Mona. "And we need to figure out what the fuck we're going to do about this mess you started."

"*I* started?" Eva stepped into the room and leaned on the table between her and her best friend and the guy who'd been following them around since college. "How in the hell is this my fault?"

Chandler smirked at her as he dropped his briefcase on the table and flipped it open. "Your little stalker friend wasn't happy when you left him."

"What makes you think that?"

Chandler pulled out a piece of paper and slapped it on the table, sliding it her way with the tips of his fingers. "He sent us a love note."

A single line of typed text sat in the center of the page.

Bring her back or I will release the personal data of each employee. You have 24 hours.

"You said only my team's data was compromised." Eva lifted her eyes from the paper to Chandler. "He said each employee."

Chandler slammed his hand down on the paper, dragging it back before shoving it into his briefcase. "Luckily I went into work early and found this taped to the door. I called our tech support and they were able to lock us down before the entire system could be breached."

"But it *was* breached." Mona's eyes were soft. "He got to all the domestic team's files."

"So they just quit?" It didn't make any sense.

"Of course they quit. We allowed their personal information to be accessed. We'll be lucky if they don't sue our asses off." Chandler dropped back in his chair, rubbing his eyes. "I told you that guy was going to be a problem."

"You told me I should move away." Eva shook her head. "I'm not letting some dick steal everything I've worked for."

Chandler held one hand toward her. "He already did." His eyes bounced from her to Mona. "Your whole team is gone. Rebuilding it will take years. Years we don't have. By the time we are ready again all our clients will have moved on."

"What are you saying?" Eva turned her attention to Mona. Her friend shifted in the chair.

"Mona and I are prepared to buy you out."

That made her take a step back. "You want to cut me out of the company?"

"We don't have a choice."

"Of course you have a choice." Eva kept her gaze on Mona. "How in the hell wouldn't you have a choice?"

"Why would you want to stay?" Chandler held his hands out. "Why come back to Ohio when you have a place like this that I'm sure would be willing to hire you." He leaned forward. "You can't tell me with your skill set they haven't already made you an offer." His head barely tipped back. "Especially considering you're fucking one of them."

"Here." Harlow stepped in at her side, holding out a brick. "Throw this at him."

Eva looked from the offered item to Harlow's face. "Why do you have a brick?"

216

She shrugged. "Why don't *you* have a brick?" Her gaze shifted to Chandler, turning icy. "Seems like you're the one who needs one."

"Who the fuck are you?" Chandler's voice was a little pitchy as he pushed up from the table.

Harlow smiled, slow and sort of scarily. "I'm your worst fucking nightmare, douche canoe." She bounced the brick a little in her hand. "I can destroy your life before you blink."

Chandler sputtered, a few almost-words tumbling from his snarling lips as he grabbed his suitcase. "This is bullshit." He pointed across the table, wagging his accusatory finger in front of Harlow's face. "Don't think for a second you can threaten me and get away with it."

Harlow looked unimpressed as she sucked through the straw stabbed into the cup she held in her other hand, the slurping sound making it clear her drink was mostly gone. "I don't need some dill hole in a suit to tell me what to think." She tapped the edge of the cup against her temple. "My tiny little female brain can come up with plenty of ideas all on its own."

Chandler straightened, one hand adjusting the button on the jacket of his expensive suit. His right eye was twitching and he looked a second away from completely losing his shit. His hard gaze snapped to Eva. "You should really consider staying here." His eyes drifted to Harlow. "You would fit in perfectly." He didn't look back as he marched from the room. "Come on, Mona. We have a mess to clean up."

Mona's blue eyes moved from Eva and Harlow to the door.

Harlow leaned back, peeking out into the hall before taking a step deeper into the room. "Go. You can always come back and talk to us later." She winked, the whole left side of her face squinching up with the move.

Eva laughed a little. "Smooth."

Harlow glanced her way over one shoulder. "What? I wanted to be sure she was picking up what I was putting down."

"I was." Mona stood, shoving her narrow shoulders back.

Eva didn't like the slightly green tone of her friend's normally flawless complexion. "You look ready to barf."

"Yup." Mona blew out a breath, her cheeks puffing, lips pursing. "Imma do it anyway."

Harlow nodded, her lips curling into a smile. "Yes. Get it." She leaned close to Eva. "She's one of us. I knew she was."

Mona pressed two fingers to her lips as she burped. "Don't get your hopes up. I might barf on his shoes and go hide in my room."

Harlow lifted both hands and both shoulders, her smile widening. "That's good too." She bent at the waist, using her brick-filled hand to emulate vomiting. "Make sure you get it all up in there."

"Yeah. Okay." Mona smoothed down the front of her sweater and ankle-cut pants. "I had shrimp for lunch, so that's good." One quick breath in through her nose and out her mouth and Mona was marching out of the room and down the hall after Chandler.

Harlow stepped out into the hall and Eva followed. They watched Mona go, arms swinging, spine straight, chin up.

"She's not usually like that."

"Probably ran out of fucks." Harlow sucked on the end of her straw again. "It happens." She shook her cup, the ice rattling around. "I need a refill. Wanna come with?"

"You guys have any alcohol in that kitchen?"

"No. The guys aren't big drinkers." Harlow led her to the large break room and went straight to the kitchen. "Something about clear heads and shit." She opened the fridge, pulling out a jug of orange juice and setting it on the counter before opening a cabinet and grabbing a cup similar to the one she had. She grinned up at Eva as she started pouring. "That's why I keep the coconut rum in my office." She filled one cup then moved to the next. "It's like a tropical vacation for my mouth."

Eva stared out the window to the frozen landscape beyond it. "I could see why you would want a tropical vacation."

Harlow shrugged as she screwed the lids onto the two cups. "You get used to it. At least most of the snow here stays white." She handed the fresh cup to Eva before replacing the juice and grabbing her own. "In New York it was nasty within fifteen minutes."

"Is that where you're from? New York?" Eva walked beside Harlow as they went to her office.

"No. I'm from Idaho." Harlow dropped into her black desk chair and pulled out the bottom drawer on the right side of her desk. "It's boring as hell there." She held out one hand, opening and closing her fingers as she eyed Eva's juice.

"More boring than Alaska?" Eva handed over her cup.

"Have you found Alaska to be boring?" Harlow added a generous pour of rum to Eva's cup before handing it back.

"Fair enough." Eva sucked on the straw, downing a few gulps of the refreshing drink. "That's good shit."

"Hell yeah, it is." Harlow poured some into her own cup then stashed the liquor back into its hiding spot. She pulled her laptop closer, straw in mouth, and started typing. "Let's see what sort of bullshit is going on in Cincinnati."

"What are you doing?" Eva moved in to watch as Harlow worked.

"I'm gonna find out who broke into your company's system." Her eyes didn't move from the screen. "Then I'm going to lock your shit down so it doesn't happen again." She spun the keyboard toward Eva. "Log in."

"How did you find that?" Eva stared at the employee screen of the database they used to store and organize the information they collected.

"A seventeen-year-old with a YouTube account could have found that." Harlow waited while Eva typed in her user name and password and hit enter.

Invalid user ID

"That's interesting." Harlow leaned against the arm of her chair, barely spinning from side to side.

"I must have put it in wrong." Eva tried again, this time being very careful to make sure she hit the correct keys.

"I doubt it." Harlow drank down more of her cocktail as she waited for Eva to finish.

She punched enter again.

Invalid user ID

"What a dick." Harlow took the computer back and started clicking through screens. "I'm gonna steal his Panera points when I'm done with this."

"Is there a Panera here?"

"Nope. I'm just gonna do it to be a bitch." Harlow's eyes moved over the screen as her fingers worked. "What kind of grocery stores do you have in Cincinnati?"

"Kroger I guess?"

Harlow was nodding. "I'm gonna get those points too."

"Then I'm gonna hack his medical records and put in that he has a family history of enlarged prostates so he gets a finger in his ass every year at his physical."

"He might like that." Eva dropped down to sit on the floor.

"Good point." Harlow didn't look her way. "Okay." She straightened in her seat. "Didn't he say he paid someone to make sure no one could get into your system again?"

"Yeah. We have a company we contract to deal with all that." Eva sat taller to look at the screen of Harlow's computer. "Why?"

"I hope you didn't pay them very much." Harlow was in the database, navigating through the tabs. "There was nothing significant keeping me out." She slowly shook her head. "I mean, they have the basics. A decent firewall. All your data is being backed up." She frowned at the screen. "But it doesn't look like they did anything I would consider high-security." She started tapping at the keyboard again. "I think Chandler-bing got taken."

"Can you tell how much information they were able to get?" Guilt tugged at Eva's gut. Her team was like her family, and thinking that she was responsible for someone obtaining their information made her sick to her stomach.

Harlow pursed her lips, pushing them out as her head tipped to one side. "Maybe?" She tapped the end of a pen against the tip of her nose as she stared at the screen. "It sounds backwards, but since there wasn't a lot of work involved in getting into your system, whoever did it wouldn't have had to leave much of a trail for me to follow."

"Shit." Eva let her head fall back against the wall. "This is a freaking mess."

"I guess." Harlow spun her chair until they were face to face. "But, I mean the ass nugget has a point."

"That this is my fault?"

Harlow winced. "Ew. No." She leaned back, propping her converse-clad feet onto the top of her desk. "Shawn hired me to help Dutch, but I don't know a lot about finding shit online and court records." Harlow pointed the end of her pen at the center of Eva's face. "But you do."

"So?"

"What in the hell do you think we do here?" Her eyes barely shifted to the open doorway before moving back to Eva. "I'm tired of being the only chick."

"You are the only woman who works here?"

"Shawn hired another woman named Bess, but she's out of town and has a kid and—" Harlow waved her hand around, "whatever. She's busy and I get it." Harlow threw her pen onto the desk. "I just can't be the one to keep these guys in line all the time."

Eva pressed her temples.

This was all making her head hurt.

The company she put everything she had into for the past decade was crumbling. Chandler was being a total prick about it, shoving poor Mona in the middle.

And now Harlow was suggesting something she didn't even want to consider.

"I can't stay here." Eva curled her knees to her chest. "I have to go back with Chandler and Mona and try to fix this."

"Pretty sure Brock's not going to be a fan of that plan."

"Why in the hell would you think that?"

They'd only spent a handful of days together, and the first couple had been rocky.

The last couple were—

Well.

And Harlow wasn't answering her.

Eva looked up at her new friend.

But Harlow wasn't looking back at her. Harlow's gaze rested on the open doorway behind her.

Shit.

Eva slowly turned. "Hey."

"Come on, Tatum." Brock held out a hand to her. "We need to talk."

CHAPTER 17

"WHERE ARE WE going?" Eva turned to look behind them as he led her into one of the glassed-in tunnels that led between the three main buildings that housed all of Alaskan Security.

"To our room." He pushed open the steel door separating the walk-way and the bunk house.

It was a term they used loosely.

"So I guess we're not going to get to go back to the cabin tonight."

"Doesn't look like it."

While Eva met with Chandler and Mona he'd had time to chat with Dutch and Shawn.

About a few things.

Eva came to a stop, eyes wide as she stared around them.

He waited as she took in the space. It probably wasn't what she was expecting.

"Who all lives here?" She craned her neck to look down the hall that led to the private rooms on the first floor.

"Probably half of us at any given time." Brock gently tugged on her hand to get her feet moving again. "The other half are either out on jobs or taking personal time."

"You guys get personal time?" She seemed surprised.

"Do you not take time away from your job?"

One shoulder lifted and dropped. "Not really."

"Seriously?" He walked through the open area that made up the kitchen and living room floor one shared. "What about weekends?"

"Don't look at me like that." Eva scowled a little. "I was trying to build a business." She pointed around them. "I bet Pierce doesn't take days off either." Her finger moved his way. "And what about Harlow? Does she just wander off and let everyone fend for themselves when she needs a break?"

They needed to get Harlow an assistant. Someone to lighten her load.

Eva smirked. "See? I'm not the only one."

"You haven't worked much since you've been here." It took shipping her across the country, but at least Eva was finally taking some time off.

Her nostrils flared. "And now I'm fucked because of it."

He hadn't caught much of her conversation with Harlow, only the last bit where the team's hacker accurately predicted Shawn's next move.

The team had been missing something, and it was only getting more and more obvious what that was. Women looked at things differently, brought a level of analytical emotion to a situation that men

227

frequently didn't. They needed that viewpoint now more than ever.

Unfortunately, Alaska was not a popular choice of residence for the type of women they were looking for.

"I'm sorry about what's happening with your business."

Her gaze locked onto his. "Are you?"

One heartbeat was all it took for him to decide to give her the truth.

"No. I'm not."

"I put everything into that company, Brock. I can't just walk away from it."

"I know that." He used his hold on her hand to get Eva moving again, this time toward the stairwell leading to the second floor. "I wouldn't ask you to."

"Good. Because I can't." Her boots hit the metal steps hard as Eva stomped her way up. "They can't just come here and tell me I'm out." She was snarling as she spoke now. "Buy me out my ass."

"Do you want me to call Charles? See if he can look into your legal options just in case?"

"Who is Charles?"

He didn't want to help her with this. If this Chandler dick got Eva to sell her share of the company then there was nothing keeping her in Cincinnati.

And she would need a job. Preferably one that paid well.

But if Eva stayed here, it would have to be her choice.

"He's our attorney."

"You would do that?"

Brock stuck the key card Shawn gave him into the door of room twenty-two and the lock clicked open. He waited until they were inside to continue the conversation. "You have a life, Eva. What kind of guy would I be if I asked you to leave it all behind?"

He caught the conflict warring in her eyes. Knew this was a tough line he had to walk. All it would take was one wrong move and down he would go.

Possibly permanently.

"My life isn't more important than yours." He stepped in close, cradling her face in his palms. "I just want you to know you have options. Go back to Ohio and fight for your company if that's what makes you happy." The thought sat heavy in his gut. "That's all you have to do. Whatever makes you happy."

He almost meant it.

Eva nodded, her eyes finally dropping from his.

The realization that she would probably be leaving him was like ice in his veins. A chill he would never be able to chase away.

She moved closer, easing in until her body rested against his, cheek pressed to the center of his chest. Her arms came to wrap around his waist.

"I like you, Tatum." He pressed a kiss to her forehead. "I like having you with me." Another kiss to the tip of her nose. "I like hearing you laugh." She gave him one as he kissed her cheek. "I like watching you give people hell." He brushed his lips over her ear. "I like watching you give *me* hell."

"Sometimes you deserve it."

He chuckled. "I probably always deserve it."

"Most people don't like when I give them hell."

"Most people are stupid."

She didn't blink. "Most people think I'm crazy."

"They might be right on that one."

Eva frowned at him.

"In a good way, though." He smiled. "It would take a woman who's a little crazy to walk into a life like mine." Brock skimmed his fingers along the neckline of her sweater. "And I like your particular brand of crazy."

"I'm not sure it's strong enough to have its own brand."

"It is. It definitely is." He started laughing. "You told Pierce your Gram-Gram was shot between the eyes."

"She was." Eva said it completely deadpan. No amusement at all.

He was going to love her. Hard and fast.

And God help him if she didn't love him back.

"Maybe I can make up for it." Brock pushed against her, moving Eva in the direction of the bedroom of the second-floor suite.

"Pierce will owe you one." She held on, letting him walk her backwards, never looking away from his face, trusting him to get her where she needed to go.

"Just one? Your standards are already slipping."

Her head dropped back and Eva laughed, a full-body, soul-deep laugh that only she could make the sexiest thing he'd ever seen.

Brock didn't bother flipping on the switch in the bedroom. The light filtering in through the open door was enough to bathe her in a soft glow. He peeled her sweater off before grabbing her around the waist and dragging her onto the mattress.

She scoffed. Loud.

He stopped. "What?"

"You didn't even look at my bra." She grabbed him by the hair and lifted his head until her eyes were on his. "You made a big freaking deal about it yesterday and now nothing?"

Was it really just yesterday? Time stopped making sense the minute he picked Eva up at the airport. It felt like forever ago that she dropped fruit punch and sushi on his boots.

Like he had known her for years.

"I'm more interested in the panties." He pushed up to his knees and unfastened her jeans, grabbing the waistband and pulling to reveal—

Eva was laughing again, her torso curling with the exertion.

"Thank God I do what I do, Tatum." He pulled her pants the rest of the way off and threw them over one shoulder. "Because you would intimidate the hell out of any other man." He dropped down, pulling her legs wide to reveal her uncovered pussy. "You can't make a habit of this." He kissed the center of her mound, working his way into position. "If I know you're walking around with no panties I won't be able to keep it together."

Her back arched a little as he probed between her labia with his tongue, finding her clit already swollen. Knowing she wanted him the way he wanted her pulled a groan from his chest.

Eva's hand locked onto the hair at the front of his head as he lapped at her, gripping her hips to keep her still so he didn't lose his rhythm.

"Brock!" His name jumped from her lips as she came, her hold on his hair tightening to the point it almost hurt.

But in a good way.

He loved her passion. The way she owned it. Unabashedly.

It made him want to pull more out of her so he could keep it for himself. Carry it with him when he was away.

Because there would be times when he was away from her.

Possibly soon.

Brock fought his own shirt over his head as Eva grabbed at his pants, her fingers frenzied as they worked the fly open.

"I want you in me." She shoved at the jeans, pushing them out of her way.

"Ow, ow, ow." Brock caught her hand right as she dragged the teeth of the zipper over his dick. "Watch the zipper."

"Well if you weren't in such a rush earlier they would have already been off." Eva pulled the zipper away with one hand and used the other to tug the pants down.

"Are you complaining that I was in a hurry to go down on you?"

Eva's hands came up to shove at his chest, hard enough to knock him to one side. "Shut up and let me get you naked." She stood up on the mattress in nothing but a plain, white bra and wrestled his pants the rest of the way off, straightening when they were free, holding them up and smiling like she'd won an Olympic medal. "Ah-ha."

He stared up at her. This wild woman would never be easy. She would never be simple.

She would never be boring.

"Come here."

Eva shook her head. "Nu-uh." One hand went behind her back. A second later the cups of her bra fell loose. Eva caught it as it slid down her arms, then pulled it tight by the straps and shot it straight at him.

He caught it mid-air. "Now come here."

Her head moved from side to side. "You've gotta come get me."

Brock didn't move. He laid perfectly still even though all he wanted was to grab her. Roll Eva's body under his and fuck her until leaving him would never cross her mind again.

Until she recognized what they had.

Eva stood straight, eyes studying his face. "What's wrong?"

"Not a thing." He pushed up to one elbow. "Except that you're up there and I'm down here."

She stabbed a finger his direction. "You're trying to make this," her hands waved around, "emotional. Stop it." Eva bounced a little. "I just want to have fun this time, Brock. Please. I can't do that right now." Her shoulders slumped a little. "I don't have it in me."

"I can be fun."

"You keep freaking saying that and I'm seriously doubting that you even know what that word means." She wiggled her brows at him. "Prove me wrong."

"Damn it." He jumped up, catching her just as she started to jump away and taking her down to the bed.

Eva laughed as his body bounced on hers. "You move fast for a big guy."

Moving fast was his MO for years. The only way he did anything. Get in and get out. Professionally and personally.

The faster you moved, the lower the risk.

But he didn't want to take anything fast with Eva. He wanted to enjoy every fucking second.

"You're looking awful serious again, Broccoli." She reached between them, her hand wrapping around his dick. "I need you to keep being fun right now."

Connecting with a woman was nothing he'd ever allowed himself to do. Did everything in his power to avoid.

And it was all he wanted to do with this woman.

But Eva was already overwhelmed.

She needed a break.

"What kind of fun do you have in mind, Tatum?" He thrust into her fist, watching as her eyes widened.

"The fun kind." Her gaze locked onto where he fucked her hand as the tip of her tongue slid across her lips.

"That's a pretty generic request." He pushed a little harder, sliding the head of his cock against the soft curve of her belly.

"I just don't want to think about things." Eva's other hand found his sack, gently working his nuts as he continued to drive against her palm.

Brock leaned down, a groan pulling free as her grip on him tightened just a little. "Then how about you let me fuck you until you don't remember any of those things."

Her head bobbed in a nod. "Let's do that." Her legs were already trying to find their way around his waist.

"Hold tight, Sunshine." Brock leaned to reach for his bag, rolling to one side so he could find the zippered compartment where he stashed the condoms.

Before he had it all the way open, Eva had wiggled her way down the bed. Right as his fingers found a packet, the wet heat of her mouth closed around him, pulling his dick deep between her full lips.

"Fuck." He dropped the condom and struggled to grab another as she pulled back to slide her tongue across the head of his cock.

"You have a nice penis." Her eyes skimmed down his length. "Maybe a little crooked."

"Crooked can work to your benefit." He laced his fingers in her hair, teeth clenching as she took him in again. The urge to thrust was almost overwhelming as Eva found her rhythm. The sight of her lips pursed around his shaft was the most fucking beautiful thing he'd ever seen.

Her ringed eyes came to his, watching as she forced him toward a climax he didn't intend to have right now. But stopping her was unthinkable. Having this woman over him, his dick in her mouth as she watched what she did to him was unlike anything he'd ever experienced.

And he'd experienced a lot.

None of it was ever the way it was with Eva. Not even fucking close.

When her hand again found his sack, he had to pull away.

Shooting off in her mouth was not in the plan for today.

Maybe tomorrow, though.

Brock grabbed her by the wrist and tugged her up the bed. "No more."

Her lips barely quirked. "Were you not having fun, Broccoli?"

"You know damn well I was having fun." He smiled, rolling them both until her soft body was under his. "But I think we need to pace ourselves. Especially considering you doubt the amount of fun I have to offer you."

Eva laughed, head tipped back, dark hair spread all around her. "I do doubt your fun abilities." She reached up, pulling his face close to hers. "But I can probably teach you some things."

"I'm a quick learner." Brock snagged the condom he'd left at the edge of the bed and ripped it open before rolling it in place. "But I have a few fun moves already."

Her brows lifted. "Do you?"

"Um-hm." Brock slid one hand behind her left knee, pulling it high as he pinned the other leg flat against the mattress. "Wanna see one?"

"I do. I really, really do." Eva's fingers speared into his hair as he dragged the head of his dick along the line of her pussy, rubbing across her clit a few times before notching it in place.

He slid into her with one easy move, shifting his hips until her body jerked a little.

There it was.

He pulled out and shoved back in, making sure to hit the spot he'd found.

Eva's back arched. "What is that?"

"The perks of a crooked dick." He leaned down to tease one nipple with his tongue. "It can hit spots a straight dick can't." He sucked the puckered peak deep as he moved, each thrust of his hips sending Eva's breasts closer to his mouth. He held her bent leg in place, pushing it wider so he could sink a little deeper.

"The fuck?" Her hands gripped tighter. "Holy shit."

"Who's no fun now?"

"I take it all back." Her eyes rolled shut as a moan slid through her lips. "Don't stop. I will kill you."

Brock let his body rest against hers, the closeness allowing him to rub her clit with each thrust. He rolled the tip of one breast between his fingers as he fucked her, the sound of Eva's cries making his balls ache with the need to come.

"I'm—"

It was all the warning he got before her pussy fisted him tight, her whole body jerking under his as she came, dragging him down with her.

He shoved into her hard and fast as his dick swelled, pouring into the condom between them.

Eva's hands dropped from his hair, falling to the mattress as she stared up at the ceiling, chest rising and falling in short bursts.

Finally her eyes moved to his.

"Maybe you're a little fun."

CHAPTER 18

"THIRD TIME'S A charm." Brock smiled at her from across the tiny breakfast bar in the kitchen of the suite at headquarters.

Eva forked off a chunk of her biscuits and gravy and shoved it in, chewing as Brock watched her.

Breakfast wasn't normally her favorite meal of the day. Usually it consisted of tea, coffee, and then more tea, most of it consumed as she ran around the office, helping her team get everything done.

But if Brock was cooking she might reconsider her opinion. "This is actually really good." She cut another chunk loose with the edge of her fork. "Did you use vegetarian sausage?"

"I used those crumble things you bought and then added the seasonings they put in sausage." His eyes still hadn't left her face. "It's good?"

Eva nodded as she chewed. "Really good."

Brock straightened, crossing his arms over his chest as he leaned back against the stove, smug smile on his face.

"You did get two trial runs though, so…" She lifted one shoulder.

He laughed. It was light and easy and so different from the way he was when she first met him. "Eat your breakfast, Tatum. You've gotta go deal with your people."

She scrunched up her nose. "Chandler's not my people."

"He's your problem, though." Brock picked up his coffee. "Unless you want me to deal with him."

Usually an offer like that would have had her spitting mad. The insinuation that she couldn't deal with this by herself would have rubbed the absolute wrong way.

But Brock knew the truth. Knew damn well she would handle this and only offered because that's what he should do. Eva gave him a smile. "I can handle him just fine all by myself."

"Didn't doubt it for a minute." He nodded to her plate. "Eat. We gotta go."

She went back to her breakfast without arguing, because damn him it really was good.

An hour later they were showered and dressed and heading across the walkway to the main building. "What are you doing while I'm dealing with Chandler and Mona?"

"We have an all-team meeting scheduled." Brock pulled open the door and waited for her to go first.

"What's all-team mean?"

"Alaskan Security is made up of four teams. "Alpha, Beta, Rogue and Shadow."

Eva lifted her brows at him. "Shadow. Sounds secret."

"It is." Brock didn't bat an eye.

She stared up at him. "Then why did you tell me?"

He didn't look her way. "Why do you think?"

"Where have you been?" Harlow came running down the hall, full cup of coffee balanced in one hand.

"That's impressive." Eva watched the rim of the mug as not a single bit spilled over the edge.

"I have a lot of practice." Harlow grabbed Eva's hand. "Come on." She started tugging.

Eva didn't budge. It wasn't hard since Harlow was a good bit shorter than she was and trying not to spill scalding liquid on her hand.

Harlow stopped pulling and turned to look where Eva was still at Brock's side. Her nose crumpled. "Just stick your tongue in his mouth so we can go."

"You aren't even going to say hi to me, Mowry?" Brock rested one palm over his chest. "That hurts."

Harlow pointed at his face. "Don't start with me right now, Brock Star. Eva and I have a whole shit show to deal with."

"Damn it." Eva turned to him. "Why in the hell didn't I think of that?"

Freaking Brock Star. Best nickname ever.

Harlow waved her hand around. "Did you not hear me say shit show?"

242

"I did." Eva reached out to grab the front of Brock's shirt, pulling him in hard for a quick kiss. "Have fun at your meeting." She let go and used the same hand to spin Harlow toward her office. "Let's go."

"I like how you did that." Harlow glanced back at Brock as they walked away. "Holy shit. He's watching you walk away like a kid watching someone carry away his puppy." She faced forward and leaned in close. "I'm a little envious." She put a hand up. "Not jealous because I'm happy for you." Her head spun back to look Brock's way again. "But you found a freaking unicorn with that one. Most men are scared shitless of a woman with balls like yours."

"You have an enviable set yourself." Eva followed Harlow into her office.

"That's why I know they scare men's dicks up into their bodies."

"Can that really happen?" Mona was staring up at them from an upholstered chair that wasn't in Harlow's office yesterday.

"Are you being serious right now?" Harlow looked to Eva. "Is she being serious?"

Eva nodded a little. "Maybe."

She wasn't the only one who'd put her entire life into building their business. Mona spent just as much time at work as she did. Unfortunately, Mona wasn't the kind who could swing a casual hook-up. It just wasn't her thing.

Harlow's eyes rolled toward Mona, her head following a second later. "Penises aren't retractable." Harlow's brow lowered. "You've seen at least one, right?"

"Yes." It was the most indignant Eva had ever heard her friend sound. "I just thought you knew something I didn't know."

"How long has it been since you've seen a wiener?" Harlow flopped into the chair behind her desk and kicked her feet up.

Mona's head dropped back. "So, so long."

"This place is crawling with them." Harlow grabbed a pen off her desk and rocked it between two fingers. "Not that I've managed to get any of it." Her eyes went to Eva. "It goes back to the balls thing."

"Didn't you say there was some sort of shit show happening?" This conversation had gone off the rails, and someone had to get it back on track.

Her business was on the fucking line.

Harlow sighed, straightening in her seat as she tossed the pen back on the desk. "So I went through everything and I can't find where the system was breached." Harlow grabbed her computer and started navigating through the screens. "I called Mona last night and had her come back to help me track down a hunch." Harlow clicked her mouse and a window opened, displaying Facebook and the photo of an unsmiling man.

A man she knew.

"That's Mike Nestor. He was on my team." Eva leaned closer. He looked even more unruly than the last time she'd seen him. His long hair was down past his shoulders now and the thick, dark beard covering most of his face had gone feral.

"Yeah. See, I'm not sure it is." Harlow scrolled down his page. There were very few posts. Just like when she'd done the background check required to be hired on at Investigative Resources. "This looks like a fake profile to me."

"He's not fake. He's real. He worked for me for six months." Eva turned to Mona. "You remember him, don't you?"

"Of course I remember him. He looked like the freaking Unabomber." Mona leaned toward Harlow. "I told her not to hire him. He was creepy as hell."

"Well." Harlow tapped on her keyboard again, this time pulling up a separate window.

This one also had a picture of a man Eva knew. "That's Howard Richards. He's the guy who stole my panties in college."

Harlow minimized the screens and lined them side by side. "See anything interesting?"

"Besides one of them is about a hundred pounds heavier than the other?" Eva shook her head. "No."

"Willful blindness." Mona pointed at Eva. "This is exactly why we had to send your ass here."

"Holy hell, Eva." Harlow pointed at a spot almost concealed by Mike Nestor's out of control hairline. "Look at that birthmark."

No.

She would have known.

"Now check out Howard's forehead."

"I don't want to." Eva turned from the computer.

Chandler might be right.

This might be her fault.

"Don't get all fucking freaked out. We have shit to handle." Harlow patted her head with one hand and continued typing with the other. "So my new friend Mona taught me some shit last night and I think we found him."

Eva pressed the tips of her fingers to her lips as her stomach rolled.

Brock would be devastated if she barfed up his biscuits and gravy, and as good as they were, nothing was ever pleasant the second time around.

"If you puke in my office I will shave your head and steal all your gas credits." Harlow didn't look away from her computer. "We found some evidence that lover boy here stuck around in Cincinnati for a while after you canned him."

Mona stood up, grabbing Eva by the arm and dragging her toward the chair. "Sit down before you fall down."

Eva dropped into the seat and leaned forward, holding her head in her hands. "I worked with him for months. Trained him."

He'd been right beside her and she had no clue.

She had paid him to stalk her. He didn't even have to work for it.

In her quest to be the complete opposite of her mother, she'd lived her life as an open book, thinking it would keep her from causing the pain

246

her mother's lies and deception brought on everyone around her. That meant Howard had been there eating it all up.

"We think he was the one leaving all those things at your house." Mona sat on the arm of the chair, rubbing her back in slow circles. "I'm so freaking sorry I didn't figure it out, Eva. I knew there was something off about him and I should have dug deeper."

It was Mona's greatest downfall. She apologized. Took on fault that wasn't hers. Carried burdens that should never be on her shoulders.

Eva straightened, ready to gently tell Mona none of this was anywhere near her fault.

"You're gonna have to cut that shit out right freaking now." Harlow pointed the tip of her pen at Mona. "Don't you ever own shit that isn't yours." She spun her computer around. "This is all this prick's fucking fault. He's the one who did this. Not you. Got it?"

Mona's blue eyes were open wide. "Okay."

"No more apologizing. Not to anyone."

Mona's gaze shifted from Harlow to Eva and back again. "What if something really is my fault?"

Harlow shrugged. "Stick your boobs out. It'll be fine."

"That why you dress so suggestively?" Eva motioned to the baggy sweater that all but swallowed the tiny woman up.

Harlow smiled. "I don't ever have to stick my boobs out." She flipped her computer around. "Back to where Mr. Richards-Nestor is now."

"Is he here?" Eva barely got the question out.

"Definitely." Harlow rolled her head from side to side, stretching her neck. "The florist who sent those flowers is old school. Uses handwritten receipts and everything." She drank down some coffee before continuing. "So there was no system for me to get into, but I was able to get into the traffic cameras set out in front of the store. Check this out."

Eva and Mona leaned forward as Harlow turned the screen their way, watching as a squatty man with wild hair and an even wilder beard climbed out of the passenger seat of a black sedan and went inside, coming out a few minutes later to get back into the same car.

"That car look familiar?" Harlow was smiling, clearly proud of all she'd accomplished.

It was impressive, but right now all Eva could focus on was the dots of dread connecting in her gut. "That's the car from the grocery store."

Harlow's smile widened. "Bingo." She sat back in her seat. "You're good at this shit."

"It's my job." Eva swallowed around the truth clogging her throat. "Used to be my job."

This was all her fault. All of it. Even the part Brock thought might be about him and Team Rogue.

"Do they all know about this?"

"They all who?" Harlow absently patted around her desk until her hand smashed onto a bag of granola.

"The teams."

Her eyes finally lifted from the screen of her computer. "Which teams?"

248

"All of them. Is that what they're having a meeting about?"

Harlow tucked her chin, dark eyes focused on Eva as she spun the chair to face her. "Which teams are meeting?"

"Alpha, Beta, Rogue, and Shadow." That was right, wasn't it? Her brain was not firing on all cylinders at the moment.

Harlow slowly smiled. "Brock Star told you about Shadow?"

Fuck. "No."

Harlow grinned as she shoved in a handful of granola. "He loves you."

"He definitely does not. We have known each other like, five days, That's ridiculous."

"Is not. Men always fall in love first. They can't help it. They're weak." Harlow looked to Mona. "Am I right?"

Mona lifted her shoulders. "Maybe?"

Harlow's head tipped toward her shoulder. "Really, Mona? You were supposed to say *hell yes*."

Mona gave Harlow a tight smile. "Sor—"

A chunk of granola bounced off Mona's forehead.

"No apologizing." Harlow tossed the next chunk into her mouth. "But I am right. Men fall in love in like two seconds, and Brock Star is definitely in love with you."

"He's not. I promise you."

"Ugh. Fine." Harlow dropped her head back. "He's falling in love with you."

Eva didn't have it in her to argue. "You never answered my question."

"The guys don't know yet." Harlow looked from Eva to Mona. "We could go crash their party. Show them what we did that they couldn't."

Eva shook her head. "Let's just wait. We can tell Dutch when the meeting's over."

Harlow was already unplugging her laptop. "That sounds way less fun then my idea." She stood up, tucking her computer under one arm. "Mona's thinks so too." She pointed at Mona. "Right?"

Mona nodded her head, smiling wide. "Hell yes."

Of all the times for Mona to find her backbone. No way was Eva going to rip it right away from her now. "Fine."

She was going to have to deal with it sooner or later. Why not do it in front of an entire room full of men she barely knew.

And one she knew well.

"Come on, girls. Time to go prove our superiority once again." Harlow pushed out both her elbows. Mona immediately linked her arm through one, still wearing a bigger smile than Eva had ever seen.

Obviously her kid glove method was not the most effective way to help Mona find her inner hellion.

Harlow lifted her brows, wiggling her other arm like a chicken wing. "You know you want to."

She did want to.

Eva laced her arm with Harlow's, being careful not to knock the laptop also tucked there loose. "Let's go tell them this is all my fault."

Harlow leaned toward Mona as she craned her neck to look at Eva. "The fuck we will." She shook her head. "I thought we covered this shit. There is one person at fault here and it's Creepy Clause."

Mona leaned forward. "Because he looks like a creepy serial killer version of Santa Clause."

"I got it." Eva wrinkled her nose. "But that's just proving my point. I'm the one who hired him. I'm the one who trained him. And I'm the one who had a protection order against him. I should have known."

"Jesus Christ." Harlow swung around so she and Eva were face to face, dragging Mona along as she went. "If you're going to consider coming to work here, then you need to understand that bad people are bad and if you are a good person, you will not automatically see them coming." Her eyes went wide. "They are stealthy as shit."

"Who said I was considering coming to work here?"

"That's all you got out of that?" Harlow's head fell back. "Just come on. We are wasting time we could be using to steal Chandler's free sub points." She took off, pulling Mona and Eva along with her.

Mona was practically skipping as they power-walked to the front of the building and down another hall.

Eva was not as excited. Harlow might not think this was her fault, but it was almost guaranteed there would be plenty of people who did blame her.

"That one." Harlow nodded to a large set of steel double doors.

Without missing a beat, Mona yanked one open, eyes widening on Eva when she didn't do the same.

"Sorry." She grabbed the handle on the other door and pulled, stepping back at the number of eyes locked onto them.

Harlow smiled wide. "Morning, boys."

A few muffled curses followed them to the front of the huge room where Pierce was seated at a wide desk. Shawn and two other men joined him.

All their gazes were fixed on Harlow.

"Is there something I can help you with, Ms. Mowry?"

Harlow pulled her arms free and stepped up to the desk, pulling the cord from the computer sitting there before pushing it into the side of hers. "We found out who breached the system at Investigative Resources." She looked up to the giant screen behind Pierce's head as the side by side of Howard Richards and Mike Nestor filled the space.

Pierce slowly spun toward the screen, but not before Eva caught the hint of a smile playing on his lips. "Who is this?"

"This is Howard Richards. Ten years ago he was arrested for breaking and entering, theft, and stalking."

"How were you able to connect him to the breach?"

"I was the one he was arrested for stalking." Eva stepped in beside Harlow. "A year ago I hired him to work at my company."

Pierce turned her way. "You hired the man who stalked you?"

"He used an alias." Mona stepped in front of her, lifting one hand to point at the screen. "Look at him. Would you know it was the same guy?"

Pierce nodded. "Fair enough." He leaned back in his seat, fingers steepled together. "Would you ladies care to pull up a chair and join us?"

Harlow glared at Pierce. "I should have already been in here."

Pierce's gaze barely shifted to the front row where Dutch was seated beside Brock, before settling back on Harlow. "Forgive my omission."

"Are you asking or telling?"

Pierce barely smiled. "Both."

Harlow stared him down for a minute.

"Fine."

Pierce stood from his chair, glancing at Shawn and the other two men at his sides. "I believe the floor belongs to them."

CHAPTER 19

"YOU NEED TO get her to stay." Shawn's eyes didn't move from the spot where the three women were presenting all the information they had on Howard Richards and his alter ego Mike Nestor.

Brock shook his head. "No."

If Eva stayed in Alaska it would be her choice. No matter what.

"Fine." Shawn straightened in his seat. "I'll get her to stay."

"Like hell." Brock checked the volume of his voice as a few sets of eyes turned their way. "Leave her alone."

"You act like offering her a shitload of money is being a dick." Shawn eyed Brock. "I would think you'd be happy to have her here with you." His gaze suddenly sharpened. "Don't fucking tell me you'll leave if she leaves."

Brock didn't respond.

"Fuck." Shawn huffed out a breath. "I swear to God if every one of you threatens to leave every time you fall into a woman I'm quitting." He reached into his pocket and pulled out a roll of antacids, popping one between his lips and crunching into it before continuing on. "And don't for a second think I will be the only one trying to keep her here."

Brock followed Shawn's gaze to where Pierce was watching the three women as they clearly and concisely laid out all the information they'd obtained. The head of Alaskan Security was completely focused on them.

But he wasn't just listening to what they were saying. He was watching them work together.

Pierce would immediately recognize the potential the three women held as a team. Add in Bess and they would be a force to be reckoned with.

One Alaskan Security desperately needed right now.

Because while this new information added up most of the recent events surrounding Eva, it didn't connect all the events.

Dutch gave Brock a sideways glance as Harlow looked out at the men seated in front of her. "Any questions?"

Brock barely shook his head at Dutch.

Reminding Eva there were parts of the puzzle still unaccounted for wasn't something he wanted to do with an audience.

"I need you three to find where Howard Richards is."

"Are you asking or telling?" This time it was Eva who stepped up to question the head of Alaskan Security.

Pierce didn't miss a beat. "Still both." He stood from his seat, smoothing down the front of his expensive suit. "And I need you to do it now."

"Kay." Mona smiled at him.

Eva and Harlow's heads both snapped Mona's way.

Pierce smiled. "At least one of you likes me." He turned to Shawn. "Move them to a bigger office. One where they can have all the room they need."

Shawn nodded silently.

Pierce turned his attention to Brock. "Walk with me, Cassidy."

Brock glanced to Eva, intending to be sure she was okay.

He shouldn't have worried. She, Harlow, and Mona were tucked shoulder to shoulder around the single laptop they brought with them, voices low.

"She's fine." Shawn stood at his side. "I'll keep an eye on her."

"You might regret the offer." Brock smiled as Eva's head tipped back and her laugh filled the large conference room.

"She's the least of my worries in that group." Shawn squared his shoulders and walked toward the three women.

"I've got places to be, Cassidy." Pierce's voice was clipped enough to get Brock's feet moving. He followed his boss out of the room and down the hall. Pierce didn't speak until they were well out of earshot. "Ms. Tatum is smart."

"She is."

"And not scared of me." His voice held a tinge of admiration.

"Definitely not."

"Is she scared of anything?"

Eva did crazy things. Things no one in their right mind would do. She ate porch brownies and airport sushi. Did donuts in snow-covered parking lots. Stood up to men that terrified most people. "Unfortunately, no."

"Shawn asked me to hire her." Pierce glanced his way. "Would you have any objection to that?"

"I doubt she'll do it." The chances of Eva walking away from the company she helped grow from the ground up were slim to none.

"I didn't ask if you thought she would take my offer." Pierce stopped walking and turned to face him. "I asked if you would have a problem with Ms. Tatum being a part of Alaskan Security. You know better than anyone the dangers this profession can carry."

His family's history wasn't something Brock made public knowledge. It was too painful to carry in his everyday life. The background check required to work at Alaskan Security was extensive, and would have definitely included the deaths of his brother and sister-in-law.

But the fact that Pierce was familiar enough with his particular life to remember that information was almost as surprising as the fact he was taking it into consideration.

"I won't ever hold Eva back. Not from anything."

Not that she would let him anyway. The woman was unbendable.

"I'm sure she'll appreciate that." Pierce glanced up as the coordinators of Alpha, Beta, and Shadow rounded the corner. "Now, if you'll excuse me, I have another meeting."

Brock watched as the four men filed into one of the smaller meeting rooms, the door clicking shut behind them.

He turned to walk back down the silent hall toward Dutch's office. Luckily Dutch was there, already parked behind his desk, surrounded by screens displaying the various cameras set up around the properties.

"The car dropping Richards off at the florist was the same car I saw at the grocery store."

"Yup." Dutch didn't look up. "But they're not driving it anymore."

"Yeah. I thought of that." Brock sat in the chair across from Dutch and leaned back. "I'm sure Reed took it out of commission."

"He did." Dutch pointed to one of the many screens and clicked a key on his board, sending a video reel playing. A black sedan flew across the monitor. "That's the car that followed you." He clicked a few more keys, speeding the action up before slowing it down. "And there is the car from the store." A tow truck moved past, pulling the Charger behind it. Dutch stopped the video. "It's at impound. Reed and Tyson went to check it out."

"I doubt we'll find anything useful." Brock rubbed his eyes.

Thinking the primary danger was directed at him and the rest of Alaskan Security was easier to deal with than what the actual truth was turning out to be. "Do we know how Richards got tangled up with them yet?"

"No fucking clue." Dutch leaned back in his seat. "If I had to guess our friends noticed they weren't the only ones keeping an eye on shit they shouldn't be and decided to use him to their advantage."

It was a good guess. Probably real damn close to the truth.

"What's our next move?"

"Finding Richards." Shawn stepped into Dutch's office. "I've got Harlow, Eva, and Mona set up. They're working on it right now."

"I'm sure their third-wheel is going to appreciate being out of that loop." Dutch scooted one of his computers over to clear the path between them. "Where is the dick anyway?"

"Apparently he got sick on the way here and is still in bed." Shawn checked his phone as it buzzed. "Probably better since he's about to be cut completely out of his company."

Brock shook his head. "It's Eva they're trying to cut out. Her portion of the company basically dissolved itself right after she left. Chandler and Mona offered to buy her out."

"I heard." Shawn stood up. "I'm just saying I wouldn't put any of my money on that being what actually happens." He slid his phone into one pocket. "I believe they are about to have another offer to debate."

Pierce.

"I don't want that fucking Chandler guy up here. He's an ass."

"Chandler isn't part of the deal." Shawn stepped toward the door. "He would be bought cleanly out."

It was a best-case scenario. Eva would still get to keep her stake in the company. She would keep everything she worked so hard for.

And she would be here. With him.

As long as she decided that's what she wanted.

"I gotta go. Pierce just met with the other team heads to fill them in on his plans and he wants me to help him work up the offer."

"Why did he need to tell the other teams?" Brock stood, ready to follow Shawn out.

"They wouldn't just be working for us." Shawn paused. "They would be company wide."

Brock froze. "Including Shadow?"

Team Rogue was known as the most dangerous branch of Alaskan Security.

The most dangerous *known* branch.

He'd worked here almost ten years and all he knew about Shadow was that it was better he didn't know shit about Shadow.

Shawn nodded. "Including Shadow."

The thought of Eva dealing with that unknown sat heavy and cold in his gut.

Her job was moderately dangerous as it was. Bringing it to Alaskan Security took that to another level.

Adding in Shadow made it unimaginable.

"You said you wouldn't hold her back, Brock." Shawn's tone carried an edge of warning. One that grated more than it should.

"She's too fucking brave, Shawn. She'll get herself killed."

"She won't get herself killed." Shawn thumbed over his shoulder. "If that was how it worked Mowry would have died her first day here."

"I can't fucking let her do that. You know I can't." Panic climbed his throat, hot and bitter.

"Brock?"

He ground his teeth together at the sound of her voice at his back.

"I'll see you later." Shawn pointed at Eva. "Don't forget. Meeting at three."

She nodded. "Meeting at three." Her eyes followed Shawn until he disappeared. Once he was out of sight her ringed gaze moved to rest on Brock. "What is it you won't let me do?"

The sweetness of her tone would fool anyone who didn't know her the way he did. "I didn't say won't. I said can't."

"Same thing."

Brock shook his head. "Very different."

"That's bullshit." All sweetness was gone from her voice now, replaced by something he couldn't stand.

Disappointment.

"I'm not doing this here." Brock grabbed her by the arm and dragged Eva down the hall, darting into the first open door and pulling her in behind him. Once the door was closed he turned to face her. "Pierce wants to buy Investigative Resources."

Her eyes barely widened.

She didn't know yet.

"What for?"

"He's been looking for a specific sort of addition to Alaskan Security." He reached for her. The last few minutes had him feeling agitated.

Out of control.

"Specific, how?" Eva didn't back away as he moved in closer.

"We needed to add another team. One that was behind the lines."

"Like Dutch and Harlow." She easily followed the path he took her.

"Mostly like Harlow."

Her dark brows came together. "He wanted women?"

Brock nodded. "Pierce knows women see things in a way men can't. That they offer a different sort of viewpoint and a different kind of intuition."

"No shit." Eva leaned back against the table behind her, resting her hands on the edge. "Harlow said she's the only woman here."

"Technically we have one more, but she's currently in Florida." It certainly didn't make up for the severe lack of women in the company.

"How in the hell do you not have any women?" Eva shook her head in disbelief. "That's the dumbest thing I've ever heard."

"It's not for lack of trying. Pierce has been attempting to recruit women, but Alaska isn't a big draw." Brock eased in a little closer. "Between the weather and the job description we didn't have many women interested."

"He wants to buy my company and bring it here because he thinks I will come with it." Eva's eyes lifted to his. "Because of you."

"I would say he's hoping that will help his case." Brock dropped her eyes, hating the next words that had to come out of his mouth. "He asked if I had a problem with you coming here."

Her eyes narrowed. "He asked your permission?"

"No." Brock reached up to smooth the line of her brows. "He wanted me to know the full extent of what your job description would be if you chose to come here."

Her head barely shook. "I don't understand."

"You would work for all the teams. Not just Rogue."

"Okay. I don't see why that—"

"Shadow Team is different from the others, Eva. The shit they deal in is so secret none of us know what it is." He swallowed around the curl of fear tightening his throat. "What they do puts anyone involved in extreme danger."

"Oh." Her shoulders dropped a little, eyes falling to one side. "Does Harlow deal with Shadow Team?"

"If she doesn't now, she will." Brock moved from smoothing her brow to sliding his fingers through her hair. The slow strokes of the dark strands helped calm him. "My guess is Pierce intends for you and Harlow to work together with Bess when she gets back."

"Will I like Bess?"

He didn't want Eva to be considering this. Brock wanted her to not think twice about it as she packed up her Gram-Gram kill-shot suitcase and boarded a plane back to Cincinnati.

But she was thinking about it.

Hard.

Finally her attention came back to him. "You don't want me to do it."

She didn't ask because she already knew.

"No. I don't."

Her lips barely lifted. "But you won't stop me if it's what I want."

"No."

Her head tipped in a half nod. Eva stood, propped against the table for a few seconds longer. Suddenly she straightened, wrapping both arms around his neck. "I really like you, Broccoli."

He held her close, the feel of her body against his keeping him centered. "I really like you too, Tatum."

"I know." She gazed up at him. "I don't know what to do."

"Talk it over with Mona. See what she thinks."

Eva's lips shifted to one side. "I'm guessing that means Chandler would not be included in this offer?"

"From what I've heard he would be bought out of the company."

"I feel bad about it." She shrugged. "But I guess he was ready to cut me out."

"What about Mona?" Brock stroked up the center of her back. "Wasn't she in on it?"

"Mona is different from me. If Chandler made her feel cornered she would go along with it just to avoid conflict." Eva's brows went up. "But she's been in a room alone with Harlow for the past hour, so who knows what could happen when Chandler drags his ass out of bed to come be a pain in the ass."

Brock laughed. Harlow was exactly what they needed and her arrival had been a fucking gift. She was smart and fearless and ready to fight anyone who dared cross her or anyone she cared about. "He should probably keep his ass in bed then."

Eva's nose lifted on one side. "He won't, though. He's got his panties all in a bunch over my team quitting."

"He's using it as an excuse."

Eva heaved out a long sigh. "I know. Mona said he's been talking about changing things up for a while now. Trying to figure out how to take the business to the next level."

"That might happen without him." Brock expected the realization to make her happy, but Eva frowned up at him.

"I'm not trying to cut him out."

"I know that, Sunshine." He pulled her close. "But you need to be prepared for him to think that's what's happening."

"I didn't say I was going to take Pierce up on his offer." She tried to push away.

Brock didn't let her. "What you do is up to you and Mona." He paused, making sure what he was offering her next was the absolute truth. It's what she would want from him.

No lies.

"I don't care where you are, Eva. Live here. Live in Ohio. Hell, move to fucking Nova Scotia for all I care."

"That's just Canada."

He laughed. "But it's the other side of Canada."

Eva leaned back to look him in the eye. "What will you do if I go?"

He stared down into the face of the woman he didn't have a chance against. Not from the first second.

He was gone before she even had her Gram-Gram suitcase off the rack.

"I want to go with you."

She lifted a brow. "You would walk away from all this?"

"In a heartbeat."

Eva rubbed her lips together. "Shit." She pushed out of his arms and fast walked to the door. "Damn it, Brock."

He smiled as she fought the lock. "Turn it to the left."

She shot him a quick glare. "Thank you."

The door was open and Eva had one foot into the hall when he stopped her escape.

"Eva."

Her back straightened at the sharpness of his tone. Slowly she turned to face him.

"I'll see you at dinner."

CHAPTER 20

"WHAT'S WRONG WITH your face?"

Harlow stared at her as Eva stormed into the room Shawn set them up in.

"Nothing's wrong with my face. This is just how it looks."

Mona eyed her up and down. "She's freaking out."

"I'm not freaking out." Eva went to flop into the chair sitting in front of her computer. "I'm fine."

Harlow laughed. "Looks like it."

"You know what he said?" Eva scooted her chair under the desk before shoving it back out and standing to pace across the room. "He said he would just walk away from all this if that's what I wanted."

"Sounds about right." Harlow's attention was on her computer now, her expression bland. Like the conversation suddenly got boring.

"How does that sound right?" Eva fast-walked to Harlow's desk and leaned over it until Harlow looked at her. "Why in the hell would he leave his whole life? That doesn't even make any sense."

Harlow leaned to look around her to where Mona sat at her own computer. "She always this dense?"

"Yup." Mona glanced up from her work. "Sometimes worse." She lifted one shoulder. "It's not her fault. She was engaged to a guy who ditched her to move to California."

Harlow's head bounced back as her dark eyes shot to Eva. "And you chose to stay in freaking Ohio?"

Eva gnawed her lip.

Harlow's eyes widened. "Oh shit." She winced. "He didn't invite you."

"He was a dick."

Both women turned to look at Mona.

"What? He was."

Eva straightened. "You never told me you thought he was a dick."

Mona's shoulders sagged just a little and her eyes dropped. "I'm sorry. I just didn't want to hurt your feelings."

Harlow picked up a binder clip and chucked it at Mona. "No apologizing."

Mona dodged the airborne office supply, leaning to the left so it sailed past her. "Sorry."

"Seriously?" Harlow picked up another clip and sent it after the first one.

Eva blocked this one, knocking it to the ground before it could gain any real altitude. "Stop. She's trying. You have to give her time."

"What about you?" Harlow sent the next clip Eva's way. "Are you even trying?"

Eva smacked the clip back at her. "Don't come crying to me when you need a clip."

"First of all, I don't cry." Harlow stood up. "Second, you didn't answer my question."

Eva groaned, letting her head fall back. "I don't want to talk about it."

"Fine." Harlow dropped back into her chair. "Be all weird and screw this thing with Brock Star up." She smiled at Eva. "I'm sure you won't regret it at all."

Mona let out a long, loud sigh from her spot.

Eva spun to face her. "Do you have something you would like to say?"

She normally watched her tone with Mona, but right now all that mattered was shutting this down. Quickly.

Mona rubbed her lips together, one foot tapping on the floor as Eva stared her down.

Just when Eva thought Mona was going to let it go, her best friend shoved her chair back and stood up. "Yeah. I think I do have something to say." Her chin lifted and her shoulders straightened.

Finally her eyes came to meet Eva's. "Your mom sucked too."

"No shit."

Mona didn't even flinch. "Your mom sucked and so did Walter. That's why you were with him. Because you knew he wasn't attached enough to care if you turned out to be like your mother."

Harlow snorted behind her. "You were engaged to a dude named Walter?"

Eva snapped her head to look back at Harlow. "He was very good-looking and had a very big penis."

"I still don't think I could do it." Harlow grabbed the edge of her desk, head rolling back a little. "Walter." She said it in a breathy voice as one hand came up to rumple her dark hair. "Fuck me harder, Walter."

"The fuck is going on in here?" Dutch stood in the doorway, all his attention locked on where Harlow was faking an orgasm with a surprising amount of accuracy.

"Deciding if I could fuck a guy named Walter." She focused on Eva. "Pretty sure the answer is no."

"Who in the hell is Walter?" Dutch's nostrils barely flared.

"Eva's ex-fiancé." Mona tilted her head at Dutch. "Do you need something?"

Dutch quickly stepped across their office and dropped a file onto Harlow's desk. "This is the information you wanted."

Harlow smiled up at Dutch. "Thank you."

Her voice still carried the breathiness of her performance a few seconds before.

Dutch stood in place for a beat. "You're welcome."

He turned and was out of the room before Eva could blink.

Harlow ignored the file, instead leaning back in her chair and resting the heels of her feet on the desk in front of her. "Back to Walter the ex-fiancé." She pointed the tip of her pen at Eva. "You picked an ass hat on purpose?"

"She did." Mona answered for her.

"Brock Star isn't a dick." Harlow dished it out like Eva didn't already realize that information.

And recognize it for the problem that it was.

Harlow didn't give her anymore time to stew on it. "Are you like your mother?"

"No." The answer snapped out. Strong, immediate, and loud.

"You're good then." Harlow dropped her sneakers back to the floor. "Let him do what he wants."

She would have followed Walter if he'd asked her. Eva would have left it all behind for a man she only liked because he was safe. Unattached.

It kept the fear she carried at bay knowing he couldn't care less if she turned out like her mother. He would simply move on unscathed.

But Brock wouldn't, and with him her genetic predispositions were only half the problem.

The rest came from a family trauma that would hang over his head forever.

"He's a grown man, Eva." Harlow looked up. "He kills people for a freaking living for God's sake. Let the man choose for himself. He doesn't need you to protect him."

"Uhhh." Mona's mouth was dropped open, her eyes moving from Eva to Harlow. "What was that last part?"

"Hmmm?" Harlow's head cocked. "The part about Brock Star not needing Eva to protect him?"

"Ladies." Pierce walked into the room and his presence sucked out what little air was left in the space. "How goes the hunt for Howard Richards?"

"He's not using his credit cards. His bank account hasn't been touched in weeks." Mona picked up a stack of papers and handed the top one to Pierce. "Credit cards are the same way. I'd say he's living on cash, but there have been no large withdraws recently to prove it."

"He could be living off money he's been accumulating." Harlow picked at one of her fingernails. "I could see him not trusting the bank with all his money."

Pierce pulled some slack into the legs of his pants before sitting on the edge of Harlow's desk. "Has he been employed since he was fired from Investigative Resources?"

"I found a short period where he was being paid by a private security company, but that ended six months ago." Mona handed Pierce another paper. "His bank account shows a pattern of deposits that indicates he was receiving payments of some sort on a regular basis."

"Maybe working under the table for someone?" Pierce took the paper and scanned it. "That's a substantial amount of money."

Says the man in the suit that probably cost thousands of dollars.

"A skill set like ours is valuable and when I fired Mi—" She stopped. "When Howard was fired from our company he had almost completed the required training."

"So he can do what you two can do?" Pierce's cool gaze shifted from her to Mona.

"No." Eva straightened. "No one can do what Mona and I can do."

It was why their business was thriving. Why they had a waiting list a mile long of companies knocking down their door trying to hire them to handle all their background checks and any other data digging they required.

It was also why they had no fewer than ten attorneys calling each day begging for their help.

Because they were the best.

"That brings me to the reason for my visit." He paused long enough to pull an envelope from the inner pocket of his suit jacket. "Part of it, anyway." He held the envelope out to Eva. "I would like for you to do something for me."

Eva took it. "We have a waiting list."

"I suppose I should share the rest of the reason I'm here." He glanced back at Harlow.

"I get it." She stood and walked to the door, grabbing the handle. "I'll be in the break room when you're finished."

The room was silent except for the soft click of the door as it closed behind her.

"I would like for you two to come work for me." Pierce stood. "Exclusively."

"We can't just shut down our company." Eva crossed her arms over her chest. "We have employees. Building leases. Contracts."

"I could make it worth your while." Pierce turned to Mona, most likely realizing she was the one who would be easier to deal with.

"We have a third partner, mister…" Mona lifted her brows.

"Pierce."

"Mr. Pierce, Eva and I aren't the only owners of Investigative Resources. We can't make any decisions without including our third partner."

Pierce's lips barely twitched at Mona's misunderstanding of his name. "I understand your partner is currently ill." Pierce paused in front of Mona. "I would be happy to wait until he has recovered to continue this negotiation."

"It's not necessarily a negotiation, Mr. Pierce." Mona stood straight and as tall as her small frame could be, facing down Pierce like a champ. "And it certainly won't be once Chandler's involved."

"I did hear something about that." Pierce was completely focused on Mona now, his eyes studying her in a way that would normally have had her shrinking and ready to disappear.

Not this time.

"I believe your friend Chandler was intent on cutting Ms. Tatum out of the business. Am I correct?"

Mona's eyes barely flicked to Eva. "It was an argument he was making, but it never would have happened. We need Eva. She is an indispensable part of our company."

"What about Chandler? Is he indispensable?"

Mona barely wilted.

"Chandler handles all of our financial matters." Eva moved in to Mona's side. "Taxes, payroll, bills, all of it."

"So a job any accountant could handle." Pierce didn't wait for them to respond. "I feel I should let you know that my offer does not include

Chandler. My interest is solely in the two of you. I don't need another accountant."

Mona's eyes bounced to Eva. "He won't be happy."

"I don't imagine he will, but it is what it is." Pierce gave Mona a knowing smile. "And money can cure many upsets, Miss—"

Mona blinked at him.

Eva elbowed her.

Her friend barely jumped. "Ayers."

Pierce held out his hand. "I hope you will decide to stay with us a while, Miss Ayers."

Mona took his hand. "Thank you, Mr. Pierce, but I'm not confident that will be the case."

His lips barely quirked. "We will see, won't we?"

Pierce finally turned his attention to Eva. "I will send over a full written offer by day's end for you to look over. I hope you will find it convincing enough to consider." He left the room, silently closing the door behind him.

They stared at the shut door in silence for a minute.

"He's—" Mona turned to her, pressing one hand to her stomach. "I thought I was going to throw up for a minute there." She laid the other hand against one flushed cheek. "Could you tell?"

"No." Eva moved Mona's chair in behind her knees. "Not at all, actually." She held the wheeled seat in place as Mona dropped into it. "That was really impressive."

"Harlow's right. I need to stop being so..." She looked to Eva to finish the sentence.

That wasn't anything she was going to touch. Mona was going to have to do that one on her own.

"Passive?"

"I think you should be whatever you want to be." Eva crouched down in front of her sweet, kind, sensitive friend. "If you don't want to change, then don't. You're amazing just the way you are."

"People walk all over me." Mona's eyes dropped to her lap. "I should have shut Chandler down the first time he said something about buying you out. I'm sorry."

Eva smiled. "You don't have to apologize to me. I know Chandler can be a dick. I don't blame you for not wanting to rock his boat."

"I know, but you were barely off the plane. It was like he'd been waiting for the chance to own more of the company." Mona looked up to the ceiling. "I know the company is doing well, but it's because of you. I don't know why he would think cutting you out would be a good idea."

Eva stared at Mona.

Why *did* Chandler immediately jump to cutting her out of the company?

Cutting out Mona or Chandler would never have been even close to the top of the list of things Eva would consider. Hell, she was still resistant to it even after he'd tried to do it to her.

"Without my team the income for Investigative Resources will be cut in half." She eased down to her butt on the ground. "Did he have anyone come into the office after I left?"

Mona squinted a little. "Lawyers. A couple that came in to go over the possible fall-out of the data breach." Her head tipped. "I think there might have been another guy who came. I'm not sure who it was. Chandler didn't schedule a meeting so I assumed it was someone he knew coming in to visit him."

"Do you think he would have had the company appraised?"

Mona's head dropped to her hands. "I don't even know at this point. He's been acting off for a few months, so who knows what he's even thinking."

Eva pulled her knees up and hugged her legs. "Off how?"

"Just way more high-strung than normal." Mona looked up, resting her chin on her hands. "What in the hell are we going to do?"

The door to the room bumped open, bouncing off the wall.

"Holy crap, Chandler. You look like shit." Eva stood up. "You should probably go back to bed."

He lifted one hand. "I'm fine. Just a little tired." His steps were slow and uneven as he walked to fall into Harlow's vacated chair. "I came to apologize."

"Oh." Eva resisted the urge to look Mona's way. "What for?"

"I shouldn't have assumed you wouldn't want to rebuild your team." Chandler slouched until his head could rest against the chair's back. "I just thought you might like the option to do something different." His eyes were cloudy with a fever when they met hers. "If you are okay with rebuilding your team, then I think that's what you should do."

This was an interesting development.

One she didn't see coming.

And it put her in an awkward position.

Chandler's drooping gaze landed on the envelope in her hands. "What's that?"

Eva held it up between them. "This is a…"

A lie sat on the tip of her tongue, teasing her with the ease it could fall free.

A lie would be easier than the truth. It would buy her more time to discuss what Pierce offered with Mona and Brock.

Brock.

He was the reason she couldn't lie. That was a slippery slope she wouldn't risk. Not now. Not ever.

Because being like her mother wasn't an option.

Whatever it took, she would make sure never to take one step down the same path that destroyed her father. Wouldn't even go near it.

"This is from—"

"Not that." Chandler pointed lower. To the hand not holding the envelope from Pierce. "That."

"Oh." Eva lifted her left hand, the fake ring Brock slid on her finger forever ago catching in the light.

But it hadn't happened forever ago. It was a few days.

Not even a week.

So much had changed so damn fast.

It was crazy.

Insane.

And nothing had ever quite made so much sense.

Which was also insane.

"I gave it to her."

Eva looked to where Brock stood in the doorway, tall and gorgeous.

Her Broccoli.

"You ready for dinner, Sunshine?" He held out one hand.

Eva glanced to where Mona sat.

They had so much to talk about and while Chandler had apologized, he was still sitting near the top of her shit list.

But cutting him out of the business felt dirty.

So did leaving Mona alone with him. Her friend might be working hard to be stronger, but Chandler could challenge the steeliest person.

And that was on his best day. Which today was not.

"Clear out boys. I've got work to do." Harlow bumped past Brock. Her face lit up when her eyes landed on Mona. "Would you be able to stay and help me?" She held her hand to one side of her mouth like she was passing on a secret to Chandler. "I'm trying to chart my cycles. They've been sort of erratic and—"

Chandler stood up. "I should go back to bed."

Harlow nodded. "Can't blame ya there." She gave Eva a wink as Chandler left. "I'll see you tomorrow, lady."

"Yup." She blew Mona a kiss. "Don't have too much fun without me."

Mona smiled. "Oh, we totally will."

CHAPTER 21

"HE APOLOGIZED." EVA poked at the lentil loaf he spent most of the afternoon assembling. "It was weird."

"Is that not something he normally does?" Brock took a tentative bite of the vegetables masquerading as comfort food.

It wasn't terrible.

Eva snorted. "Uh. No. Chandler has never apologized for anything in the ten years I've known him."

"Why in the hell did you go into business with this guy?"

"We were still in college. None of us thought it would go anywhere and he was the only person we knew who could handle the finances." Eva finally ate a little of her dinner. "Holy shit, Brock. This is fantastic."

"Don't act so surprised. I told you I could cook." He smiled as she shoved in a big bite.

Eva pointed her fork at him. "You said you could cook breakfast." She grinned. "If I remember correctly it's because that's where most of your experience is."

Brock sat down on the stool beside hers at the short breakfast bar in their suite. "You are the only woman not related to me that I have ever made dinner for."

"I feel special then." She smiled as her eyes went back to the plate piled with lentil loaf, mashed potatoes, and green beans.

"You are special." Brock reached out to tuck a strand of hair behind her ear before it could end up dipped into the gravy he'd worked up from a carton of vegetable broth. "Did you talk to Pierce?"

"I did." She glanced his way, smile lingering on her lips. "Mona thinks his name is Mr. Pierce."

"I'm sure he loves that." Brock had known Pierce since their days in the military. He'd always been serious. Focused.

Unshakable.

Eva lifted a shoulder. "He seemed to think it was funny."

"I don't doubt that for a minute." Pierce was intimidating as hell to most people, and only surrounded himself with the select few who stood their ground when facing him down.

People like Harlow and Eva.

"He said he would send a written offer over tonight." Eva was back to poking at her food.

"He doesn't waste time."

"Are you going to ask me what I'm going to do?" She didn't look at him, but the hand stabbing her dinner was perfectly still.

"No." Brock leaned in. "It doesn't matter to me what you do."

Eva's head barely dipped in a nod.

Brock went back to his own plate of food. Thank God it was edible. Cooking two meals every night would be a pain in the ass.

Not that he wouldn't do it if he had to.

Cooking for women had always been an act of apology. A way to make him avoid the feelings of guilt that tried to push into the corners of his brain.

None of the women he bedded ever made him feel it. They all seemed perfectly content with what he offered, limited as it was.

He was the one who struggled.

Cooking for Eva was completely different. It was an act of service. A way to show his appreciation to her for being all she was.

"Thank you for dinner." Eva peeked at him from under her lashes. "You didn't have to go to all this trouble."

"I wanted to." He reached out, letting his palm rest on her back.

They were at a crossroads right now and pushing her wouldn't do him any good.

Not now, not ever.

"Would you really come to Ohio?"

"I want to go where you go." It was a truth he never imagined would be his. "I can't imagine being somewhere you're not."

In such a short time Eva had permanently altered his reality. Shifted the world as he knew it.

"Okay."

Her response surprised him. "Okay?"

She nodded a little. "Okay."

A heavy knock on the door saved him from the temptation to ask where they would be this time next week.

Brock opened the door to Shawn's face. The team coordinator's gaze moved to the inside of the suite where Eva sat. "Did you forget our meeting?"

He didn't. There was no meeting.

Brock checked his watch. "Time got away from me I guess."

"Stop lying." Eva bumped him with her hip as she crowded her way in between him and Shawn. "What's going on?"

Shawn pursed his lips and rocked back on his heels.

"Might as well tell me. If you don't I'll just go ask Harlow and she'll tell me." Eva leaned against the door frame, crossing her arms over her chest as she stared Shawn down.

"I need a fucking assistant." Shawn raked one hand through his hair. "We think we found where Richards is."

Eva didn't move.

Didn't say a word.

Which was a pretty good indication she was freaking out.

Brock wrapped one arm around her, pulling her body against his. "I'll be down in a minute."

"We move in ten so don't drag your ass."

He closed the door, pulling Eva fully into his arms. "I'm going to go."

"I know." She wrapped her arms around his waist, squeezing tight. "Is this how it will be if we stay here?"

"Yes." He leaned down to press a kiss to the top of her head.

All he'd ever focused on was what would happen to him if he fell in love.

And what would happen if he lost it.

Never once did he realize there would be another side to the coin. That a woman might feel the same about him.

"Good to know." She pushed out of his arms, giving him a smile that was nowhere near real. "You better get ready or you'll miss out on all the fun."

"Are you going to be okay?" He'd never hesitated like this. He was always the first one out the door, chomping at the bit to go do what needed to be done.

"Are *you* going to be okay?"

She was scared. He knew that.

And it made him happier than it should, especially considering the fear he'd let rule his own life. "I'm going to be just fine."

"Good." Eva's chin tilted up. "Me too then." She opened the door. "Go."

Brock grabbed her, pulling her close, one hand tangled in her hair as he took one last taste of her. He forced his mouth from hers and locked eyes. "If you need me go to Dutch. He will find me."

She nodded, pushing up on her toes to press another kiss to his lips. "Now go. I want this over."

Eva gave him a push out the door as his cell started to ring in his pocket.

Brock jogged down the hall as he answered Shawn's call. "I'm coming."

He glanced back as he reached the top of the stairs. Eva's head was poked out the door, watching him go. She smiled and gave him a single-finger wave. "Be careful, Broccoli." Then she disappeared and the door clicked into place.

"Five minutes." Shawn disconnected the call.

Brock rushed to gear up and was running out the back door six minutes later. The door to the black van they used for night ambushes was idling, the back doors open. He jumped in, taking the only empty seat, settling into place between Tyson and Reed. "Thanks for waiting."

Tyson grinned. "Figured you'd want to be there when we find your lady's creeper."

"I do." Brock adjusted the holster across his shoulders then turned his attention to his boots. "Are we confident he's here?"

"Yup." Dutch's voice was hollow in his ear.

Brock pushed the piece in, shifting it around until it was in place. "Good."

"Where is he at?"

"Downtown Fairbanks." Dutch's answer was clipped.

"Where, downtown Fairbanks?" Brock looked around the faces of the men crammed into the back of the van with him. "Where the fuck is he?"

"Across the street from the place Eva rented."

"How the fuck did you not find this out before now?" The urge to hit something was strong as he thought back to the morning Eva spent God only knew how long in front of the window in her underwear. "How long has he been there?"

"Long enough." Dutch barely paused. "Pierce would like for him to be brought back in one piece, so check yourself."

"Pierce can kiss my ass." Brock yanked the laces of his boots as he tied them. "It's bullshit that you didn't find Richards before now."

"We didn't know his alias, Brock." Dutch's voice muffled for a second.

"Who are you talking to? Is it Shawn?" Brock pushed his ear piece deeper trying to hear the smothered-out conversation.

"You probably need to calm down, Brock Star. You're getting Eva all worked up."

"Harlow?" He sat straight. "Is Eva there with you?"

"Of course she's with me. You didn't think she was going to sit in your room all by herself while you went and had all the fun, did you?"

He rubbed his eyes. Knowing Eva was there, listening to everything added a whole level of stress he didn't need right now. "Can you just take her somewhere else?"

"I'm trying to make an educated decision, Brock. I can't do that if I don't know what this would be like."

Her voice was strong. Clear. Confident.

No trace of the fear he saw in her eyes when he left her.

"Alaska is cold, Sunshine."

The rest of the team lined in the van seats avoided his gaze as they messed with their gear and checked their phones. Probably not enjoying being a part of this conversation.

Too fucking bad.

"If we stay is this what you're going to do every time I go out?"

"Probably. It makes me feel better." He could hear the smile in her voice. "I'll let Dutch take over now. He looks super irritated."

"Eva?"

"Yeah."

There was so much he wanted to say to her. Wanted to thank her for.

"I'll see you soon."

"You better."

"It looks like Richards just had some food delivered." Dutch was back. "He should be good and distracted. Make it easy for you to move in."

The van turned onto the road that ran parallel to the one where Richards' rental was located. They pulled into the parking lot of a row of commercial buildings, taking the drive down the side of the end building before parking at the rear of the dark lot.

"I'm going in first." Brock pushed open the back door and jumped out, pulling the knit mask down over his face as he ducked against the privacy fence lining the back of the property. He waited for the other five men to unload and find their positions. Nate and Abe held back, sticking close to the idling van while Brock, Tyson, Reed, and Jamison made their way toward the house.

The place was lit up, with light spilling from every window. It made it easy to peek inside, but the added illumination increased the risk they would be seen.

Not that it would matter as long as they moved fast enough. The Alaskan Troopers couldn't keep up with their workload and frequently made off-the-record calls to Alaskan Security.

It was a useful relationship for both of them. One neither would be quick to compromise.

"He's an ugly mother-fucker, isn't he?" Tyson was at the corner of the house, tucked tight against the brick wall as he peered through the window.

"Where is he?" Brock crept toward the back door.

"Northwest corner. Back to you. Shoving wings into his face." Tyson ducked down as the headlights of a car swept down the street.

"Blue Civic." Reed was stationed at the front corner, watching the street.

Brock slowly twisted the knob of the back door.

"It's unlocked."

The balls on this guy.

"I'm going in."

"Copy." Dutch went quiet in his ear.

Brock silently pushed the door open, letting Jamison hold the screen door as he stepped inside with Tyson coming in right behind him. The two men walked in tandem, moving through the kitchen at the back of the house.

The only noise came from the television in the front room and it was loud enough to provide all the cover they needed. Within seconds Brock was stepping in behind the chair where Richards was parked. He leaned down just as the show on the TV cut to a commercial, the black screen reflecting his form behind Howard.

Richards yelped as he tried to spin in his seat. Brock caught him with an arm around his neck, pulling him up and out of the chair as he pressed the smaller of the two guns he carried to Howard's temple. "Shut up."

Howard's eyes bulged as they moved around the room. "Who the fuck are you?"

Brock pressed the gun harder against the man's skull. "I said shut the fuck up." He started dragging him toward the back door. Howard was short and wide and weak, making it easy to maneuver him out the door and into the cold, silent night.

Unfortunately it wasn't silent for long.

"Help!" Howard sucked in a breath, ready to let out another howl.

Jamison stepped in close, shoving a gag into his open mouth. "You want to be quiet buddy. There's not much keeping you alive right now."

Brock tightened his hold on Howard's neck, cutting off most of his airway. "I can move you dead just as easily as I can move you alive, Howard." He paused. "Or do you prefer Mike?"

The man went still.

"Smart choice." Brock started dragging him again, moving toward the van as quickly as he could make the smaller man's stumpy legs go. "You play nice and this will go much better for you." He stopped as Nate and Abe moved in, each one wrapping a set of zip ties around Howard's wrists and ankles.

Abe stepped back. "Get him in."

Brock hefted Howard up and onto the floor of the van before climbing in after him. "We've got him."

"Load up and get out of there." Dutch's voice held an unusual amount of edge. Probably because he had an audience for the first time.

The rest of the team was in the van within seconds, pulling the doors closed as Rico took off.

Brock leaned toward where Rico sat. "Are we in a hurry?"

Rico's eyes met his in the rear view but he stayed silent.

Brock turned to the men lining the seats. "We're on our way back, Dutch. Ending communication."

They each pressed the disconnect buttons on their earpieces, cutting off the line to Dutch and the women who ambushed his office.

"There was a black sedan cruising the street in front of the house." Reed shifted in his seat, pulling out his cell, thumbs tapping out a message. "It looked similar to the others." He slid his phone back in place. "I sent the photos to Dutch."

Brock bent over Howard. "Who's keeping an eye on you, Richards?"

CHAPTER 22

"THAT WAS FASTER than I expected it to be." Eva sat on the couch in the suite she shared with Brock. "And sort of anticlimactic."

"Right?" Harlow took a drink of her cocktail. "I was really hoping for more from that." She heaved out a loud sigh. "Maybe just a little excitement."

"You work for a team of mercenaries. How much more excitement do you need?" Eva scooted down into the plush upholstery of the cushions.

If there was one thing she could say about Pierce, it was that the man had good taste and didn't mind spending money. Everything in the tiny suite was high-end. From the stove to the mattress, nothing was base grade.

It was a little nicer than her apartment.

"What the heck are we gonna do?" Eva nudged Mona with her knee.

Mona held up a finger. "I'm still stuck back where you said mercenaries. That's twice now you've mentioned Brock killing people and I'm starting to think you're not kidding."

"Not technically mercenaries." Harlow was kicked back in the large armchair sitting to one side of the sofa, her socked feet up on the coffee table. "They just kill people when they have to." She straightened when Mona's eyes widened. "And only bad people. Like, they don't kill people who are nice and law-abiding."

"I don't know that it makes it any better." Mona was obviously struggling. "Killing is killing."

Harlow shrugged. "Everyone is capable of murder."

"I'm not sure I agree with that." Mona turned to Eva. "Right?"

"Well." She fished around her brain for a good answer to give Mona. One that wouldn't give her nightmares.

Or reduce her interest in possibly moving here.

Because the more time Eva spent in Alaska, the less awful it seemed.

And the less appealing Ohio sounded.

"I think there are times where you just don't have any other option."

Mona's lips flattened and her nostrils flared.

"Say, for instance, someone was trying to hurt a baby and the only way to stop them was to kill them. You would do it to keep the defenseless baby safe." Eva held her breath, waiting for Mona to process.

Finally she lifted one shoulder. "I guess if it was to save a baby." She lifted the other shoulder.

"Maybe a dog." Her lips rolled together as she thought a little more.

"My mom."

"And my brother."

"Definitely my dad."

Eva nodded along with each addition Mona made. "Don't forget your Oma."

"For sure my Oma."

"Damn, Mona. You've got a kill list a mile long already." Harlow downed the last of her drink. "Remind me not to fuck with your Oma."

"I've met her Oma." Eva grinned. "That woman could probably handle the killing herself."

"I want to be a badass old woman." Harlow stood up and went into the small kitchen, pulling the orange juice from the fridge. "Anyone want another?"

"I can't imagine you not being a badass old woman." Eva stood up, setting her own empty glass in line for a refill.

"Shit." Mona jumped up from her spot on the couch, staring down at the screen of her phone.

"What's wrong?" Eva scooted her glass closer to where Harlow was pouring.

"Chandler went out to smoke and got locked out."

"Probably because the whole place is non-smoking and Pierce doesn't fuck around." Harlow unscrewed the lid from the coconut rum and tipped it up. Nothing came out. "Shit." She plunked it down on the counter. "Let's go let dumb ass in and then we can get the other bottle from my office."

"How long do you think it will be before the boys get back?" Eva grabbed Brock's coat off the hook by the door and shoved her arms inside.

"They will be back soon, but I bet they'll want to have a little chitty chat with what's-his-nuts." Harlow's brows came together. "I can never remember which one is his real name."

"Howard." Eva snagged her own coat and held it out to Mona. "You want a coat?"

Mona took it. "Thanks."

"Wimps." Harlow opened the door and went into the hall ahead of them. "We aren't even going outside."

"The tunnel isn't heated, jerk." Eva followed Mona out, pulling the door closed behind them. "Us Ohio girls aren't used to the bullshit they call weather yet."

Harlow turned to face her, walking backwards in her socks. "Does this mean you might be deciding to get used to it?"

"You know?" Mona's eyes were wide.

"Pshh. Of course I know. Pierce would be stupid not to try to seduce you into coming." She turned to walk forward alongside them. "And he is definitely not stupid."

"What was inside that envelope he gave you?" Mona pulled out her phone, frowning at the screen as it buzzed in her hand.

"I forgot to look." Eva worked her way under the heavy fabric of Brock's coat and started patting the pockets of her jeans, sliding it free of the back left where it was stashed. She tore open the flap and pulled out a single slip of paper. A

297

name was written across it in the neatest handwriting she'd ever seen.

Anthony Sanders

"It's just a name." Eva slid the paper back into the envelope and tucked it back into her pocket. "Maybe we can see what we can find tomorrow."

"Which door is he at?" Harlow squinted down the first floor hall. "I don't see anyone outside that door."

Mona typed a message. A second later her alert dinged. "He says the one at the back of the main building."

"That's why you shouldn't sneak around. You get locked out in the cold." Harlow led them down the connecting tube to the main offices. "Pierce will lose his shit if he finds out Chandler was smoking on the property."

"It's really that big of a deal?" Who cared if someone else smoked? Especially if they did it outside.

"He's weird." Harlow pushed through the door and into the warmth of the big building. "Hot, but weird."

They finally made it to the door where Chandler thought he could sneak out to smoke unseen. Eva pushed it open and peeked out.

No freaking Chandler.

She tucked her head back into the heat. "Are you sure this is the ri—"

A hard grip grabbed the front of Brock's coat and hauled her out the door and into the freezing cold night. She tried to fling the door shut as her body was dragged into the darkness. A shadowy form stepped in before the locks could keep Mona and Harlow safe, grabbing both women and pulling them out.

"What in the hell?" Harlow's voice cut through the night, reminding Eva she was making this way too easy.

"Get off me, dick." She swung an elbow right into the gut of the man holding her.

He grunted but his hold on her didn't budge.

So she fought harder. "You are the dumbest mother fuckers in the world if you think this is a good idea." Eva raked the sole of her snow boot down the man's shin, shoving as much of her weight into it as she could.

"Stupid bitch." The voice was a low growl in her ear. It was menacing and dark and deadly.

And obviously didn't know she had fully embraced the bitch life long ago.

"You're going to have to get way more creative if you want to insult me you piece of shit." She swung her arm, trying to work free of the hand clamped so tight it was cutting off her circulation.

"Gag this one. I'm tired of her fucking mouth."

A second later one of the men shoved a wad of something so far into her mouth it made her choke.

"That's much better." The man grabbed her by her hair, pulling her head back so she was forced to look at his masked face. "You must be Eva." His grip tightened, moving her head from side to side. "You're just as pretty as he said you were."

Harlow's yelling had stopped too and the night was eerily quiet.

Her mind was not.

Eva counted the men around them. There were five. All dressed head to toe in black, faces covered with masks as they quickly and efficiently zip tied each of their hands and feet.

What the fuck was going on?

A sound she recognized was barely audible in the distance.

"Time to go." The man holding her stepped forward to look around the bend in the building, nodded to the rest of the group. Then he bent, shoving his shoulder hard into her stomach before lifting her up and taking off at a full run.

These were not normal men.

Her head bounced as snow kicked up into her eyes, making them burn from the cold.

The open space around them shifted to trees.

They were taking them to the woods.

She didn't want to die in the woods. She didn't want to die at all.

This was exactly what Brock was terrified would happen. He didn't love her, but he definitely liked her.

And now she was going to die.

Eva fought to lift her head, looking for her friends. Harlow and Mona were both in the same situation she was, their bodies blurred by the snow clouding her vision.

Suddenly the world shifted and her body hit the ground, the impact knocking what little air she had left in her lungs free. Eva rolled to her side, trying to knock the gag choking her loose enough she could at least breathe.

Another body hit the ground beside hers. Mona's eyes stared into hers for a second before rolling to peer up at the men standing around them.

"Hold still." Mona was the only one who had been quiet during their abduction and had also been the only one to come out gag free.

She shifted closer, watching the men as she barely moved.

Her mouth pressed to Eva's, biting down on the bit of fabric peeking out. Slowly she pulled back, taking the gag with her.

Eva sucked in a full breath and swallowed down the saliva collected under her tongue.

Thank you.

She mouthed the words at Mona as the final man came up and dropped Harlow between them. "I think your friend is cold."

Harlow's lips were pale around the gag they'd shoved between them. Eva scooted closer, trying to block as much of the wind and cold as she could. Harlow was the only one of them not wearing a coat and it wouldn't be long before she would be in a very, very bad situation.

"They're almost here." One of the men stepped through a gap in the metal fence surrounding the property.

No. Not a gap.

There were parts of the fence missing. They'd cut their way in.

These men came here specifically to take them.

Eva leaned in, resting her head on Harlow's. The sound of snowmobile engines muffled the sound of her whisper. "Where's Chandler?"

Mona shook her head. "I don't know."

They were being kidnapped and Chandler might be freaking dead at this point.

All because fucking Howard Richards had to have her panties ten years ago.

Eva went still.

Something moved in the trees.

Something big.

Something fast.

And it was moving like it was ready to kill.

"Shut your eyes, Mona."

Mona stared at her a second longer.

"Everything is going to be okay, but you're gonna want to close your eyes." She caught a second movement. "Now."

Mona held out a heartbeat longer. Her eyes squeezed shut just as the first silenced shot came.

Four more followed it, each one deadly accurate.

Bodies fell around them heavy and fast.

They never knew what hit them.

She did.

Boots crunched through the snow as another group of men dressed head to toe in black moved in around them.

"Harlow's not wearing a coat." Dutch yanked the gag from Harlow's mouth then pulled up the mask covering his face. "What the fuck were you thinking, Mowry?" He shucked his coat and carefully wrapped it around her, scooping her up right after and tucking her close to his chest. "I swear to God you're going to make me lose my fucking mind."

"Stop b-b-b-being mean t-t-t-to m-me." Harlow's voice was broken by the shivers wracking her body.

"Someone has to." He tipped his head back to yell toward where Shawn was pulling up his own mask. "I'm taking her in."

Shawn dropped down to kneel beside Eva, pulling out a knife to cut the ties binding her wrists.

Eva rubbed the irritated skin. "Where's Brock?"

Shawn's eyes rested on hers just a second before dropping to where he was cutting her ankles free. "There were sleds en route."

Eva nodded.

"Someone tried to take you, Eva. Brock's going to do whatever he can to make them pay." Shawn stood, offering her his hand. "He knows you're safe and he knows you are strong enough to be able to handle this." His lips barely lifted in a smile. "It's probably why he likes you in the first place."

Mona sat silently as one of the other men cut her free. Even once she was on her feet, Mona still didn't say a word.

Eva moved in to wrap one arm around her. "You okay?"

"No. Definitely not."

Eva nodded.

"Yeah. That's what I thought."

CHAPTER 23

"WHERE IS SHE?" Brock rushed down the hall, adrenaline and frustration pushing him faster.

Shawn stepped right in his way, blocking the path to where he knew Eva would be. "Calm down."

Brock didn't think, just acted, shoving both hands into Shawn's chest and knocking him back. "You calm the fuck down."

Shawn regained his footing almost immediately and lunged at him, one shoulder hitting Brock square in the sternum. The impact took them both to the ground.

Hard.

Anger still crept along his skin, frustration riding right behind it, and the combination had him lashing out. "See how calm you would fucking be if someone took your woman." He rolled, trying to gain the upper hand with Shawn. The team's coordinator was at least five inches shorter than Brock's six-six frame, but right now you wouldn't know it.

Shawn was coming dangerously close to getting him pinned.

"You think those girls only matter to you?" Shawn grunted as Brock caught him in the gut with a knee, a move that only made the smaller man more aggressive.

A second later Shawn rolled, legs locked at Brock's waist as he worked both his arms around one of Brock's in a perfectly executed Kimura. "Don't fuck with me Brock. I've had a bad day."

"You've had a bad day?"

Brock rolled his head back to stare up into the face peering down at him. "Hey, Sunshine."

Eva's brows came together. "Why is Shawn kicking your ass?"

"He's not kicking my ass." Brock tried to work his arm free of Shawn's hold, but the other man only tightened his grip. "Ow. Fuck, Shawn."

Shawn leaned into his ear. "I will pull it out, Brock. I swear to God I will." He twisted a little more, straining Brock's shoulder joint as far as it would go without dislocating. "Tap out, Cassidy."

"Jesus Christ." Eva reached down and dug her thumb right into Shawn's eyeball. "Let him go. We appreciate and admire your manliness."

"Goddammit, Tatum." Shawn's head jerked as he tried to get away from her assault, but Eva moved with him, pressing harder.

"Let him go, Shawn."

Brock let out a groan of relief as Shawn's arms dropped his, allowing him to roll away from the team lead. "You're an ass."

"You're both asses." Eva glared at Brock as he pushed up into a sitting position. "What in the hell were you two fighting about?"

"Nothing." Shawn pressed the heel of one hand into the eye Eva gouged.

"That makes it even worse." She toed Shawn's butt with her boot. "Get up. Mona needs a suite."

Shawn squinted up at the two women. "Yeah. Okay." He pushed up from the floor. "You want her in the room next to yours?"

Eva scowled at him. "Of course I want her in the room next to mine. Why would you not put her in the room next to mine?"

"I was just asking, Tatum." Shawn's single eye moved from Eva to Mona. "You're staying?"

"She has to." Eva's gaze fell on Brock. "They can't find Chandler."

Mona's lips flattened into a thin line. "I think I should stay at least a few days. Hopefully he's just—"

Eva wrapped one arm around Mona's shoulders. "I'm sure he's fine."

Chandler was most likely not fine.

"He's probably been left somewhere." Brock stood up. The faster he could get Mona calm, the sooner he would have Eva to himself.

And he fucking needed her to himself.

"I'm sure we'll find him before morning."

Mona's head bobbed in a slow nod. "That would be good."

Eva smoothed down the white-blond strands of Mona's hair. Both women looked worse for the wear after their close call, but Mona was definitely not taking it nearly as well as Eva was.

Shawn tipped his head toward the tunnel leading to the bunk house. "Come on. I'll get you moved to a suite."

Eva started to walk with them but Mona stopped her before Brock could. "I'm okay."

"You're sure?" Eva didn't look convinced. "I can come with you."

Mona glanced at Brock. "I'm fine." She gave him a small smile. "I'm sure Shawn can help me with whatever I need."

"You're sure?"

Mona's smile moved to Eva. "Positive." She grabbed Eva in a quick hug, whispering something in her ear before letting her go and walking down the hall with Shawn close at her side.

Eva watched them go, waiting until they were out of sight before turning to face him.

"What did Mona say to you?"

"She said you needed me more than she did."

"She's right."

Eva barely smiled. "I know."

He couldn't hold back any longer. In two steps he had her, pulling Eva tight against his chest. "I don't know that I can handle this, Tatum."

"You have to." She held him as tight as he held her. "I have to stay."

"Shit." This was the worst case scenario.

This wasn't about Howard or Chandler or even Eva.

This was about Alaskan Security and whoever was out to take them down.

And tonight they made it clear what they were willing to do to make that happen.

Anything.

They were willing to risk breaking into a place they would almost certainly never get out of, to take the one thing that would guarantee an immediate use of deadly force.

Because they believed the potential gain was worth it.

"I can't leave Harlow here to deal with this alone." Eva sniffed a little. "And she won't leave just to prove she's not scared."

He held onto Eva as the truth of everything pushed in on him from all sides.

Eva wasn't safe.

Harlow wasn't safe.

At least Bess and Parker were away from all this.

"Brock." Shawn's tone was clipped and short.

He looked to where the team coordinator stood at the end of the hall, his jaw tight. "What's wrong?"

"Chandler's room is empty."

****

EVA STOOD IN the doorway to the room where Chandler had been staying since his arrival in Alaska.

It was a mess. The mattress was sliced open, pillows were emptied of their stuffing and flung around the space, the walls were covered in some sort of brownish streaks. "That's not shit, is it?"

"Based on the smell, probably." Shawn stood at the entrance to the bathroom of the hotel-style space. "The toilet's overflowed and he stuffed towels into the sink and left the tap running."

"He was part of this." It was an easy conclusion to come to. All Chandler's belongings were gone. Computer, suitcase, everything. "How did he sneak out without anyone seeing him?"

"He's there on the cameras, but Chandler left right after we moved out to get Richards. Everyone was focused on that." Shawn raked one hand through his hair. "Not that we would have been watching him closely anyway. He wasn't an issue."

"Obviously not true." Eva's head dropped back. "God, he's such a dick."

Brock pulled her in close. "If it makes you feel any better they'll probably kill him once he stops being useful."

Did that make it better?

"I don't necessarily want him to die." Eva scrunched her nose up as the smell from inside the room started to waft out. "That's definitely shit." She pinched her nose together. "Who does that?"

"He's pissed." Brock pulled her into the hall. "I'm taking her upstairs, Shawn. Call me when you go to talk to Richards."

"I'm not talking to Richards."

Brock paused. "Who is?"

Shawn stomped across the room, pulling the door closed behind him. "I believe Pierce has claimed that prize."

"Pierce wants to be the one to question Howard?" Eva looked between Shawn and Brock. "Is that normal?"

Shawn shook his head. "I think normal is not anything we're going to be enjoying for a while." He walked beside them down the hall. "And honestly Howard is the best shot we have right now. He's the only one who might be able to prove we're right about the connections."

"You mean that Howard and Chandler were both working with whoever it is that's trying to take down you guys?"

Shawn pointed at her. "Bingo." He kept walking toward the connecting hall to the main building as she and Brock turned toward the stairs to the second floor. "If I hear anything I'll let you know."

Eva moved up the stairs alongside Brock. "Who's going to clean that mess up?"

"Which mess are you talking about?" Brock pulled her in closer. "The one inside or the one outside?"

She barely shivered. "I was trying not to think about the mess outside." Eva swallowed hard. "Was it you?"

"I'm proud you believe that could have all been me, but no. They all had to be taken out at the same time."

"So that means you're only up to nine." She forced in a deep breath. "That's good. Better than hitting double digits, right?"

Brock stopped at the top of the steps, turning toward her. "That will not be one that keeps me up at night, Sunshine. I will never feel bad about what I did tonight and neither will anyone else." He pulled her close. "Any man here will protect you no matter what. No questions asked."

"I can't believe that asshole tricked us into coming out there." She rested her head against Brock's chest, listening to the steady beat of his heart as her eyes drifted closed, an oddly heavy exhaustion pulling at her. "What the fuck was he thinking?"

"He was thinking there was going to be a whole lot of money in his future."

Eva blinked her eyes open and found Pierce standing right beside Brock. "I figured it was about money."

Pierce's cool gaze rested on her for a second before moving to Brock. "I need Ms. Tatum for a bit."

Brock's hold on her tightened. "She's tired, Pierce. She needs to sleep."

"I don't disagree, but I believe she might be our best chance to pull useful information from Howard Richards." Pierce turned back to her. "I assume you would like to know what your business partner was up to."

Damn it.

She did.

Slightly more than she wanted to be curled up in bed with Broccoli. "Fine." Eva straightened. "Let's make it quick, though. I'm over this for the night." She grabbed Pierce by the lapel of his expensive suit and pulled him along with her. "Did you hear Chandler spread shit all over his room downstairs?"

Pierce let her drag him down the stairs. "I had not heard that." He pulled out his phone and tapped through the screen before putting it up to his ear. "I need room fourteen handled tonight." He slid the phone back in his pocket. "Do you know where you're going, Ms. Tatum?"

"Eva." She glanced his way. "Or just Tatum is fine. And no." She dropped his coat. "Lead the way."

He nodded, eyes barely shifting over her shoulder to where Brock was behind her, strong and solid. Supporting her in the decision she made, even though it was the last thing he probably wanted to do.

Eva reached back, sliding her hand into his. "Come on. Let's go see if Howard is happy to see me."

He was.

"Hey." Howard smiled across the table at her. "Did you get the flowers I sent you?"

"Yup." Eva shifted in her chair. Now that she knew just how crazy this guy was he made her uncomfortable as hell. "So you were hanging out with Chandler, huh?"

"Yeah." Howard lifted one shoulder. "We're friends."

"Cool. Cool." Eva glanced to the dark corner of the large room where Brock and Pierce were tucked into the shadows.

The set up was a cliché if she'd ever seen one. A single table set up in the center of a black room with a light shining down into Howard's ruddy face.

"I think Chandler left." Eva sighed. "All his stuff is gone.

Howard's unruly brows came together. "What?"

"Yeah. Just packed up and left with some guys in a black car."

Howard frowned. "Oh." He reached out to pick at a mar on the table with his zip tied hands. "I'm sure he'll call me soon."

Probably not.

"Yeah. Of course. Because he'll want to talk to you about…"

"The job and stuff."

"Totally." Eva nodded. "When are you starting?"

"Well." Howard glanced up. "Don't be mad at me."

Eva shook her head. "Never."

"I'm going back to work at Investigative Resources." Howard held his hands up. "But Chandler said you would be fine with it because you would have all the money from the buyout." His eyes were wide and open. "Did you get your money?"

"I didn't get my money, Howard." She sighed. "I think Chandler might have been using you."

"No." Howard shook his head fast. "We're friends. He helped me come up here and find you so I could make sure you were still happy." He smiled. "That's why I sent you those flowers."

So Howard Richards was definitely still sort of misguided.

"They did make me happy, so thank you for that." Eva plastered on a smile. "But I'm worried about you, Howard. Why would Chandler just leave you like that? He knew you were here."

Howard's expression sobered. "He knew I was here?"

Eva nodded. "He's the one who told those men where to find you."

Howard barely shook his head. "No. He wouldn't do that. He's my friend."

Eva leaned closer, resting her arms on the table between them. "Who were the other men, Howard? The ones who took you to the flower shop?"

Howard's lips pressed together.

He was not as stupid as he might be pretending to be.

Actually, Howard might be way smarter than she'd given him credit for. "Who were the men in the black car?"

Howard crossed his arms over his chest as his entire expression shifted. "How do you know about them?"

"I saw you on video with them." Eva watched him for a minute, trying to gauge what of this conversation was real.

And what wasn't.

Because Howard was absolutely trying to manipulate her.

Howard's eyes barely narrowed. "You should have stayed out of this. Everything would have been fine."

So there was the crazy.

"I'm not very good at staying out of things."

"That's why you're here. So we could make sure this would run smoothly." His lip curled. "But you still managed to fuck it all up again."

"Again?"

"You shouldn't have fired me, Eva. You should have let me be. Then you could have been a part of it." His gaze raked down her. "We could have done it together." Howard's lip moved to a snarl. "Instead it had to be Chandler."

"He was always your best bet, Howard." Eva smiled sweetly. "I would never have been a part of this bullshit."

Howard smiled back at her. "But here you are." He leaned in. "They won't be happy they didn't get what they wanted."

Eva eyed the wild man across the table from her. "What did they want?"

"They wanted Investigative Technologies, and Chandler was going to give it to them." Howard's gaze carried no small amount of disgust as it rested on her. "He knew you wouldn't understand. Would act all fucking righteous. So he had to find a way to remove you from the equation."

"What about Mona?" As disturbing as all of this was, the thought of Mona being left sitting in the center of this without her bothered Eva the most.

"Mona does what she's told. She knows her fucking place."

A hand came down between them, hitting the table hard enough to make it rattle on its feet. "Enough."

Eva stared up at Pierce.

She'd never seen him anything but cool and calm. Collected.

But right now the man looked as capable of killing as the rest filling the buildings around her.

"Take him somewhere." Pierce jerked his chin toward Howard."

"What? Who they fuck do you think you are?" He kicked at two large men as they came toward him. "You don't know who you're fucking with. They'll come for me." He fought against their hold as they locked onto his arms. "They will take you down. They won't stop till it's done."

The two men didn't react to any of Howard's antics as they picked his feet off the ground and carried him toward one end of the room.

"They will destroy you!" His short squatty legs swung in the air. "All of you." His eyes landed on Eva. "Bitch."

She let out a sigh as the doors closed out his continuing yells. "Can someone call be something besides a bitch for once?"

"You did well, Tatum." Pierce stepped in beside her. "Thank you."

"I think he's crazy."

"I believe that's an accurate assessment." Pierce nodded as Brock came to her side, his arm immediately finding its way around her. "She is all yours, Cassidy." Pierce barely smiled at her. "For now."

CHAPTER 24

"WHAT IS THIS?" Eva leaned over the counter to peer down at the plate he put in front of her.

"French toast." It was a pretty self-explanatory dish. One he figured a vegetarian would eat. "It's the second best breakfast food."

Eva lifted her brows at him. "Did you determine this through a survey?"

He grinned. "Something like that."

Eva picked up her fork. "I guess we'll see if I agree with the masses."

"They weren't masses."

"Not judging, Broccoli." She chopped a chunk free and stuffed it into her mouth. "I have masses of my own."

He straightened behind the counter, sending her into a laughing fit that led to a choking fit.

Brock rounded the counter and was about to pat her back just as she held up one finger, stopping him dead in his tracks.

That's how easily this woman could rule his life. Already did.

"You okay?" He leaned against the counter as she swallowed some coffee on top of the problematic bite of toast. "If you choke to death on a breakfast I made you I will—"

She reached up, her hand curling around the back of his neck to pull him down to face her. "I'm gonna tell you something right now, Broccoli, and I want you to listen to me very carefully. Got it?" She didn't wait for his answer. "I don't plan on dying anytime soon. I will not step foot out of this building until you tell me it's safe." Her ringed eyes were wide on his. "But someday I will die. It's just the way shit goes."

"I don't want to—"

"I don't care." Her hand came to rest against his cheek, palm cool against his skin. "I might die before you." Her eyes skimmed down his body. "Probably not given your choice of profession, but it could happen." She stared up at him. "What happened with your brother is a tragedy." Her head barely shook. "But most people find a way to go on. It's not fun and it's not easy, but most people do it." Her hand skimmed down his chest to give him a single-finger poke right between his ribs. "And you would be like those people."

"I don't plan to find out."

"Then that means I'll be the one to find out." She lifted her shoulders. "Does that make you feel better?"

He barely smiled. "A little.

Eva's head bounced back. "Ouch. You would rather I be the one left here to suffer without you?"

He grabbed her from the stool and pulled her body against his. "I like hearing you say you would suffer without me." He nuzzled her neck. "I like that you're talking about us being together until one of us dies."

Her body stiffened for just a second before softening. "Damn it, Broccoli." Eva's arms wrapped around his neck. "We were having a perfectly fine conversation and you had to go and make it serious."

He laughed loud. "You were talking about death. How am I the one who made it serious?"

"You just were." Eva was smiling when she leaned back, but it faltered as soon as her eyes landed on his. "Serious is hard for me, Brock."

"Weren't you engaged once?" He tried not to sound as irritated as the fact made him.

"Yeah, but it was," Eva rolled her eyes, "I was young and it wasn't really..." She blew out a breath, lips flapping together in a raspberry. "It wasn't like this."

"Good." He caught her lips in a kiss that tasted faintly of French toast and coffee.

Eva pushed up onto her toes, arms holding him tight.

She might be acting brave now, but last night scared her. It's why she was happy to stay here under lock and key.

And he didn't doubt for a second that sacrifice was only for her benefit.

Eva pushed against him as the whole kiss shifted to something more.

Brock gripped her hips and pushed her back. "Nope. Not until you've eaten your breakfast."

She'd skipped enough morning meals this week and this one was not being added to the list.

Her lower lip pushed out. "Please?"

He shook his head at her.

"I guess I was right." Eva turned from him and plopped back onto her stool, shoving up the sleeves of his shirt as she faced her breakfast.

"Right?"

"Um-hm." She took a bite, keeping her eyes straight ahead as she chewed. "You're no fun."

"I'm fun." How many times had she made him say it over the past week?

Too many to count.

"Whatever makes you feel better, Broccoli." Her bare feet hooked over the bottom rung of the stool as she continued to eat, refusing to look his way.

Brock stepped in behind her, leaning over one shoulder. "You have a very narrow definition of fun, Sunshine."

"I really don't." She tilted her head to look at him. "It's very, very broad."

"Be careful, Tatum." He rested his palms on her bare thighs. "If you're too fun I might not tell you when it's safe for you to go outside."

She laughed deep and real, head falling back against his shoulder. "If you're fun enough I might not mind." She smiled up at him. "It's cold as hell out there." Eva rested one hand on top of one of his, guiding it higher as her legs pushed apart. "I might be happy to stay inside if you gave me incentives."

Brock skimmed his lips along her neck as Eva moved his hand where she wanted it. "Don't I remember you saying something about not being satisfied by—"

Eva's arm wrapped around his neck as her hips lifted into his touch. "Shut up, Broccoli. I know what I said."

He barely brushed against her. "Do you?"

She nodded, eyes falling closed as he probed deeper. "Prove me wrong."

****

"HOW IS HARLOW?" Mona chewed her lip as she watched Eva come into the room Shawn set up for them to use.

"Brock says she's resting." Eva flopped into her chair. "We need to find out who the fuck these guys are before they do something else."

Mona stared at her computer screen. "I'm not sure I even know where to start."

That was the understatement of the year. Eva was used to starting at a target and moving out. This was the complete opposite.

And unfortunately it wasn't their only pressing problem.

"What are we going to do about Investigative Resources?" Eva rubbed her eyes as she waited for her computer to power up.

Now that Chandler was MIA, she and Mona had to make some tough decisions.

"The first thing we need to do is make sure Chandler can't get into the system."

"I handled that last night." Dutch stood in the doorway.

"You did?" Eva stared at him as Dutch came in to sit on Harlow's desk.

"I know how to hack." He tipped back a drink of the coffee in his hand. "I'm not as good as Harlow, but in fairness, no one is as good as Harlow."

"So the system is safe." Eva took a breath. "That's good."

"The system is safe for now." Dutch shrugged. "I would imagine it won't be long before our friends are trying to get into it."

"Why?" Mona looked from Eva to Dutch. "There's nothing in there that could be useful to them."

"Not true." Dutch stood. "They were trying to lock down Investigative Resources." His expression was serious. "They are looking for people capable of digging. Chandler was supposed to give them that."

"But he can't." Eva stared at Mona. "They are going to try to hire your team."

Mona's eyes widened. "But..." Her head barely shook. "No."

"Unfortunately, yes." Dutch crossed to stand between them. He tipped his coffee toward Eva. "They will go after your team too."

The thought of the people she worked side by side with for years being lured in by the same men who tried to take her and Mona and Harlow last night had her stomach rolling.

Because for many people, money talked.

"So what do we do?" Eva stared at Dutch, needing some sort of direction in a situation she could never have imagined being caught in.

"Call them." Pierce stepped into the office.

"What do we tell them?" Eva stood. "We can't just say someone bad is trying to hire you so please don't take their pile of money."

Pierce dropped a paper on Mona's desk, his gaze lingering on her as she picked it up and stared at it. "You offer them a pile of money from me." His eyes pulled from Mona and he handed Eva the second paper in his hand. "I will hire anyone you believe will be a good fit for your team."

"Our team?" Eva stared at the sizable figure on the paper.

"My offer stands, and unfortunately I'm not sure you have a choice in taking it at this point."

"We could walk away." Mona's voice was soft, but solid. "From all of it."

Pierce shook his head. "What happened last night will happen again." He moved in close to Mona. "Now just to prove they can." One hand tucked into the pocket of his pants. "I won't have you put in danger." He cleared his throat, stepping back, head nodding Eva's direction. "Either of you."

Mona's eyes held Pierce's long enough to make Eva proud. Finally she looked Eva's way. "We will discuss it and get back to you, Mr. Pierce."

Pierce's lips twitched. "I would appreciate it if you could do that soon, Miss Ayers."

Mona gave him a single nod, staying silent as Pierce and Dutch left together. She stood and quietly closed the door, turning to face Eva. "We have to try to get as many of them to come here as we can, don't we?"

"We do." Eva pulled out her phone. At least she could have that again. It was no secret to anyone where she was now. "Start calling."

****

HARLOW PULLED AWAY from the feel of something rolling against the skin of her forehead.

"Good morning."

She barely lifted her lids, squinting up into Eli's smiling face. "It's not. Not even a little bit."

The resident physician at Alaskan Security kept smiling. "Well you're not dead so I would call it good all things considered."

"Stop being dramatic." She batted at his hands as they felt just beneath her jawline. "I'm fine."

"Your temperature was 94.8 when Dutch brought you in last night." Eli lifted the edge of the blanket covering her. "May I?"

"I guess that depends what you're asking permission for." Harlow snorted a little.

"I need to check your toes. Make sure none of them are frostbitten." Eli pulled the covers back and tugged off the thick sock covering her foot before checking each of her toes, taking extra time on her baby toe. "I was worried about this one last night, but it seems to be doing okay."

"Good. That's my favorite toe."

Eli glanced up at her. "You have a favorite toe?"

"Of course I have a favorite toe." She scratched at her head. "You don't?"

The doctor shook his head. "Can't say that I do."

"I think you've been feeling her toes long enough, Hart."

Harlow's stomach clenched at the sound of Dutch's voice. "Eli can fondle my toes as long as he wants." She wiggled them as she glared up at the man standing in the doorway to her room.

Nope.

Not her room.

Harlow looked from side to side. "Where am I?"

Dutch took a sip from one of the cups in his hand, his eyes never leaving hers. "You're in my bed, Mowry."

****

Printed in Great Britain
by Amazon

59917021R00194